# Ojimbo and the Tembo

-L.R. Claude

Cover  Design:

Heidi Hobe Dailey

A Special Thanks to:

My Son for always being my reason to aspire

to be a better person

May you find:

Smiles in the flowers and faces in the clouds,

Comfort in thunder and love that abounds,

Laughter in the raindrops and joy in the trees,

Warmth in the sunlight and faith in the breeze

-Carol M. Dailey

# Ojimbo and the Tembo

        Let me tell you about a boy names Ojimbo, a tale of how a small meek teen that hardly weighs sixty kilos has managed to carry an entire continent as he worked his way from Africa to England. This boy has quite a good story and for those that seem to soak in what he has to say. I was skeptical about the walking for days through a desert, his run in with elephants, sailing with pirates, and wrestling with sharks, it all seemed a little far-fetched for me to believe all of this from some bush kid, at first. Ojimbo had caught the ears of high end scholars; he's spoken about conservancy and about truly having encounters with elephants in his homeland. Through the good deeds of good people that believed in his tale he has traveled all the way from South Africa to England. Ojimbo is of small frame, he has a thin face and high cheek bones, but his small body carried him thousands of miles and held the strength to endure more than the journey he set out for.

        I was beginning my career in finance when I decided to join a mate of mine for a guest lecture that was gathering a rather illustrious crowd at a speaking hall at the University. I was young and motivated when I decided to go into trading stocks and bonds. I was aware of the abilities that having a high paying job could afford me and I said cheers to plenty of late nights of studying and examinations. My name is Peter Bateman and I was raised on the outskirts of London, I love the busy streets, football days and the busy goings on of all the people all the time. My story fails in comparison to what I am about to tell you. As I stated; I joined a mate at the University to attend a lecture by a guest speaker, we were to visit a pub afterwards so even if the speaker bored us to tears, a few pints after would bring us right back to our formidable selves, and the tab was on him for my going.

The guest was just a mid-teen boy, he was thin framed and a meek looking fellow. The reason the boy was being hosted was for his struggle and his purpose, he was telling his story in many places, most places he was merely camping out of random people's homes and some of those people were helping to book lecture halls for him to stand up and tell his story to larger and larger crowds.  Ojimbo Clarke was a small teen; he was passionate as he spoke in broken English about his home and his journey from it. Ojimbo was very rigid when he spoke; he leaned forward on a podium and spoke into a microphone to amplify his soft voice, he stood tall and statuesque as he narrated his tale. Ojimbo was wearing a red and white plaid shirt, khaki pants, and dirty white sneakers, he had narrow shoulders and long fingers that held him to the podium as he spoke, he looked timid staring out at the people staring back at him, but he felt compelled to continue to speak.

After listening to Ojimbo's story I hardly felt changed, this boy had been through hades and back and has had his entire life changed, and here he was, standing up in front of a few dozen chaps and speaking passionately, thousands of miles from his home. I didn't really stray far from home, even for my collegiate experience of briskly walking through large arches between university buildings and clock towers. Ojimbo had traveled from the southeast portions of Africa; leaving behind his tribe and family to find himself, he has also taught many as well. This smaller dark skinned young man might only be able to carry a few jugs of water at a time, but somehow he has also carried his continent.

My parents were loving adults, in my youth they taught me how to be a courteous neighbor and to always care for the elderly. School taught me about geography and what it might be like in many other countries. I remember meeting a Yank when I was a young adult, the bloke called a few men "Limey's" while in a pub one afternoon and they shared some pints and that was that. London is a magnificent people market, many people come and go and few stop for long but you can always spot the tourists and travelers, people with bags on their shoulders or milling around and standing in the way asking directions to "Big Ben", or even in their dreadful accents trying to impersonate the song that is our native language. Anyways, I rode some of the railways at the metro stations to some of the adjacent counties with mates and pals back in school, we all had our small adventures through our childhood and further dreams of exploring more of this globe as we aged and once our finances afforded us more of the grand luxuries from our dreams.

Ojimbo looked like some Zulu lion hunting tribesman, he was almost midnight dark in skin, his eyes were a dull yellow, and he had sharp cheekbones and choppy English when he spoke. I disregarded the small framed bloke when I took my seat, I didn't mean to be rude but if he wasn't going to offer some tips for making a thousand percent return on an investment, then I was wasting my time. Some of the local journals had written columns about this lad, he had spoken in many cities and walked to almost everywhere he needed to go. By the time Ojimbo had gotten near our city, his fellow man had fed him, clothed him, sheltered him, and many people went out of their way to taxi him to many of his destinations. After I heard Ojimbo speak; I wasn't moved to help, I had a little scratch and didn't feel that it would be better off in anyone else's hands than mine but I still felt the philanthropic needles poke at my heart. Ojimbo spoke passionately about his home, he had a fire in his heart and a slight tremble in his voice but he still stood tall and delivered his message.

After the speech I was almost dying of thirst. My mate Thomas and I slid out of the back hall as people stood and cheered for the speaker, I attended because Thomas said the first round was on him if I joined him, he went because he was finishing up at the university and as an elective, he opted to listen to the chap speak and tongue click whatever for two hours and call it a night. Thomas and I discussed our standpoints about the lecture, we debated if the kid actually did all that the columns in the papers said he did. Thomas and I were skeptical as to how the boy traveled: from the South African villages and plains, up through the continent, through Egypt, and without papers or proof of who he was, guest lectured in his broken English to dozens of large institutions all over Europe, it seemed a little far-fetched for either of us to believe.

Thomas and I parted ways once the late hours passed in the pub, we had a few pints, shared some laughs, and even entertained an intelligent bit of conversation pertaining to the lecture we attended and everything we had heard. Thomas hailed a taxi and as the light drizzle of the rain muffled some of the cars motoring passed, I walked toward the bus stop to wait for the late night shuttle. The bus box was a simple three sided glass enclosure, it shielded enough of the weather to stave off much of the cold or rain while waiting, it sat between two overhead street lamps so there was sufficient light for safety to anyone waiting for a motor coach. As I stepped closer and closer to the motor box to see someone laying on the bench inside, inconsiderate seeing's how many people come and go from these boxes whilst waiting for a shuttle to their home. The drizzle in the air became illuminated as it fell under the street lamps, the forming puddles on the ground reflected the lights from many different angles and rippled in the back lights of cars that drove through them while heading back to their home, splashing outwards onto the street, then gathering back to make puddles again.

I stepped just inside the motor box to catch a small bit of reprieve from the rain, cars still zipped by, the splashing spread across the wet pavement. I did my best to avoid making eye contact with the homeless person sleeping on the bench; there are homes or boxes under bridges for these people to live, not in the way of hard working society. Over my left shoulder I saw the pile of person covered in a dark makeshift blanket. I kept my eyes trained over my left shoulder to prepare myself in case this bum wanted to try and roll me for my billfold. Through the corner of my eye I could see a person lying on the bench sat up, the mound rose up and caused my hands to begin to clench without my intent.

"You can sit" a soft voice with thick accent broke the sound of the rain dripping overhead. The interruption startled me enough to turn my head but quickly whip it back forward. I was in my youth, making good money, on my way to a life of wealth and beautiful woman to accompany me on holidays, the last thing I wanted to do was get stabbed over a few pieces of paper in my pocket. I shook my head in response to the question that was posed to me. My heart beat harshly in my chest, I stared at the rippling puddles, slowing in their motion, so did my heart beat a little. The quick actions of the mound rising just to my left replayed in my mind, flash after flash until I realized I recognized what I saw, and heard. I recognized the red and white plaid shirt, it was just the collar under the makeshift blanket but the collar, coupled with the thick accent, made me realize it was Ojimbo lying on the bench.

I sat down beside Ojimbo, I explained that I attended the days lecture; Ojimbo properly introduced himself, as did I. He pulled his coat up towards his neck, there was a bit of a chill in the air and as he yawned I could hear the shutter in his voice because of the lower temperatures. I broke my silent stature and had to ask; "is it all true?" his chin was resting towards his chest, he must have been exhausted to have almost fallen back asleep in such a fast moment, his head jerked upright, I apologized for surprising him. "It is true" Ojimbo assured me. "I miss my mother, my home, it is far far from me" Ojimbo continued speaking to me; I could feel my guard begin to ease, I still had many questions but the shuttle was rounding the corner. I was at an imposition, I hated being stuck, like when a beggar pins you down and you just don't want to give them any of the money you worked for, even if you can afford a few pounds.

The shuttle drew close and the sense of dread struck me; my small voice of compassion in my mind began to speak, I stepped towards the opening in the motor box, the few millimeters I moved made the noise of the rain turn to a siren in my ears. I let my heavy head hang, and without rehearsal my mouth let out an invitation to join me for a dry place to sleep. "Are you certain my friend?" the broken English emerged over the rain; I turned to see his white teeth appear from his dark presence in the shadow of his coat. I stretched out my open hand to help the newly acquainted associate to his feet, the man hardly pulled nor weighted much as he steadied himself with my assistance. "My mother told me, do not pull someone down to pull you up" Ojimbo said as he stepped closer to the opening I was standing in. I suspected that he had learned to navigate buses and such fairly well, I had heard that he traveled from South Africa on his own wind and ended here so far away in jolly old (England.)

Ojimbo sat beside me on the shuttle as we passed side streets and tall buildings, he looked out the windows, still in awe of where he was and what he was seeing, he turned to me a few times to see if I was seeing what he was, he had a bright smile on his face. Ojimbo looked ever so much younger with a gleaming smile on his face, experiencing everything as if it was still new and he hadn't been hardened over by it yet as I had. It was a bit of a putter through the drizzle, I told Ojimbo that my flat was up a lift and of small space, I wasn't expecting to host or have a guest over but this was a sudden circumstance. Ojimbo told me that he would have even been fine on the bus bench, he is thankful for everything anyone has ever done and without the kindness of everyone he's ever met, he may not have ever seen the things he has seen.

Ojimbo bows his head a little when he speaks, he seemed to be carrying around a deep burden in his heart, for a man not much older that fourteen or fifteen I'd guess. Ojimbo was ever so much more mature than any of the students I had ever met at school or even in the country. Our final stop had come, I warned Ojimbo we had to still take a lift up but that he'd be able to sleep soon enough. Ojimbo followed close on my heels, from my periphery I could see him looking around and taking in all sorts of sights and smells, he didn't shutter or hide under his jacket from the rain; it wasn't an inconvenience to have him. Ojimbo and I made it up to my flat; I let us in while he let his eyes wander the new quarters for the night. I offered the man some tea as I put the kettle on, I had some crackers and meat to snack on while my guest sat with me at my small table and thanked me repeatedly for my kindness. I felt a slight tinge of guilt that I had dismissed him earlier in the day.

Ojimbo had dark brown, almost black skin, his eyes were also dark brown with the yellowed whites, his hands were speckled with bits of scars and scrapes, I thought to imagine how much different our lives were, he was born and raised in a small African tribe while I was born to the city of London, I had meal makers on every street corner, he had to get up early every day and work for something to eat, and even that wasn't ever a certain. Ojimbo asked if I had any Honey Main graham crackers; "I like them very much, I first hand them in Spain" he told me. I was several years older than this *kid* and yet he had already traveled ever so much more of the world than I had, and without the concept of money to fund his mission. I had worlds of questions whirling in my mind, I wanted to pepper him all night to know everything about him but he continued to pop his head up from nearly falling asleep as he sat across from me at my table as we ended the evening.

I woke up mildly early for a Saturday, my usual day to sleep in after a late night at the pub with Thomas or any other friends. I let myself out of my room to discover that the guest I had let sleep on my couch, was not there. I looked around for a moment to discover Ojimbo on his hands and knees wiping not only my kitchen floor, but the six last tenant's worth of dust bunnies out from under the stove and icebox. I addressed Ojimbo to let him know I was up and ready to see what he needed for the day and to find out where I could take him in the afternoon to continue on with whatever it was that he had planned. I cleared my throat as I turned to enter the kitchen, I found Ojimbo on hands and knees and reaching well under the refrigerator. I asked what he was using to clean with and tried to explain that it wasn't necessary. "My mother, she tells me to work, if I can't pay for couch to sleep on, or food to eat, I can clean, its ok" he told me as he turned to reveal his left hand hidden within a sock.

I felt my eyes open a little wider at the sight of a sock covered in all manner of dust, hair, hardened food particles and whatever else migrates under appliances in a kitchen. I asked my guest turned maid where he managed a sock to use to clean and before I finished saying "so." I glanced down to take notice that the bloke was only wearing one. The cheeky devil was using one of his very own socks to clean my grimy nasty kitchen floor. I failed at my attempt to dissuade him from continuing, "is OK, I am almost done my friend" he responded, he had a smile on his face as he swiped his hands back and forth. I turned myself around and headed back to my dresser for a fresh pair of socks for him. I stepped in behind Ojimbo and lit the skillet, I asked if eggs were ok for our morning meal, "most definitely yes please, I like eggs, eggs are good."

I tried not to let my mind wander for a moment but in that instance before I snapped out of it, it almost was akin to having a pet, learning what he did or didn't eat, trying to judge how much his small frame might eat or not eat. I didn't really have any zebra or ostrich, or bugs or whatever but I had some eggs. I offered Ojimbo the restroom if he wanted to clean up or anything before I served us breakfast; he parted my presence for a moment as I scraped out a few eggs onto plates for us. Ojimbo and I sat and ate, he nodded and smiled as he ate, he repeatedly expressed his gratitude and appreciation with "thank yous" and moans to show his enjoyment with his meal. Ojimbo let his lips curl around his fork as he ate, he was a slender boy, he must have been hungry but he ate slow enough to appreciate each bite he took, a lesson I might have to learn.

I asked my guest where he had to be, he told me that he didn't want to take up any more space or my time, he wanted to make his way back towards Cairo, he liked the weather more than here, which was still lightly raining. I told

Ojimbo that I wanted to ask him a bunch of questions, I had ample plans for the day but hearing his two hour speech wasn't nearly enough, I wanted to hear everything about where he was from, what it took and how he ended up on my couch. I asked his permission to journal his story, ensuring it wouldn't be too intrusive to copy down everything he says and try to better get the whole picture. Ojimbo smiled a very large toothy smile; he reached out with both of his hands and shook vigorously while simultaneously bowing his head in thanks.

The speech I had listened to while sitting with my pal Thomas was geared towards elephant conservation. Thomas was finalizing his master's degree in environmental law; he was making headway towards a career of wealth just as I was. Thomas wants to sit in courtrooms or just in mediation rooms while large corporations feed him large sums of money to make their problems go away. In his pursuit of his degree he had to take classes that were meant for either side of the law, pro or con of one view or another and the University had put up Ojimbo the night prior to his speech. Ojimbo traveled and spoke about how the elephant is a magnificent creature, how compassionate they are and how they symbolize how great and caring this world can be. The university offered courses that detailed how the environment was being altered and affected by our action. Ojimbo had first-hand experience with the large elephants and made for an interesting and cheap guest lecturer, which was why he was asked to speak.

Ojimbo opened up his speech with an old joke he came across on his travels, it was cheesy but because it was an elephant joke he told it anyways. Ojimbo then spoke about how as a boy in his village it was the job of the women to cook and of the children to attend to many chores with the women while the men left for days or weeks at a time to hunt, and then to bring back enough food to cook, eat, and store by drying it over a smoke rack until they needed it again. Ojimbo loved his life in his village, he was part of the Kuzi people, they farmed a small bit of potatoes, peppers and grains to supplement their hunting. Ojimbo had a best friend named Teeta since birth. Ojimbo and Teeta would often feed together from either of their mums; there was no one woman to nurse one baby, any woman that could nurse a baby would nurse all that she could when they needed it.

The tribe in the village all worked together, there was no ownership, there was no big world mentality like there is everywhere else he has traveled. Ojimbo said he learned a lot as he reached further north into Africa, he learned what "mine" meant and that the more people had, the more they kept it to themselves. Ojimbo often missed his mom Bendu and quoted her very frequently as he spoke, her wisdom and teachings have carried him across a continent and through many countries so she must have been a wise woman. Ojimbo felt it in his heart when it was time to head out for his adventure, his childhood was certainly behind him and he stood tall and stared at manhood before him. Ojimbo stood quietly, he glanced around to take in his surroundings but hardly said much without being asked or spoken to. Ojimbo stood with good posture but he mostly kept his head bowed, it was hard to tell if it was habit to keep the hot African sun from his eyes or if he was just tired from his travels.

I cleared my schedule and asked Ojimbo to stay the rest of the day and night and perhaps another day so I can get as best a picture of everything I could, I was intrigued. I wanted to hear more of his travels, I wanted to take a safari and see some of his own sights with my own eyes. I intended to find a young vixen and head off to faraway lands and make the kind of love you would only hear the sounds of in a jungle. I wanted to chart a yacht and sail to the Cape of Good Hope or East

London, a few tanned bodies lying out on the deck with me as we ate fresh seafood from the drink below. I thought it might come in handy having some first-hand descriptions of what types of things I might come across. I still had ample work ahead of me but a fella can dream.

I began taking some small notes in my mind while we headed down to the market to gather up supplies to carry us through the weekend. I set up my laptop and began to organize this stranger's story. I wasn't sure what I was going to end up with but the wide eyed, wide smiled face of the stranger was somewhat contagious. I almost cast Ojimbo aside back at the bus stop, it was always dutiful to donate a few pounds to the red kettles but out of the blue I brought this man to my home and was sitting in my living room penning his story. I thought about retiring in the mountains of Italy or Spain, high enough to herd a few sheep and hide away from the hustle and bustle of the city below, perhaps farm enough grapes to press my own wine in the fall. I wanted to spend some time on the Mediterranean, wander around the smaller towns and eat some of the freshest seafood to be pulled from the blue waters. I wanted to meet girls in towns for a while before deciding to look for the kind of girl to make my wife, then sit back and sip wine in the evenings and grow old on large investments I had accumulated.

I encouraged Ojimbo to take a seat on the couch while I sat in my chair and readied myself for a long weekend of writing as he told me his story. I asked him to begin by giving me some background, what types of chores they had each day or tasks that they enjoyed or disliked. Ojimbo raised his eyebrows to some of my inquisitions; "chores? Did not like?" he tried to figure out what I meant and I stuttered a little trying to explain what I meant by the phrase. I tried to explain what chores were but he rebutted with "there are no chores;

everyone has work they must do," and "didn't like? We had our games and there were some games we enjoyed and then there was work to be done." I spent just as much time trying to wrap my head around why he didn't understand some of the terms as I did explaining what they meant. We were from opposite hemispheres, different countries and extremely different lives, but I was intrigued to learn from Ojimbo.

There was a slight disconnect when it came to small talk, some common phrases I expressed fell upon him without any meaning, he continued to smile and nod his head as I struggled to bridge the gap between our languages. I explained that the Jolly'O was just a slang term for London, that "the pond" meant any large form of water but mostly an ocean. Many phrases that I grew up with, he hadn't been exposed to during his few months of traveling. Ojimbo worked a few small jobs to get around; he helped to cook a little while in Spain, it turned out mostly to scrub some pots and pans for a nice man. Ojimbo expressed over and over how nice people have been to him and how he can't wait to tell his mother when he returned to her as a man of the world. Ojimbo wanted to make his mother proud, she raised him to be smart and hardworking and to teach others the knowledge that he had learned, and I was learning it from him.

Ojimbo was born in a small village, the men hunted while the woman cooked and cleaned. Ojimbo was much like another boy just a little older than he was, named Teeta. Ojimbo and Teeta often played around, they would chase and catch bugs, howl and yelp at the larger animals nearby, run to help bring back the meat that the men's hunting group had brought back to feed everyone and spent a lot of their time gather wood to cook. Ojimbo recalled stories of he and Teeta being lively little boys, swinging sticks their mothers were trying to use to build a fire or pulling the longer hair of some of the girls that they grew up with .Ojimbo was born to a woman named Bendu, she had a soft pleasant voice, and even when agitated, her voice became stern but she never yelled or shouted from her anger; "Why waste more energy being angry, it takes less energy finding peace" his mother used to tell him.

Ojimbo wanted to be a man like the men in the hunting group ever since he can remember. Ojimbo and Teeta used to run with their sticks and then drop down and crawl to hunt animals; they would crawl through grasses or dirt to get good and close before shooting at the animals that would become their meal. Ojimbo and Teeta were often inseparable, much like other young children around them, many people paired up out of nature, just that one person that you could often help and also rely on. The tribe had a few mud huts that people slept in, everyone had their roles in the village and no one laid around and then still ate. Everyone knew what it took to make sure that everyone went to sleep with food in them, and everyone got their share. Teeta was always just a little bit taller, he seemed to be able to run just a little bit faster or jump just a little bit higher than Ojimbo.

Ojimbo was very nimble, his actions were animated as he showed how he would squat down to follow animals or his hands would sway back and forth describing the way the grass blew, he raised his arms to show how large the big mountain would be and how the birds flew around overhead. Ojimbo was still very young at heart, he smiled well enough even if he didn't raise his head and holds it very high. Ojimbo had light pads on the palms of his hands, the pink of his under hands were coarse and callused from his working, he rubbed his right thumb into the left palm as he sat leaning forward, his elbows keeping him braced on his knees. Ojimbo stared mostly at his hands and he rung them together, his voice was solemn, there wasn't much change in the pitch when he spoke to me, much less energetic than when he gave his lecture.

Ojimbo told me about his buddy Teeta having many of the same small scars on his arms and leg from carrying sticks for fires and he and Teeta swinging sticks at each other while playing when they were younger. The corners of Ojimbo's mouth curled upwards a little as he spoke of his home, his memories were small treasures and he kept them tucked in his heart for when he was feeling homesick. Ojimbo would look at some of the darker spots on his skin and think about how each one was caused, if he could remember how he got each one then each small scar was a reminder that he has had a fun life and how many great memories he has. Ojimbo would occasionally stand to stretch, his long body would unfold underneath him and then he would smoothly rise up and outstretch his arms and recoil them back to his chest before folding back up to sit down.

Ojimbo chuckled at little bit talking about Teeta jumping and trying to jump over tall grass but never quite making it. I asked Ojimbo where Teeta was now; he turned and asked me: "do you want me to tell you from beginning or no?" I puffed out my cheeks with air as I had to answer, he was correct in stopping me but it only raised more questions than it answered. I continued to jot down questions on a yellow sheet of paper while typing to follow on with Ojimbo's story; I tried my best to relay it as appropriately as possible while interpreting it. From Africa to London by way of passion and good will, this is about Ojimbo Clarke.

There aren't many babies born a lot in my village, it is small and there is not enough food to go around to feed a big amount of people, there would be aches and hunger. The men hunt and the rest of the village works to survive. I was born not long after my friend Teeta; he was a little older than me. Teeta could walk before me, he could run before me, he could even talk before me; it was good that he was my friend. One time Teeta and I wanted to be with the men and go hunt, we were not very big, we were almost as small as a ndege (bird.) The men were hoping to bring back pundamilia; it is black and white lines (a zebra). Teeta and I wanted to hunt with the men, we tried to lie on the ground and follow them away from the village. Me and Teeta crawled like snakes, we tried to be still in the grass to make no noise but one of the men, they see us and come to set us back to our momma's. Me and Teeta wanted to hunt with the men, to be men and to bring back food for our families.

As small boys Me and Teeta had to help with the tubers in the ground, we had to help dig lines in the dirt and plant seeds in the lines, we had to help pick up and carry sticks, everyone had a job to do. Me and Teeta would race to see who had the biggest or longest sticks, and we would run to see how fast we could bring back enough wood for cooking fires. Sometimes it was hard to find sticks, Teeta and me would have to take out a basket to fill with kinyesi. Kinyesi is dried browns lumps, if not dry is very dirty and fall apart. Kinyesi is not so easy to find, sometimes the Kinyesi is small or stepped on by animals and no good. One time me and Teeta, we was bringing big basket of kinyesi, it was full and heavy, I was trying to walk as fast as my friend Teeta but he was walking to fast, I tripped and the basket spilled kinyesi all over me. Sometimes the kinyesi has small bugs in it, it burn real good but has a lot of smoke and when it smokes, the bugs on the inside, they come out. Teeta laughed and laughed, I did not like him laughing but he laugh and then he fall too. When Teeta fall, I begin to laugh, he did not get mad but together, we laugh a lot. When we bring kinyesi back to our momma's, they laugh a little but then we had to wash up, the kinyesi is stinky.

Teeta and I liked to splash in the water, when we washed as little babes we both like to clap our hands to the water, our momma's used to use less water because we splashed so much of the water. After we rolled laughing in the kinyesi our laughing and playing did not stop, we go to a small amount of water and began to splash again, it was only when my mother came did we stop. My mother knew that children were children and she was not stern. My mother was always smart when she told me what I was supposed to do, she tell me that everyone has their share of the work to do, the men hunt, and the woman raise the babies and keep up a good village for the men to come back to.

My mother made things fun, she would ask me and Teeta to gather grasses for the huts, we did not like to gather the grasses, it took a lot of bending over and at the end of the day it hurt my back. My mother told us that because we were smaller it was easier for us to pick the tall grasses because we were close to the ground. One time I try to tell my mother that the picking hurt my back and that the adults should help, they had larger hands to hold larger bundles of the grasses. My mother pointed out that the grass only comes out from the ground a little at a time so bigger hands would not pick bigger amounts of grass. My mother, she was right and many days Teeta and me would have sore backs and itchy skin from the grass. There were many trails worn through the grass and into the dirt, sometimes the men would go out the trail that faced the rising sun and to the large grass fields, other times they would go out the trail that points at the setting sun and to the trees in the far far away.

Many times the men would go out and hunt for days and days, sometimes they would come back with enough nyati meat for everyone to eat until they could burst, other times they would just come back. My mother said that we would just eat our viazi vitamu and some of the bugs we could find but that the moms with babies inside of them needed the meat that the men brought. Sometimes after the rains came, the nyati would fill all the grass you could see, they were big and moved fast, many many of them. The men knew to hunt the large nyati soon after the rains came back and turned the brown grass green once again. After the grass turned brown and the men were away longer and longer to bring back food, we could begin to prepare for the rains, and then we prepared for the rains, we also prepared for a big festival.

The festivals were very much fun, the men would bring back ngiri or Siwalla, both animals that could be found closer to the far trees when the nyati went away for a very long time. When the skies above would grow dark in the day, when usiku (night) would replace mchana (midday) and look angry, we knew it was a good night for a festival. The men could be seen in the distance carrying back lots of meat. Me and Teeta knew when it was time to hurry and gather supplies for fires and for cooking, we would get so happy we would dance a little as we looked around for what our mother's would need from us. Teeta would lots of times tell me to gather the wood or kinyesi so he could run and help the men carry their meat back. I wanted to hunt with the men, I did not like Teeta getting to help them before me, we did lots of things together, but not that, not yet.

Teeta would run and run down the path to greet the successful hunters, one day, I would run to join them and they would know my name. The paths that led into or out of our village were light brown, sometimes the dirt would show our footprints from walking but sometimes it would not. I liked walking down the paths and stretching our my arms like a ndege and trying to touch the grass on both sides, I was not able but I would tell myself that one day I would be big and then I could feel the tips of the grasses flow under my fingers while walking down the pathway. Sometimes a long nyoka would be seen down the pathway, my mother did not like them but Teeta and I liked to hunt them. The pathways seemed to stretch out far far away, some of the men told stories about the path that pointed out to the rising sun, others talked about traveling the pathway to the great hill to see the top of the world. Some of the men would not agree how long it would take to climb the great hill, some men said it would take a whole life time, others' would say more than one lifetime, the younger men always stood tall and puffed out their chests and boasted that they could climb it and come back down in time to join the next hunt, all the older men would laugh.

Festivals signaled the return of the rains, they were full of drum music and the women singing while the men used big knives to cut away meat to hang by the fire to cook. The festivals were great fun, everyone would stay up late into the darkness and eat and laugh, many of the smaller babies would cry along with the song, some would wobble and dance as best as they could, many of the rest of us would sing and dance. Our singing and dancing would make the skies smile and then the rains would fall to the land and refill them with life. Sometimes from the small hills Teeta and I would look in the far away to see if we could see any of the great beasts from the stories we heard, large long spotted creatures that swayed along the great grass plains, or the magnificent gray beasts called tembo that let out a loud call from the long nose on them, me and Teeta wanted to hunt all of the animals that the men spoke of.

The tembo were great bit animals, they had a long nose on their face that swung as they walked, they would swoosh their ears back and forth to cool themselves and also kick up dirt as they walked. The tembo had a loud call that could be heard for many kilometers away, it was very loud. The tembo would sometimes trample through the big grass plains, me and Teeta would sometimes sit on the big hill and try to spot them in the distance to see where the loud calls in the distance were coming from. The elders and out mothers always said that the tembo was a special animal that should never be hunted. The tembo takes a very long time to have one small baby, and it takes a very long time for that baby to grow up, and that there are not very many of them. There were always many other animals to hunt for food and the tembo was not food.

The pathway that pointed to the rising sun was said to lead to a water that lasted forever. I asked how the men knew that it went on forever and who went on that long and still came back to say that it did, the men just called me a young boy and told me to wait and see it for myself. I wanted to be just like my friend Teeta, we hunted nyoka together and bring the long bodies animals back for food, it was good practice and we hunted together, just like we would when we grew old enough to join the hunters. Sometimes some of the men would gather up many of the animal skins that we stretched out and dried from the hunts and one of the younger men would carry them towards the great water. Loza was only with the hunting group for one or two rains before he made the journey to the great water. Loza was much taller than me, he had bulges in his arms that I did not have and he had great strength.

Loza used small rope to bundle up the furs and began walking towards the morning sun. I walked with Loza for a day last time, he was excited to see the great water the men spoke of, I wanted to go with him all of the way on his journey but my mother would not allow me. I was allowed to walk with Loza and carry his small water until we reached the first split in the pathway, I was to turn back around and come home while he took the pathway on the side of his shooting hand (Ojimbo raised his right hand) and continue on until he found a trader named Teran. Teran was not like us, he was a different man but spoke our language and it was a new hunters job to walk for six days and find Teran, then walk for six days again to come back. I did not understand what my mother meant by saying that Teran was a different kind of man, I wondered if he had many more arms, or stood as tall as a tree, or maybe even covered with hair all over like a mbwa-mwitu. My mother just told me that the man was a different kind of man than what we were used to and that I would be the one to carry the skins to him one day.

Loza was only a few years older than me, when I was very little he still played with me and Teeta, we liked him very much and he was very nice to us. Loza would build mud huts with us in the rain or show us what some animals were by drawing their shapes in the dirt on the ground. Loza would try to catch chuta alive instead of kill them so we could see how they slithered in the dirt. Loza taught me and Teeta what tracks and dirt prints meant what animal, we would walk all the way towards the water ponds to look at different tracks in the mud or even find animals out watering themselves. Loza was aware of what he was doing when we all went out, he would walk softly and keep his head held high to watch out if there was anything that might harm me or Teeta. My mother Bendu was very nice to Loza and knew that he would grow up to be a very nice man.

As I walked with Loza I talked, I talked much more than he did. I asked if the tall pile of skins were heavy, how he would know Teran when he saw him, if he was scared to find out what another kind of man might be, what it felt like to get to join the hunters and if it made him happy. Loza also knew that it took everyone to do their jobs, if one person did not than it would make everyone else work harder, this was just his job. Loza lifted the big pile of skins up and down as he walked, the hair was soft on some of them but they still looked very heavy. I asked Loza why he lifted the skins up and down so much, I did not know why. "Pika likes my arms when I do it" Loza told me, Pika was a girl about his age in the tribe, they like each other and one day Loza wanted to marry her, and she wanted to give him children.

Pika was born a little after Loza, like me and Teeta they grew up together. In our tribe there are only a few babies born between rains, it depends on how well the hunters do; if the hunters are out a lot then they bring back plenty of meat, which meant a few more babies. Sometimes the hunters did not do so well and then that meant one or two babies the next year or no babies at all. Loza wanted to prove that he was a man, he also hunted nyoka in the grasses, just like me. One time Loza was out hunting and came upon a ngiri (boar,) they have big teeth by their nose and raise their head up and down trying to cut you with those long teeth. Ngiri grunt and roll in the dirt when the sun is really hot. Most of the time it takes two men or more to spear down a mad ngiri so no one gets hurt. Loza saw the sleeping ngiri, he watched it move its body up and down breathing but not moving, it was asleep. Loza wanted to prove to the men that he could hunt so he used his nyoka killing stick and then he made a plan.

Loza crept around the back of the lying animal, he knew that the teeth in its mouth were the dangerous parts, he thought if he could get to its back legs and grab it that he could keep it close enough to stab it. Loza was brave, but also not smart to creep up to a sleeping ngiri, very dangerous. Loza slowly put each step forward towards the beast, he reached his shaky left hand towards the back leg of the animal, he planned to lift the foot and reach around and stab the creature in the ribs to kill it, then he would prove that he was a man and could join the hunting party. Loza was frightened as he reached his hand near the back foot of the sleeping ngiri, he said that his chest burned like the sun but on the inside. Loza grabbed onto the foot and braced his own feet onto the ground and waited for the beast to try and stand up and run away, it rolled onto its feet before trying to turn and start swinging its teeth at Loza. Loza said the power of the beast knocked him to the ground most easily and that he did not know what to do. The beast tried to get its leg back from Loza, he dropped his stick in order to keep hanging onto the angry animal.

Loza continued to speak about how he had to crawl really fast on his knees to stay behind the animal before finding enough footing to stand back up, the beast pulled and pushed against him and let out a terrifying shriek as he reached in for the other hind leg. Loza reached in for the other hind leg when it kicked its leg back near his hand, Loza said he felt his arm begin to burn like his chest, he grabbed the leg to see that the foot had cut his arm open. Loza stood up and pulled the beast backwards enough to turn it to its side in the dirt filled air. Loza dragged the animal in a circle until he could find his stick to stab it with. Loza had to move faster than the animal to keep it from bloodying him more; he finally found his sharpened stick, only half of it. In the fight the stick was broken, Loza didn't know what he could do; he picked up the part with the sharpest piece and stabbed deep into the belly of the animal.

Loza said that the skin was harder to pierce than that of the nyoka, the animal let out an even louder shriek once Loza got a good enough angle to stab deep into the animal. Loza said that he pushed so hard that his whole fist entered into the animal, the animal kicked and grunted for a long time, Loza was too scared to let go of the animal and unsure of what to do next so he hung onto the back leg of the creature and fought it trying to stand up to run at him, or away. Loza was a brave boy but a scared boy, my mother told me that often times scared and brave are the same thing, but brave still does what it is scared to do. The animal finally stopped kicking, grunting, and howling, Loza said he was too scared to let the leg go in case the animal was trying to trick him, he also wasn't sure what to do next with the animal.

Loza thought back to having seen the same animal many times hoisted up on the shoulders of some of the men, the animal tired him from the fight and Loza couldn't carry the animal that was much bigger than he was. Loza pulled the other broken half of his spear from under the dead animal, he shook the leg in his hand a few times and with no sign of life, he knelt onto the topside of it and tried to plunge the sharpest part into the chest of the animal. The stick broke and pieces stabbed into the tough skin but only under the skin, not into the chest as it was supposed to. Loza pushed his hand back into the belly of the animal, the blood splattered, pooling onto the dirt underneath and the course hairs on the belly began to point up with the blood dripping off, he put his hands together and pulled the belly open a little to let more of the blood out.

Loza said that he did not know how he was going to manage to get the animal back to feed everyone but he was feeling the pride of a mighty hunter begin to give him strength.

Loza searched through some of the grasses to find a hearty stick but did not have any luck. Loza knew that fresh kill often meant mbwa-mwitu or chuta might smell the blood and give him even more trouble than the ngiri did. Loza took off his cloth that was draped around him, he tied an end to each long tooth and around its nose, and then he placed the middle over top of his head and leaned forward and began to walk back to the village. Pika was one of the first to shout that naked Loza was walking back into the village, Loza said he tried to shield his body from the grass whipping at him but he had his good hand clenched over the gash in his arm from the sharp tooth. Pika and Loza had seen one another without coverings on several occasions but this time he was concerned that she would see his chuta. Pika ran to help Loza finish dragging the beast back in, she smiled as she ran towards him and when he saw her heading in his direction, he stopped pulling.

Loza untied the animal as fast as he could as Pika neared, she slowed her pace and spoke loudly to him, offering her help and to see what it was he was doing walking into the village without any clothes on. Loza said he stood up quickly and tried to keep his back to her while he fumbled with his kanzu. Loza was struggling to get his kanzu up and tied back around his waist then Pika suddenly bent down next to him, she picked up his kanzu and helped him to tie it back where it belonged. Pika saw his trying to protect his injured arm, she helped to take care of him and in that moment, he knew he wanted for her to be his wife. Pika still teased Loza a bit as she tied his kanzu, she tied it rather tight and then giggled as he had to walk with a wide stance as they worked together to finish dragging his kill the rest of the way back to the village.

Loza was tall, he was a fast runner and also had long arms, he also liked Pika. Pika had small holes by her mouth, she was very beautiful and everyone told her. I remember a few rains ago when Pika was taller than Loza, he was older but she grew taller than he did, that was when he still played with me and Teeta, showing us how to hunt nyoka in the grasses. When Pika began to grow she no longer joined him in splashing in the water but instead stayed near her mother to learn more about cooking and listen to the older women tell their stories. Loza missed Pika on days and we would watch him as he would crawl on his hands and knees up behind her hut. Loza would reach in through the window in the wall of her hut and scare her, sometimes she would be asleep and he would hold a mouth full of water to spit on her, he then would run away laughing while she would holler at him. Loza was very much fun.

Loza and Pika grew up at almost the same age, they both helped to gather wood and kinyesi for fires together, threw mud in the rains together and searched through their imaginations together. Pika was a little younger than Loza but as she began to grow taller, she would sometimes be mean to him, especially when he was playing with me and Teeta. Loza sometimes would hold water in his mouth for a very long time after we visited the watering hole, he would not speak but make motions with his hands and arms for us as the three of us would walk back to the village, Loza would hold that mouth full of water only to finally spit it out on Pika when she was not being very nice. The girls grow taller than the boys for a little while and when they do they begin to spend less and less time with the women that watch over the boys and spend it with the women that guide the girls to grow into women. Me and Teeta liked having more time to play with Loza when Pika spent more time with her mother, but he did miss having her as his friend.

Loza waited for his turn to join the hunting party, he had killed a ngiri on his own and once he realize that he wanted Pika to be his wife, he focused more on waiting for his place with the men. Loza impressed everyone with his kill, especially Pika. Loza and Pika worked together to clean the meat, stretch the skin to dry and put the rest of the animal to use while everyone waited for the hunting party to return. The night Loza killed the ngiri on his own there was a small feast, there was plenty of meat for everyone, we did not have to dig up any of the tubers for the meal paste, or pick from the garden that we often had to protect from creatures eating it. Loza smiled really big that night, his teeth did not hide under his lips at all, and Pika smiled at him. Loza made it into the hunting party once the men returned, there was no gun for him for a while but he got one soon enough, he was very happy.

In the hunting party there was only one firearm and one big knife for each man, any man that did not have both to help was only eating meals that could feed the hunters, the men often hunted for many moons or until they had enough to feed the village with. Loza joined the hunters without either a knife or gun because he proved he could be a good hunter with just a stick, and he was a strong young man and could help carry more meat back to the village. I enjoyed hearing the story of Loza and the ngiri, he moved his hands and arms wildly whenever he retold what happened, it was very enjoyable. Loza was proud to join the men and was also excited to take the saved skins to Teran. It was a long journey but once he navigated his way to and back with the supplies, he could then be given permission to wed Pika. Loza took his mission to meet with Teran seriously, he saw it as his proof that he can navigate life for himself and be a good husband, and he wanted to be a good husband.

I thought about the day when it might come that I might get to meet Teran, I still wanted to know what a "different kind of man" meant. I walked all day with Loza, he told me about the first long hunt he went on with the men, what it was like and what he got to experience. "It is new and exciting, different than staying back with the women" Loza told me. Loza must have felt my wondering face staring at his back as we walked, I did not even have to ask, he told me more about it. On the first night they all lay down and sleep after having walked all day, with small stops for spotting smaller animals to eat before sleeping, most of the day is made up of a fast pace, there are many animals out there but none of them wait to be hunted. Loza explained that he had to learn a new way to walk; I did not know what he meant so he explained. "See how your foot slaps onto the ground when you walk?" I stared down at my feet for a few steps, sure enough the bottom of my foot made a small clap noise when it landed.

Loza showed me that when you step with your heal and roll your foot on the outside that your step is much more quiet and less animals can hear you coming. I knew I might upset my mother if I continued with Loza longer but I was learning to become a hunter, I might even become a better hunter than Teeta, maybe even Loza himself. The back end of the pile of skins swayed as Loza walked down the path, I watched the loose ends bounce off of him and watched his leg muscles flex as he walked, I looked at my own legs, they did not indent with muscles like his. I often tried to notice many small things, I was taught as a young boy that looking for things was how you stayed safe and watched out for dangers, a skill that is a must when you grow up to become a hunter.

I watched Loza's feet as we walked, I lost focus for a moment on what he was saying until he called my name; "Ojimbo, are you listening to me?" he asked. I told him I was distracted for one moment, "when hunting you have to watch the whole world around you, you cannot get distracted" Loza explained that animals often have larger eyes and ears than us, and that makes them better at hearing or seeing than us, so we have to use better skills, which is watching and listening while walking slowly and carefully, and working together. Loza continued to tell me how some of the men would split into smaller groups to surround larger nyati or Siwalla, animals that are large or fast need extra care when hunting, some men would drive an animal to a few of the men that were waiting and hiding.

Loza told me that at night far from the village the howls and yelps of the mbwa-wmitu could be heard in the distance, they don't like the fire or people so they stay away from the village but when you take the path towards the great hill, there are many more sounds than you are used to back at home in the village. Loza's first hunting trip was several days long, Loza said that he was surprised that you could walk for so many days and still not reach the end of the world, he told me that he was surprised to see how far this path would take him and what it might be like when he reaches Teran. Teran was supposed to trade Loza for all of his skins, he was supposed to bring back bullets and hunting supplies from the trader for our hunters to use to continue to work and feed the village. I wanted to go with Loza the whole way, it was his journey but I wanted to see what other kinds of men there were. I wanted to see the great water that went on forever and I wanted to see all of the other types of animals there were in the world.

As the sun fell behind us Loza and I laid the pile of skins onto the ground, I collected some sticks for a small fire on the path for the night. Loza was fast at making a fire for us to sleep next to for the night. I had a hard time sleeping that night, the skins were soft and the air was clear but my mind went further than my body ever had. I thought about the great water, I wondered how far away that great hill was, I wondered if the world was really as big as some of the men said it was. Occasionally in the village we'll meet a traveler, some men from other tribes that ask for a place to stay and food to eat, some men have shirts or pants from other places in Africa but they just pass on through. One time a man was kicking a white ball, it looked like fun and he used his foot to kick this ball around. Teeta and I thought the man was very funny, he had a white cloth on his head and would jump about very fast to kick the small ball over and over and over, the ball did not even touch the ground, every time it came down he would kick it again and then it would go up again.

The traveling stranger let Teeta try to kick the ball to keep it in the air and Teeta did not. I had one try to kick the ball, I had watched very closely as the man was kicking the ball and when it was my turn I was ready. I kicked the ball very quickly, over and over and over. I kicked the ball a few times before the ball finally fell to the ground. I was very proud of myself, I did very well. The man was impressed at my talent and rewarded me with the very ball, he told me to continue to practice the football and to teach my friend. The man had a white cloth on his head and he wore long clothing on his body but he had two eyes, one nose, one mouth and some hair on his face, he was just a man. Teeta was jealous when the man patted my head and told me to teach my friend (Teeta).

Teeta had fun with me kicking the ball, it made be very happy that the strange man thought I was very good at it. Teeta did not like when the man told me I was very good, Teeta wanted to be better than me. I liked being told that I was better than Teeta, he jumped higher and ran faster, but I was better at the football than he was.

I wanted to ask Loza many more questions, the stars in the sky grew brighter and many many more of them appeared as the sun went away. I had a hard time sleeping, I watched the small fire send crackles and small orange flecks way up into the air as the heat warmed my feet. I strained to listen for any unfamiliar animals or different men, I was not sure of what I was supposed to be hearing but part of me was curious while another part of me was afraid. I wondered many many things that night, I wondered if I could count how many things I had learned since I was born, had I learned as much as Teeta, or Loza? Would I suddenly realize I already know the girl I might make my bride? There are a few girls in the tribe close to my age but they all stick together or with older girls that have changed.

I was curious about Teran, I wondered what others kinds of men were out there, was it like birds? Many, many kinds of birds that look different but are still birds? I hardly slept that night, Loza didn't budge, he was like a log on the ground, I wondered what else was out in the world, I thought about when it would be my turn to bring the skins to Teran, would I come straight back or perhaps keep going? I know my mother Bendu would worry, I care for her and would not want her to be sad but I could also explore during my journey and bring back even more knowledge and wisdom to her, stories of my travels or even to describe what the great water is really like. I wondered if Loza was going to miss his family on his travel to Teran, how many nights would he have to spend alone.

I was missing my mother, it was very late when my eyes finally began to close, I still felt my mind wandering from side to side but my eyelids closed anyways. The next morning I awoke to hear Loza saying my name, I forgot for one moment that I was to return to my mother and the village while he continued his journey to prove to Pika that he would be a good husband for her. I bowed my head to my chaperone and stood for a moment as he continued on towards the rising sun, the skins bouncing against his back as he walked. The hue from around Loza was magical, the orange ring that circled the sun made me feel as if I were getting older, wiser, more mature and ready to become a man myself. I stared and watched as Loza grew farther from me, I hoped he would turn and wave to thank me for keeping him company during his first day of walking, he did not.

I turned so that the sun was on my back and began walking towards my village and back to my role as a young boy. I thought a lot about when I would make the journey towards the morning sun, to meet this different kind of man named Teran. The sun rose high above me as I walked, the grasses were fading into brown while I was keeping my eyes open, looking for something to eat. I wondered if Loza was going to miss Pika, did my mother miss me? Will my interest in Loza and the journey keep me from joining the men and hunting? I wanted to see the great water; I wanted to see water go far out in front of me, like the grass, but water. One of the elder men spoke that farther down the path, past Teran and near the great water, there were boats, boats sat on the water and would take you to other lands, to see many different people, with many different looks.

I often hung on the words of the older men when they told stories, often daydreaming about what the world was like. Teeta sometimes would laugh at me, he wanted to hunt, he wanted to be a great hunter like Loza and bring back big beasts to feed our village. I always knew Teeta would make a very good hunter, we would hunt small animals in the trees or grasses by our village, he was most often the one of us to make a kill first, sometimes I could only find eggs, but it was still something for the village to eat. Sometimes Teeta would talk on and on that he had a bigger kill, how he was a better hunter or had faster legs than me, I did not like it very much sometimes. One time an elder man named Zada spoke about when he saw the great water, he said it could not be seen across, it was cold and almost as dark as the night sky, that boats looked like giant beasts that crawled across the top of the water, and that many of the men on the boats wore many different clothing.

I liked to try to imagine these giant things called boats, he said they are sometimes small but men get inside of them but are still on top of them and sometimes with sticks the push themselves through the water to move around, I was excited to see the great water. I thought about the great water as I walked back to my village after Loza carried on towards Teran, he kept the pile of hides above his shoulders; they looked heavy as his arms moved and flexed keeping them straight and from falling. Many nights passed, Teeta and I worked around the village, at nights we would make the calls of the wild dogs in the distance, we would howl and laugh while keeping the village fires behind us. Many animals hunt at night, many dangerous animals but we wanted to see some of them, we wanted to see how they hunted and then perhaps it would make us better hunters ourselves, watching one animal hunt another, you learn what you can do better. Teeta and I watched as often as we could, we would watch animals move to know when to strike them with a spear or a gun, where to shoot them and how to cut them to carry.

Hunting is a big part of our tribe; it is what the men mostly did. The woman reared the children and did so together, each child spent as much time with a lady that was not their mother as they did with their own, everyone was family and friend, it took everyone getting along together to live peacefully. The animals feed and cloth our village, we farm plants to eat as well, everybody in the village takes turns growing and doing their part to make sure that nobody feels the pains of hunger. Every child born into our village is a member of the village, a vital person to be welcomed and loved. Around the land where we have our smalls crops growing we take extra care, some of the animals like to come and eat them as well so we have to keep strings tied with tin cans around. The tin cans make loud noise when the strings are tugged and they clang together. The men also bring back logs and heavy wood for the homes that we build and live in, there is always work to be done, but there was also many large feasts and festivals that we gather around to eat and laugh together.

I liked hearing stories from Zada more than Teeta did, I liked the idea of a boat, I liked the idea of water stretching out into the sun and I liked the idea of going to strange new lands. Teeta wanted to be a hunter so very bad, there weren't enough guns for all of the men so young boys could only join the hunters when there became a gun available, except Loza, they let him join without a gun because he was a very good hunter. Loza had not been with the men all too long when he finally earned himself a rifle, it was to be waiting for him for when he returned from taking hides to Teran. My mother, she told me that Loza may not come right back, he may get to Teran and find more things that he likes and stay a while. I did not think so, he had to come back to Pika, she was the most beautiful girl in the village, next to my mother, and she was so very nice and they like each other so very much. Pika was a very good cook, she also knew very much about gardening for the crops that the village grew. Pika was excited for Loza to come back, she wanted to be his bride and when he returned we would have a big celebration.

Pika was glad Loza chose her for a wife, he was tall and very strong, he was a fast runner and very much fun. Loza played with me and Teeta when the traveling man brought the white ball for us to kick with our feet. Pika and Loza looked at each other a lot as they passed in the village, out village is not very big but there is room for everyone. The children are in charge of helping to collect fuel for the fire, the women clean the huts and everyone helps with the elders, most elders move into the hut with their child and their family; we all take care of each other. I have crossed paths with many people on my journey and not all of them are very kind like Pika and Loza, some of them were not very nice at all. Teeta and I looked forward to being able to join the men, we wanted to make our mothers proud and make the men proud. Sometimes the men would all join together for one big hunt when the nyati were near, it is a large animal and they take several men to bring all of the meat back to the village, sometimes half of the men would bring back one animal while the rest hunted another and then they would bring that back also, many many times the men would see so many nyati that they could feed the whole village forever.

Teeta and me always wanted to join the men, when I followed Loza toward the morning sun I asked him what some of the hunts were like, he told me that a lot of the time it was a lot of walking, some men would go in different directions to see what they could find, sometimes there would be animals near one water or another, then some of the men would take cover in the tall grass and aim their rifles or ready their spears. Sometimes the men would only shoot a small animal, and eat it among them because there wasn't enough to bring back to the village for everyone. The men would scavenge for small animals to feed themselves along the hunt but when they finally found something large enough to feed the village, they cut it up well enough to carry and then they would make their way back to the village with their bounty. My mother always told me to be thankful to those who do work for you, the men killed to feed everyone, and we always thanked them.

# CH. 3

Loza was away for many days, three weeks maybe went by before he was seen coming back with the morning sun behind him. Pika was most glad to see him and upon his return, we had a celebration for him. Loza earned his place with the hunters for sure, everyone was glad to see him. Teeta wanted to be missed so much too, he wanted to come back and for everybody in the village to come running to him. Teeta would take a big breath in and make his chest big and walk slow and swing his arms every time he would talk about coming back from his journey. Teeta talked about when he would take his journey, joining the hunts was only part of becoming a man, the bigger part was taking the journey to Teran, doing what was needed of you for the village was the way everyone was brought up, when you take the journey to meet Teran, you find the man inside of you. You take the hides to Teran to trade for supplies and from there you decide if you turn around and go back to the village right away or spend time further exploring.

Teeta always talked about carrying the biggest load of hides to Teran of all the loads, he always talked about getting the biggest muscles and being the strongest of the village and that he would run all the way to Teran and drop off the hides and then run all the way back, all in one day, he was funny. I wasn't so certain that I was going to be in a hurry to go back, Teeta was going to be a good hunter, he would be joining the men before me so there would not be so much need for me to join them right away. Teeta did not understand why I wanted to explore the world; he did not understand why I did not want to join the men quickly to hunt. My mother tried to explain to me how large our world is, she tell me that there are as many people in this world as there were stars in the sky. I had a hard time believing her, she was my mother and never tried to trick me, she was very smart but it was hard for me to think of so many people. I watched the grass wave back and forth when then light winds blew, the tips of the grass seemed to turn silver as bent to touch the grass they were close to and when most of the grass was blowing, I tried to imagine if they were all people instead.

In the far far distance on clear mornings the big mountain could sometimes be seen if we traveled for a while, sometimes we would travel out to find supplies for our village, stuff to repair our homes or to go to the trees to bring back more wood for the fire, we were always walking, I liked the sun on my face and the wind on my fingertips. A lot of the time I would keep my arms spread out like a ndege (he flapped his arms like a bird) and run my fingers along the grass tops. My mother would shout ahead to me and tell me that she did not remember finding me in an egg. Teeta would flap his arms to joke at me but then I would run in large circles like the animals above and I would call out, many others would laugh when I do this. I liked my life, I loved my mother and Teeta, I loved that older boys like Loza were fun to be around. I loved that most nights, when the sun sank in to the far away and the night bought out many different sounds, that that was when I was at the most peace. I knew my place in my village, but not in the world, I knew that nothing would ever be so simple or comfortable in my life as it all was when I was a young child and could run to my mother and she would make it all safe for me.

*We sat in my flat for the better part of the morning; Ojimbo liked talking about his childhood, and especially about his mother. Every time Ojimbo spoke about things from his youngest of days he would re-live them, he would smile largely while recanting his tale. I wanted to capture as much of what Ojimbo had to say as well as follow his journey to where he was now, on my couch, bouncing up and down as he spoke. I had to begin to plot out the midday meal for myself and my guest, I often just assume to dine out on Saturdays, get a window booth and gaze among the passersby but I didn't want to stray far from my laptop in order to continue to chronicle Ojimbo's travels. I warmed the skillet and poached some eggs while Ojimbo continued to tell me his tale. I was still dumbfounded how a small village kid from somewhere south in the sub-Congo area of Africa was plopped down here in the heart of the Queen's jewel, I'm not even sure Churchill traveled that much, at least not as young.*

Teeta finally had his dream come true, we were still both sort of young boys a few years ago but one of the men could not return to hunting. Binbe had injured his ankle on a hunt and even long after, he had troubles walking on it. Binbe was off with two other men when the crossed paths with nguruwe-mwitu, it was protecting its babies when the three man group followed it through some of the thick brush. Two of the men were going to come up on it while it began to defend itself from Binbe. Binbe was stepping backwards to ready to spear the angry animal when he stepped into a small animal hole in the dirt. Binbe fell backwards and almost broke his foot off. The men had to help Binbe out of the hole after spearing the animal; Binbe was almost more injured by the mean teeth of the animal as it charged for him. The two other men dragged Binbe and the animal all the way back to the village; it was not a triumphant hunt that day. The men could not leave Binbe alone, when there is fresh blood around the duma come around, they are very mean and want the animal you killed, they will attack  you for it if you do not build a fire or keep guard.

It took a whole day and a night to get Binbe back to the tribe, the men pulled on his foot so it faced the right way and braced it with some sticks and long grass to tie it back together, but he could not walk on it for many weeks. Everyone took care of Binbe, when it was my turn to help him with his days he would tell me about his favorite hunts. Binbe's favorite hunts were the herds of Nyati, the large groups of beasts would thunder down the lands, thrash and climb through the streams and kick up large dirt clouds that it looked like the plains were on fire. I had seen a few of the great herd migrations, they swarmed like birds in a flock or bugs in a pile, so many of them and they run for so long. Binbe told me that often times the weak ones might fall in the herd, it was easy to pick up the ones that died but you also had other predators out to eat also, so it was much better to let the mean animals eat the dead ones and to hunt a stray animal further away to keep the duma or fisi away, animals with mean teeth were much better hunters, no good fighting them for meat.

My mother told me that all animals need to eat, when we hunt we take the food away from another animal, if we hunt another animal we take away another animals food again, if we were not careful and we take away too much food, then we might become food when other mean animals don't get enough to eat also. There had to be a balance to everything we did, if we took too many trees for our homes or wood for our fires we wouldn't have enough for shade or food or for protection from the mud when the rains came. I listened a lot to my mother Bendu, she knew a lot of things. I was going to miss Teeta when he went and became a hunter, I was left behind. Teeta was always faster than me, had longer legs than me and when we were out collecting food or any of our other duties, we had different dreams than each other. I wanted to see the great water so very much, Teeta wanted to be the best hunter anyone had ever seen, he even joked about hunting a great tembo, one so large that our village could eat for a lifetime.

No village hunted the great tembo, they took a very long time to grow and have babies, if even one was hunted, it would change the entire herd and the small herd might die off. The great big animal could be heard from many kilometers away, they had long noses that swung around when they walked and they also used it to move branches or to pick up food to eat. The tembo had great big feet and they would step on plants or leave big holes in small muddy patches in the dirt. Our small tin can alarms hardly deterred the tembo, sometimes when one of the animals was hungry, they would ignore our alarms to keep them away and they would reach in with their long noses and pick some of our food.

The men shared stories of crawling through the tall grass to get close to animals, spending many nights in different areas near a small fire with Siwalla or kima on the fire, just enough food to feed them for the day. Binbe told me about his father, a great hunter named Misu. Misu was known to hunt with a very long spear; it was longer than his own body. Misu could run and throw his spear and take down a mbuzi of kondoo from very far away. "Many animals don't see as well if you throw a spear form the angle of the sun, it blinds them" Misu said to Binbe on their first night out hunting together. Binbe had always wanted to join his father in the hunts and he finally had his chance. The next morning while on a hunt Misu was walking with his long spear, Binbe was trying to see over the tall grass but it was difficult. Misu stopped walking and told

Binbe to stop moving too, Binbe did not understand why his father was keeping him still.

Misu told Binbe to turn around and head back towards the rest of the men and to go quickly and not to look back. Binbe saw the terror in his eyes, he was afraid and it made Binbe afraid. Misu began to shout at the grass and swing his long spear, the "swoosh" sounds made Binbe more afraid, he turned to look to see if his father was coming behind him, he was not. Binbe turned to watch a large angry simba leap from the grass and land on his father, knocking him to the ground. Misu tried to kick and scream until the angry beast stopped clawing at him but it did not work. Binbe said he was so afraid that he could not move. The simba were around, many times you could see them just meters from where you were, and they were never really a problem as long as you knew not to play with them. Binbe watched in terror as the simba bit and clawed at his father, the dirt ran red with all of his father's blood. The face of the simba wore his father's blood and it finally stopped killing him. Binbe was terrified, he froze in shock, not from fear of the simba, but in horror of what was happening to his father.

The simba did not wait around that long; it circled Misu a few times and then returned to the grass, leaping almost silently into the grass. Binbe heard the voices of the other men coming to see what the shouting was all about. Binbe did not respond to his own name right away, he said he was just frozen and watched as the simba took his father. Binbe was not much older than me when he watched his father die. The simba was hungry and it had to eat, Binbe was very sad to lose Misu and also he understood that there was nothing he could do. Binbe picked up his father's spear and began practicing how to throw it, he could never throw it as far as Misu could but he still liked hunting with it sometimes. Binbe's story made me sad to hear,

I worried about Teeta hunting because I wanted for him to be ok. Binbe told me that he hunted more and more, he was always watching for that simba in the grass, the one that hunted hunters.

I talked to Binbe more than when it was just my turn to help him in his days. I wanted to know everything he saw on hunts, I wanted to know if he had ever seen the great water or climbed the big mountain in the distance.  Binbe said when he was my age, before he joined the hunters that he had taken to his own journey, he stood on top of a big hill and for a whole day, he looked around the horizon. Binbe wanted to see every direction in all of the lights before deciding which way to start walking. Binbe walked towards the big mountain, he walked for days and days, he ate, slept, and everything else while walking towards the big mountain. Binbe walked for many many days to get close to the big mountain, he said that as he got closer and closer, it took up more and more of what he could see.

Binbe did not climb the mountain, he got close and when it touched the sky where he could no longer see the top, he felt he saw enough of it. Binbe found peace in his time walking to the big mountain, he also found it funny that from far away everyone just called it a big mountain but if they lived closer they might call it a giant mountain. Binbe liked walking for a very long time, he knew his legs were strong, his hunting skills were getting better and that he had a family back at the village that cared for him. Binbe missed his father, he decided that while he walked he would still talk to him, like he was there with him, it made him feel better. Binbe cried and felt sorry that he could not help his father when the simba killed him. Binbe was angry with himself that he froze in the eyes of the beast; he could not have been that great of a hunter if he froze. Binbe was sorry to his father, he was angry with himself but not with the simba. The simba was only doing what it knew, it killed for food or to protect itself, animals only do what they know to do, they could not be blamed for being animals.

Eventually Binbe forgave himself, he walked through the great plains, passed the big mountain and when he returned to the village, he was a man and ready to take a wife. Binbe had been with the hunters for many years, he had many successful hunts and he knew that someday the time might come where he wouldn't be able to hunt any more. Teeta thanked Binbe for the chance to join the hunters, Binbe was glad to see a good hunter go and join his friends. Binbe knew that to be a good hunter with the rest that they all had to work together, in hunting and cleaning the animals, everyone in the village works together. The first animal Teeta killed on his very first hunt was a ndege (a small bird) and some of the men laughed because he told them all he was going to be such a great hunter. Some of the men knew not to laugh, most of the men had small animals that they hunted and food was food, but some laughed at Teeta anyways. Teeta did not like being laughed at until he remembered many of the times he laughed at me for things, like having shorter legs, and he laughed with the men, it was still food.

When Teeta came back from his first hunt he was so excited, the men carried back meat from a few small animals for the village to eat. Teeta strutted around and talked about some of the animals he had hunted; many of the women sat around the fire and compared his stories to some of the stories from the other men on their first hunts too. Teeta did not listen to the laughter, he was finally being taken as a man and he liked it very much. Teeta sat by me and told me that someday I would be a man too; he put his arm across my shoulders and pulled me side to side as he laughed. I told Teeta

50

that someday I would be a man too and that I would travel and explore the great water and maybe see many different kinds of men. Teeta told me that there were great beasts to be hunted in the great water and that hunting was our roles as men, well his as a man and mine when I became one. I did not find Teeta as funny as he did, he had a big laugh when he was making jokes at me but that was just Teeta.

Mmsu was one of the older hunters, he was finding himself more tired after long hunts as well as unable to carry as much meat as he used to when he was younger. Each of the men can feel in their bodies when it is time to let one of the eager boys become one of the hunting men. Each man knew when it was time to return back to the village and help the woman with the field work and let the younger men haul and clean the large animals and large amounts of meat to feed the entire village. Mmsu had gray hair on his head; he had deep wrinkles around his forehead and eyes and spoke more quietly than most of the other men. Mmsu was glad to speak with me, he wanted to share much of his knowledge and his stories he was fond of. I told Mmsu that I was excited to get to hunt with Teeta when it was my turn to go out to Teran and then return. Mmsu enjoyed his last few hunts and counted down until it was no longer required of him.

Teeta and I grew, he wasn't with the hunting group for very long before it was his turn to go and meet Teran with the hides. Mmsu was getting older, he was willing to show me the ways of the men while Teeta was to be gone and then when Teeta returned, me and him, we would hunt together. I wanted to hunt with Teeta, he was my good friend and he wanted to be a great hunter. I wanted to gather many hides and when it was finally my turn to follow the path that lead to the rising sun, I would have many skins to haul to Teran, and then I would finally get to meet the different kind of man.

Mmsu was willing to share with me all of the skills he had learned while hunting, he also wanted to tell me about all of his favorite memories of his life, he liked to talk.

The night of the celebration was a great feast, everyone ate until their bellies were full. The sun went on its journey far far away and each member of the tribe sat around and told stories. Some of the men told of Teeta and his first official kill. Teeta was unsteady with his rifle, there were not so many rifles that the boys get much practice, so when it was time for Teeta to take his place in the hunting group, he too had to learn how to shoot. Nga was the leader of the hunting group; he was a strong man with a wide chest. Nga handed Teeta his rifle, he told Teeta how to look down the top and put the small point at the far end, on what he was going to shoot. Teeta took aim; Nga raised his arms up to show everyone what Teeta had done. Nga made his hands shake to show everyone that Teeta's hands shook while I was getting ready to shoot. Teeta crossed his arms and mumbled that his hands did not shake like that.

Many of the other men began to laugh; Nga paused for a moment and told them to hush while he tells the story. Nga raise his arms back up, he told everyone that he counted in Teeta's ear and when it was time for the right shot of the beast. Teeta pulled the trigger. Nga stood next to Teeta, as he told Teeta when to pull the trigger and kill the beast; he heard the big bang of the gunshot. One moment Teeta was standing next to Nga, and the next minute, no Teeta. Teeta stood up and tried to speak very loudly that Nga's story was not true and that no one should listen to his tale. Nga continued speaking that Teeta was so shaky when he tried to shoot that the rifle shoved him to the ground, his eyes began to look at each other as Nga stood over him to make sure he was OK.

Nga almost fell over because he laughed very hard. Everyone sitting around the fire let out very loud laughs, everyone, except Teeta. Teeta sat with his arms crossed; he did not find it as funny as everyone else. Nga bent his wrists and held them to his chest and turned his head back and forth and made a funny face with his mouth down and eyes small. Teeta jumped to his feet: "finish the story, finish the story" Teeta shouted as he tried to make everyone stop laughing at him. Nga moved his hands up and down to get everyone to quiet down a little so he could finish telling his story. Nga continued to tell that the big Siwalla jumped away, the gunshot had scared it and as the men neared where the animal stood, Ziza, another man in the hunting group, he stopped all of the men.

Nga was trying to reassure Teeta that no one can shoot that well the first time, Teeta was too mad to listen, he wanted to be a great hunter and that was that, he was very unhappy that he did not make a successful kill on his first shoot and he did not take it well. Ziza popped up from the grass; "Hooray the mighty hunter Teeta" he exclaimed with great joy. Ziza raised his arms up and in his one hand, was a small ndege (a bird) he found it in the grass, it was small enough to fit into his hand but Teeta shot and killed it off the back of the Siwalla. Teeta raised his arms as Ziza showed everyone how small the ndege was, Teeta shooed his hands towards Ziza and everyone began to laugh again. Teeta raised his hands high into the air, he raised his head to look up and then threw his arms down to his sides, he did not find the story funny and did not like everyone laughing at him but it was very funny.

Nga honored Teeta, he finished the story of his great first shot killing a small bird, it was a moment later when the men were still laughing and shaking the small animal that Teeta raised his rifle one more time; the men stopped laughing right away. Teeta fired, the men were fast to cover their ears and scattered away from the barrel of the gun as it thundered out a cloud of smoke. Nga said that when he looked at what

Teeta had shot, he watched an even larger Siwalla stop running and then collapse. Teeta smiled so very big, he shot the animal as it was running and sure enough, Teeta became a great hunter. The men all patted Teeta on the back for a great shot. Teeta told the men that he shot the ndege on purpose; he wanted to show them how good of a shot that he was. The men skinned the animal while Teeta watched, he knew how to but he was so happy and out of honor, the men cleaned his first kill for him. The group brought the large amount of meat back and that is what leads to the large feast for everyone in honor of Teeta joining the hunting party.

I think about that night of the feast for Teeta's first hunt, everyone patted him on the back and told him he did a good job. Teeta was not very happy about Nga telling everybody about the bird but it was quickly forgiven. My mother always told me that forgiving was like letting go of a big rock you carry around, once done you no longer are burdened with it. Ziza whistled out the call of a bird each time Teeta would stand up or start to talk, Teeta would look at him and scowl, Ziza would whistle louder and open his big white eyes and stare back. It was a very fun night, everyone worked together to get hides stretched to ready them for Teran and the night drifted away. Ziza knew that Teeta did not find him very funny, he did not like Ziza always staring at him with his big white eyes, Teeta did not like the attention. The hunters knew that when a new hunter would join the group, like me, then Ziza would turn his focus on the new hunter and that Teeta would then find him funny.

I miss my family very much, I miss my mother and I miss my friends. When I arrived in England I was greeted very nicely, everyone wanted to know who I was and why I had come. I have come a long way from everything that I knew when I was a boy and I want to return to there very soon. I spend a great deal of time remembering and missing my mother, she was always very wise and comforting when she spoke to me and I love her very much. I look very forward to the day when I get to tell her all of my adventures from my travels as a man. I miss my warm sun back home, here it is very grey very much and the air is very cold. The food has new tastes, the chips I have eaten are mushy and taste very good but I miss the skin warming sun very high in the sky and the tips of the grass on my outstretched fingers.

The next day Teeta told me all about hunting, he told me like he told the much younger boys that had never hunted before, I had to tell him many times that I was a man like him and knew how to hunt, I just had to wait until there was a rifle so I could join the hunting men. Teeta stood much taller, he made sure to stand tall when he was by me so it made me feel smaller. I did not like that Teeta talked to me like a small boy, I was happy for him but did not like the way he spoke to me. I told Teeta about Binbe telling me stories about Misu. Binbe gave Teeta his rifle and let him into the group of men.

I talked about Misu getting married, about him traveling and seeing the great water and the giant hill, and walking for days upon days and passing some of the many different kinds of men. Teeta told me that men hunt, and only boys wanted to see the world. I wanted to stand on top of the great big mountain in the distance and see half way around the world. I wanted to see what the great water was like and how it tasted. Teeta did not agree that having a big adventure would be all that much fun, I told him he was wrong and that it would be a great adventure. Misu told Binbe about going off and seeing much of the land, he traded furs with a man named Foral, he spoke different than everyone in the village, he had hair on his upper lip and when he spoke it sounded like he had food in his mouth.

Teeta did not understand my desire to travel, the ndege had wings and could fly anywhere in the world they wanted to, the Siwalla were very fast runners and could jump very high, many people in my village never left, sometimes a few of the women would go together with one of the men to show them the way, they would spend a few weeks making the journey to and from the trader, they would go in small groups and slowly take in information about what they saw or heard on their way to get more supplies for the village. No one really left the village, few men were gone for long stretches as some wandered off in search of new watering holes of supply paths, others were not gone very long, nobody really left, they always returned back to the village, some with interesting stories and others without.

Teeta told me that I should be the man that could guide the wandering women to and from Teran's, sometimes he would tell me that I could join them when one of the men could take us. I did not laugh when Teeta would tell me to only think about hunting, it was for me to think of what I wanted to think about. When it was Teeta's turn to take the hides to Teran he was sure he going to make it there and back in no time at all. There was a small moment I thought about joining my friend like I did with Loza but I did not want to slow him down on his travels. The boys are not allowed to join the women when they go to Teran, the boys must make the journey alone and prove that they can navigate the world by themselves, like a man.

I could not wait to see Teran, to meet this strange mysterious man I had only heard a little about. When a boy sets off down the path that leads to the rising sun, he is simply told to follow the path and take the small path on the right at the end of the first day; that was where I left Loza behind when I headed back to my village and he to his destination. Loza and

Pika were very happy, they were never far away from one another unless Loza was hunting, and then Pika would be sad and miss for him. Each time a boy set out to Teran, Teeta and I would talk about when we went, Teeta talked very much about coming back fast and being a man that got to hunt for the village rather than a small farmer with the women and elderly men of the village. Me and Teeta spoke about some of the previous men that had gone to trade the hides, how each got their turn and at different ages than what we would when it was out turn. I wanted to hunt with Teeta, he was my best friend and it would be much fun. When Teeta left to hunt I found myself learning much more, I did not have him to play with so I visited with more people and listened to more of what they had to say. In Teeta's absence I found myself a little different, I felt a little more grown up.

I dreamed that I would make it to the great water and peer out into the forever and see what called to me. Loza returned quickly because he had Pika to return to, he spoke briefly about Teran and what happened there but he wanted to be beside the woman that became his wife. I couldn't wait for my turn to carry a big pack of skins and head off to the morning sun. Most men return and talk about the walk, there were hardly discussions about the destination; it was always about the walk. Men described walking for many days, through tall grasses, through a jungle of trees, seeing many animals along the way and having to search for food. The biggest part of the trip was the journey itself, Teran's was just a small building with many things inside, he took the hides even further for what he needed as the traveler turned around and headed towards the afternoon sun and back to the village.

When Loza returned he ran to greet Pika, she was very glad to see him, each day when he was missing from her, she would walk down the path a little to try and see out in the distance if he was within sight, her mother would yell to her to let him become a man by himself. One time Pika shouted back: "if he could become a man without a woman, why did a woman have to give birth to him?" most of the village stopped at the same time, many people could be seen thinking about what she had said. Pika's mother did not wait too long before responding: "yes, only a woman can give birth to a man, but if a man doesn't realize he needs a woman, he becomes stupid and does not learn respect or appreciation for the woman and then treats them poorly." Pika shrugged her shoulders and thought about what she had heard, her mother was not wrong and she had chores to do.

I had heard what was shouted to Pika, about how men need to learn to respect a woman. Loza spat a mouth full of water on Pika many times when we were boys, he would smile right after and even though she would not be laughing or think it was very funny, she knew he was playing and maybe even showing off for the younger boys, like me and Teeta. Loza knew that once he decided to make Pika his bride that he would treat her differently, they had a loving relationship together but it was after his journey that it was much more respectful between them. Loza took his time to be gone, he wanted to truly miss Pika when he was gone, not just miss her a little but to spend enough time away that he could feel it in his heart that he was meant to be with her. Loza knew that he would be leaving Pika plenty whenever he would go out with the men and hunt, he wanted each time he came back to her, to be just like when he returned from his journey and that their love be strong and true, not in a hurry and not thought out.

Teeta did not spend as long exploring our world as many of the elders suggested him too. I got to join the men on two hunts before Teeta returned. I walked beside Nga and Ziza as we headed towards the big mountain, I was a little afraid to get to grow up and join the men; I wanted to be a boy for a while longer. When I was a boy, me and my good friend Teeta would play with sticks and not have to worry for weeks or even years, as I get older I have more that I have to worry about, it is less fun. On the first hunt we walked for a long ways, there was a big amount of Siwalla and ndege far away; we were to hunt many of them for the hides and to bring back plenty of food for the village. Ziza crawled beside me as we snuck up on some of the animals we were going to shoot, I locked my eyes on the animal, I was nervous. I did not have a gun with me because when a boy becomes a man, he spends a hunting trip helping the men while the newest man to hunt goes to trade the skins. As I was watching the men I held very still, I was told to be quiet and still so I did not scare away the animals.

I felt something brush my ear, I slowly brought my shoulder to my ear to swat at what it was and then I felt it again. I tried to make the itchy tickle go away from my ear but it continued to fly by my ear. Suddenly something landed *IN* my ear, it felt like a big bug flew into my ear hole; I swung my head to try and begin to swat away the bug that was trying to fly into my ear. I began to be scared, I did not want a bug in my ear but was trying to be most very still, I let my head down and brought my hand up to begin to paw at my ear to get the bug out and I felt the prickly brush hit my hand. Ziza was using a piece of grass to tickle my ear when I was not watching, he laughed a little but I did not. Ziza always tried to play, he was always laughing, even if nobody else did. Ziza sometimes likes to drop pieces of grass or small seeds on people's heads to see how long before they catch him, Nga does not tolerate Ziza and his tricks but he will smirk break a smile when Ziza picks on the younger boys, especially when there is a big pile of seeds and grasses on someone's head and they do not know about it.

My second hunting trip was much better than the first; we returned back to the village for only a day before heading back out. When we came back I knew that Teeta would not have arrived back but I had to walk around and ask some of our friends just in case he really did make it out and back within a day like he bragged that he would. When we went back out we had a much more fun and much better hunt, we headed in another direction to find the animals we needed to provide food for the village. When I came back from my second hunt, Teeta was already there. Teeta did not like missing a hunt, he wanted to be back in time to go back out with the men and take his position back up with the other hunters. During the few days before we all went back out on a hunt together, I peppered Teeta with questions about his travels.

Teeta did not like that I asked him so many questions, he knew I was wanting to go out and meet Teran myself, I wanted to see the great water and he knew that, but he did not understand why. When we were small, Teeta and I would raise our arms out and pretend we could fly, we would run down the paths of our village or through the tall grasses the surrounded, I wanted to fly real high and look down on the people or the animals, I thought Teeta wanted it too. Even as we all packed up and headed out to our hunt, it was the first time me and Teeta would be out on the same hunt together with the men, I still asked him what it was like.

I often think about the first night me and Teeta were out with the big hunting group, I kept asking him what it was like to get so far away from the village, what it felt like to walk for so long and know that he could keep going. I asked him if he was excited about making it to Teran and if he even thought about keeping going. Teeta was pretty quiet about his travel, he said that the men told him that it was during the travel that you find out what kind of man you are, the walking gives you time to find peace with yourself. Teeta said that he had time to figure out what kind of man he wanted to be. Teeta said that the hides grew heavy, sometimes he couldn't keep carrying them and needed to stop for a moment, he did not like that they grew so heavy, "Loza would not have put them down" he said to himself, and that was when it hit him, he wasn't Loza.

Teeta left in a hurry to endure his journey to become a man, he wanted to run full speed to Teran and back and magically be welcomed as a man and be the image he idolized since he was a young boy with me. Teeta came back and was much more quiet about himself, he did not speak as much and I wondered if perhaps he saw the men as more quiet and wanted to be like them, or if maybe he just did not speak to me as much because he still saw me as a boy while he was a man. Teeta followed the same path as many of the men before him, his feet touched the same dirt and his eyes saw the same sights. I wanted to feel different dirt, see different images and animals and touch many different things with my fingers, and my heart. I love ,my friend Teeta, we grew together like brothers and I wanted many more things for him than he wanted for himself, but he was not easy to tell him things because he thought he knew more than me.

Teeta did not come back looking very different, he did not change his looks or even stand taller like Loza or anything. I only noticed some of his quiet and wondered what he had seen. Teeta spoke very little about his journey before we went out to hunt, and during he told me that the days seemed very much longer going to Teran than they did coming home. I did not know what to think about what Teeta said, I just remembered it. Teeta told me that after a long day of walking alone and having to find your own food, you appreciate being able to get the help of others, he missed the village a little but he was also sure he was going to keep up a steadfast pace and hurry back.

I wondered what kinds of things I would further learn about my own self. I already learned long ago that even though Teeta was my best friend that we did not agree on everything. I learned from watching Loza and Pika that being apart can make a loving couple, love more. I learned patients from my mother, she always told me to take a deep breath before doing something, sometimes a second deep breath if it might be something important. In my life I have learned how good people are, in my village, everyone takes care of each other and we all work together. In my travels I have since learned that not everyone is as good as they can be, or should be. I remember laying in the grass and staring into the night sky, I wondered what more I could learn when I went to Teran on my own, I got to join in one hunt when Teeta returned, then I would have to go back to waiting until a rifle became ready to open up a place for me.

I thought about all the many paths that I could walk, I could walk towards the afternoon sun and have no idea where I would end up, and what if I made it to Teran and kept going to the big water, then from there maybe find another path. I knew I wanted to take my place with the men that hunted, I wanted to be one of the men that brought back food for the village and get to walk back to the village and be greeted by everyone smiling at the meat we carried and then sit around a fire and tell stories of our trip. I stared up and the dark night sky and pictured all of the different animals in the distance, I wondered if they knew what path they took, or if in the rumble of the herd, they just followed any path they could run down.

On my own walk I thought about animals, did the great herds know of being alone or were they just in the big group because that was all they knew? Did any of the younger
62

animals think about getting away from the herd and exploring on their own or did they just hide within the safety of the herd? Many animals stayed in large groups, some in small groups but not many lived alone, some that did like snakes, did not move very much to explore the world, and did a snake really need to see the great world around them when they lived so closely to the ground?

I began walking to Teran, I wasn't sure where I was going and that was half of the purpose of the walk, if I were to become a man I would have to figure out my own way. I was scared and afraid and had many feelings inside of me. I thought about Teeta a lot, I thought about when we were small children and playing in the tall grass or making the noises that many animals did. I walked for many days, it was a long journey and it was very hard. I had a different walk than anyone else did, I had a heavy heart and many things weighing on my mind.

I spent a great deal of time on my own, I knew I had my village back home to think about and the smart words of my mother to keep me brave when I was feeling scared. There were days I was so focused on walking that I forgot to eat, not eating after a day of walking made it very hard to sleep at night. The nights were very hard for me, I had visions of Teeta in my head, the late night howls from the darkness made me uneasy and also kept me awake in the night. I did not know how to feel after I began my walk, it was my walk that I had looked forward to when I was younger, but everything was different. I walked for many long days, most days the sun kept me warm and sometimes the land kept me fed, I felt the ground below my feet as I walked but I did not feel my body most of the days. I walked and walked, I passed many animals in the distance, past water, past, trees, past the views of big hills and the great mountain in the far away distance. I did not know what I was searching for but I continued to walk.

I began to see other people, people I did not recognize, there were clothes that were different and the further I walked; the more and more people I saw. I stayed one night just away from where I found there to be many people moving about, I decided I would enter the town in the morning. In the morning I continued to walk towards the town, I had heard from some of the elders that there were places that men could go to that would feed travelers if they stopped in and asked for it, I could see many big homes, many of them were bigger than the tembo and I looked for the sign the elders spoke about, I was very hungry. There were many people walking around, looking at me as I walked closer to where many of the people were. There were very many people around, some walked down the large wide paths, others stood near buildings to watch as other people bustled with their days. I was unsure of many of the things I began to see, but I was on my journey.

I did not know where I was, I did not know what all of the people were doing but many of them moved about, all over the place, some of them spoke but I did not understand what their words were. I saw the cross on a building that I was told about, it had a round ceiling and a cross on top, I knew that there was a place that I could find a meal and maybe someone that I could understand and talk to. The building was brown, light in some places, dark in others, it was not very big but I still hoped that there were things to eat inside. I did not know what to do, I knew that being afraid and still doing what I had to, was part of being the man.

A man walked out of the door of the building I decided was the one I was looking for, I decided to walk around the building a few times before beginning tell myself that I should sit on the seat by the side. I wanted to look around and see more but I was tired and hungry from a very hard journey. The man was wearing long dark clothing, he let a wind out of his nose when he looked at me, I was covered in dirt, the red tint on my legs looked like long socks. I felt my hands tremble, and my mouth was so very dry. The man in the long clothing walked over to where I was seated, the sun was high and growing hot when he tried to speak to me. His lips moved but I did not know the words he spoke. I watched the man and as his lips parted, wiggled and strange words came out, I waited until he spoke

The man sat down next to me, he continued to speak until I recognized him say "this?" he was speaking some of the languages that he could speak until he found one that I could understand. The man did not speak so understandably but I got most of what he meant. My mother always told me that I might meet new people in my life and I looked forward to it, but I was struggling to understand but still very willing to try. The man told me his name was Father Shumbin, he was in charge of the small church, he liked to help people and he often met new people that came across his door. Father Shumbin was very friendly, he had new food for me to eat, he called it a sandwich, the bread was dry and so was my mouth, but it did not matter, I was very hungry.

Father Shumbin was very nice to me, he gave me clothes and then explained how to straighten up my pants or button my shirt, clothes I did not have back in the village. I had to learn a lot from the Father, I stayed at the church for a few days, the Father showed me around the town, there were markets where you could trade paper slips called money for items like clothing or food, it was all very interesting things to see. I had never seen so many different foods in the market, we grew many back home in the village but there were so many foods and so many colors. I did not like to wear the shirt for a while, it was strange to have to button the shirt and then have the collar choking on my neck. Shoes were very strange, I could not feel the dirt beneath my feet, I could not wiggle my toes and it made walking very hard. The roads were hard packed, the hard dirt made my feet hurt to walk on, Shumbin showed me so many things that I had never seen before.

Father Shumbin showed me a television box, it was a small black box that had a hard wall on it that made pictures change over and over again, and it was most interesting to me. There were many people, everyone seemed to be in a rush or have some place to go, I never felt the hurry when I was back in the village, everyone worked, everyone worked together to support each other. In the town I watched people walk into one another, and not apologize; many people were just in a hurry. Father Shumbin taught me how to help him clean the church, the long wood benches needed to be cleaned and I was glad to work for the food I ate and the bed he let me sleep in. Father Shumbins wife was named Arbroa, she was very pretty and very nice, she did not speak my language but she smiled very much and brought me food to eat when I was hungry.

Father Shumbin let me work for my food while I stayed, I was glad to work for him. I learned how to clean the floors and clean my clothes with his small machine that he had. I tried many new foods, his wife Arbroa cooked very good, it was very tasty and I thanked her very much. I learned many new things in my first few days with Father Shumbin, he explained to me what the bathroom was for and told me how to work a shower, the water fell from a wall and it was much warm, this was very new. In the evening we would sit and I would tell him the story of how I came to his church, I told him about hearing about Teran and wanting to go there. Father Shumbin did not know Teran but he did know a man with a truck and that he could take me to a bigger town, I saw some motor vehicles and was a little nervous to ride in it to anywhere. Father Shumbin and Arbroa were really interested in my journey, I was not where I was supposed to be and my path to get to them was very hard, but I told them all about it.

There was much more noise in the night in that town, there were motor vehicle noises all around, and they moved so fast. I could hear people coming and going outside, all night. In my village most everyone slept when it was dark, it was quiet and calm and the only real sounds that you could hear were of the animals and the nature around you. I missed my friends, I missed my village, and most of all, I missed my mother. My mother always told me that when I journeyed out to become a man that I should stay away longer than I thought I should, she said once I missed her so much that I wanted to cry, that was when I knew I wasn't gone long enough. I did not understand what she meant, I thought that missing someone was proof that you should be with them, but I also have come to know that missing someone, is different than just being without them. I loved my mother and being back at my village but I also know that I do not miss them because I am alone, I miss them because they are all my family and I would like to go back to them, after my journey is complete, not before.

It was hard for me to sleep those first few nights at the church, the new place was very new and I was not used to it. I had a straw bed back at home, we would lay down a layer of grass to soften lying on the dirt and we would lay a cloth over us to keep away the biting bugs. The church had a mattress that was like a few blankets lay on one another, it was nice and soft but different. Arbroa was very nice to me, I did not understand her much when she talked to me but Father Shumbin was very nice and tell me what she said. Arbroa was a young girl when she first met Shumbin, she wanted to help in the church and he liked her very much also. Father Shumbin and Arbroa had met many many people traveling through their town and it was their job to help the tired travelers. Many travelers, Father Shumbin told me, were from small villages, just like me, others were from different parts of the continent. I did not understand what a continent was.

Father Shumbin found a round ball, much like the one the traveler gave to me and Teeta, but it had colors on it. Father Shumbin called his round ball a "globe" and spent most of a day teaching me that the world was a great big ball. I did not understand how it was a ball; we had the skies above our heads and the land below our feet. I spent many nights telling father Shumbin and his wife Arbroa about my life in the village and about wanting to travel, he told me that with the globe, I could see where I wanted to go and even find out how I might get there. Father Shumbin showed me a picture on the globe of the great water; it was very very big on the very small globe. Arbroa was very kind to run into another room and bring big pieces of paper; father Shumbin called for more and more maps.

Each map had different lines and squiggles; some were blue, green brown, some black and white or red. I did not understand what all of the colors meant; he slowly explained how to look at a map and what I was looking at. It took me most of a night to begin to understand, none of it made sense for a very long time but with my church friends trying to help me, I slowly began to understand. There were sometimes new people coming into the church, some women came in, wearing long dresses, and they would cry or others would come in, sit alone and then wave their hands across their chest and bow their heads down. I did not understand what the visitors wanted but the Father explained that people came in to pray and have their prayers heard. I did not understand who was hearing their prayers but Father Shumbin reassured me that prayer was for a lot of things inner strength and inner healing; I was still very confused but he told me not to worry about it so much, I had peace with me.

The church had many long wooden benches for people to sit on, there were some windows that were very dirty until I got the climbing ladder out and washed them. The town had dirt roads and when people or animals passed by they kicked up small puffs of dirt, when a motor car drove by there would be a trail of dirty air following behind and the dirt would then settle back onto the windows again. The town was not so big and many of the people knew Father Shumbin when we walked to the market. I was impressed by the buildings, many of them were much bigger than out small homes back in the village. Sometimes I would smell some foods that someone in their home was cooking and it would smell really good to me, other times I was not sure of what I was smelling but it did not smell good to me.

The more I looked at the maps with Father Shumbin and his wife Arbroa, the more I learned that there was much much more to the world that I wanted to explore. Arbroa kept a smile on her face the whole time I was there, she and Father Shumbin seemed most happy together. One morning Arbroa tapped on the door that hid me and my sleeping bed, it was early in the morning but she wanted me to wake up and sit with her for a moment. Arbroa was much younger than Father Shumbin, she did not speak my words well so I do not know what she tried to say most of the time but she held books in her arms. Arbroa was wearing a long light yellow dress and she was wearing a big white hat, she looked very pretty. Arbroa sat down on my bed beside me, I took a moment to sit up and try and understand what she was saying.

As I remember what Arbroa told me, I did not understand then but I recognize some of the words now. Arbroa opened up some of the books she sat on her lap, she slowly turned each page, and each page had beautiful colored photographs and pictures, bright greens and blues and colors I had only seen in my dreams. Arbroa showed me more pictures from around the world, Arbroa wanted to travel to some of the places she discovered within the pages of her books. Arbroa spoke about reading the pages and tracing her fingers over the pictures of lands and dreaming all night of smelling the air or feeling the earth with her own fingers, but for real. Arbroa understood that her place was with her husband serving god and the people of her town but she dreamed of seeing many of the sights with her own eyes and touching them with her own fingers.

Arbroa showed me pictures of Ireland, the bright green grasses that filled hill after hill and large stone buildings that were hundreds of years old. Arbroa showed me many many pictures; she wanted me to see a bit of what could be out in the world waiting for me. Arbroa smiled as each piece of paper from her books turned, her eyes grew big and wet with tears at the beauty within the pages, she wished that she had the ability to see things and she told me that my story and want to travel and adventure relit the fire in her heart to see the world. I saw beautiful pictures of large buildings Arbroa called "Pyramids" and a long stone chuta called a "great wall" and many more kinds of animals. Arbroa wanted to see of the things but knew in her heart that she never would, she was meant to stand by her husband. Arbroa wanted me to visit all of the things that she wanted to, and then to return one day and describe them all to her. The pages in the books were lightly cracked and the color was fading from being turned many times, it was easy to see that she spent many days looking at the pictures she held so dearly.

I did not want to tell her I would visit the places she wanted to see, her life was for her to live just like mine was for me but I nodded just to reassure her I understood what she was saying. My mother always told me that I was the only one that could live my life, no one can taste food for me or smell something for me, although sometimes if you find an animal that has been dead for a while while out walking, I would wish that someone else could smell what I smelled instead of me. I missed my mother very much, the farther away from home I seemed to get, the more I missed her. I thought a lot about my hunt, Teeta was happy to be back hunting with the men, he did not want to answer all of my questions about his travels but we were good friends. During my journey I had really missed my good friend, we only had the one night to hunt together and I missed him.

The town had a few small stores, I was curious to how they got such things, when the men went to trade hides with Teran they often came back with rolls of cloth that was cut and divided among people, it came back in big long rolls and there was always enough to go around, everybody worked together. Some of the shops had small shiny gadget things, some people had small white things in their ears and those things made noise when they walked by. There were so many new things and new people, I tried my best to say hello to everybody that I walked passed but there were so many people so I just smiled at everyone I could. After I stayed and learned from father Shumbin how to clean and what some new foods were I began to feel that it was time to continue my journey to the great water, I had to see it before I felt that I could think about going back to my village. I knew that the village needed me to come back and help hunt, I needed to take my place with the men and bring food back to my village but I had the rest of my life to do that, I owed it to my friend and my mother to explore more of the world than they did.

One morning Father Shumbin and Arbroa walked with me down a few roads, the motor vehicles were so loud and so fast, I was a little scared to be too close to them, Father Shumbin warned me not to get in the front of them. Father Shumbin told me that he knew a man that was taking a truck and some animals to a town a little ways away and that I could get a ride with him to carry on my journey. When the motors drove by they put the red dirt into the air and it made my clothes a little dirty. It felt strange wearing a shirt as I was only used to my cloth wrap around my waste, the shirt made my skin itch a little and I felt like the collar was choking me a little, Arbroa swatted my hand away each time I tried to tug at the shirt a little, It was a nice shirt and it was a gift from my new friends, but it choked on my neck and I was not used to it.

The motor was called a truck; it was grey and very dirty. The man driving the truck was called Whutta, he had gray hairs on his face and his shirt was very dirty. Whutta and Father Shumbin shook hands and exchanged some words, I tried to listen to what they were saying but there were many noises around me. Whutta had a box that had four ng'ombe in it, they were black and just stood in the box and stared around, they made a funny noise that sounded like the nyati when they ran in their great herds. The ng'ombe are called cows up here but back home, they were very uncommon outside of the cities, they ate a lot and were a lot of work to grow them and feed them. Our village had smaller animals to kill when the men were unable to bring back meat for everyone. Whutta reached out and shook my hand; he smiled and exposed his yellow teeth when his lips parted. I looked at this truck, I did not know what to think about it, and he pulled the side open and waved his hand at me. I did not know what to think, Whutta put his hands on my sides and set me to sit inside and then he shut the door.

Whutta was an older man, he had a round belly under his stained gray shirt that had holes near the neck, I suspected from tugging at the choking collar. Whutta had small grey hairs sprinkled around the sides of his head in his hair, he had a few hairs that stuck out from his face and when he spoke, his voice sounded raspy and he wheezed a little when he laughed. Whutta had a motor truck and a small box on the back that had some animals in it. Whutta wore dark blue leg clothes and they had more holes in them as well as lots of dirt. I did not understand Whutta's words when he spoke but he seemed to be a funny man, he was in good spirits and laughed very much. Whutta had big hands and on the back he had lots of dark black spots with scars, sort of like mine. There was much trash looking papers in the motor truck, the floor by my feet had crumples on it, and the seats inside were very dirty.

Whutta jingled some metal and then the truck began to shake and rumble, the cows in the box on the back made more loud noises. We began to drive and I did not know what to think, I was a little cared to hear the motor make the loud noise and shortly after we zoomed down the road. I felt like I was running very fast, the motion of the bouncing made my stomach feel unwell but I tried to enjoy watching the grasses on the sides of the road zoom past. Whutta knew a few words of my language but not very many, we had a hard time trying to talk but he mostly smiled as we motored. We made a lot of travel with the motor truck, we journeyed a very long way, I saw more homes and buildings along the side, there was a great amount to see and I could not wait to get back to my mother and tell her all about it. My mother did not know of motors, she never told me about engines that would zoom you along the path, some of the men had seen the metal contraptions out along their hunts but it did not come up back in the village. Whutta drove for very long while, the sun rose high into the sky and began to fall behind us as we drove, it was much fun to get to motor, but my stomach did not like it, it made me feel sick.

I had to ask Whutta to stop the truck by waving my hands, my stomach could not handle any more motoring, it was most urgent that I step out of the truck to be sick. Whutta laughed at little when he spoke, I did not find it funny and it hurt very bad to be sick. I thought back to times when I was ill as a child, my mother would spend the day rubbing my back and making sure that I had water to drink, even If it made me more sick. The air seemed to smell different; it did not smell like the motor trucks that drove by in the town where I had been staying. The motors did not smell good and they puffed out black smoke, like a fire, but no fire. The smells that came into my nose when I was being sick standing in the grass was nice smelling, it smelled a lot like food but we were a ways from another town, but I hoped that we might be close. Whutta worked himself out of the truck and walked over to me, he asked if I was feeling any better, I stayed bent over with my hands on my knees trying to make sure my stomach was no longer going to be sick.

Whutta handed me a small bottle, he said to drink to feel better, it was water and it did help my stomach not be sick. I tried to stretch for a few moments before we got back into the truck and motor along. I did not like being sick, Whutta wanted to get to the bigger town to sell his cows; this is how he made his money. Whutta drove cows from some small towns to bigger towns, then he would turn around and go back. I asked him how he could motor for so long and not get sick like me, he said that he was used to it and it did not bother him. I liked to motor a little but too much made my stomach sick and I was not sure if I wanted to do much more of it. We drove towards a small hill and when we were on top, I could see a very big town rose up before my eyes.  There were more buildings than stars in the skies it seemed, they were in many shapes and grew bigger and bigger as we motored closer. I was a little scared of what I might find in the city, there were so many buildings. I asked if it was Teran, Whutta raised his shoulders and shook his head, he did not know Teran. I tried to ask many questions but Whutta raised his shoulders to many of them, I do not know if he understood many of my questions, I did not speak the same as Whutta, just a few words.

It was beginning to get a little dark, the town I left behind had lamps and small lights that lit up when it was dark, Whutta clicked some clicks and then there was light shining on the path as we drove, he said lights help to see the way. The many lights of the town grew more and more, we began to pass some homes that also had lights inside, it was amazing to see so many lights, I thought maybe everybody in this town had a light for themselves; there were so many. With the sky almost dark the outlines of the homes and buildings stood as big black shadows, I wondered how many people lived in the big ones and where they all might be. There were lamps over the roads to better see as we motored, Whutta yawned and that made me yawn, we were both tired men, my stomach still hurt a little but now it was just hurting from being empty. My stomach grumbled like the truck did, we did not motor as fast when we made it to the big town, there were many more streets than the last town I was in, and it was much much bigger.

Whutta turned down one road and then to another before we finally stopped, he turned his truck to face a home on a small path by the home. Whutta asked me to pull the cows off of the box and pull them to a small pen for the night. We pulled four cows from the box and the big animals pulled me back a little but they were not as big and mean as the nyati, they groaned and slowly moved along to the pen for the night.

Whutta told me that we were at his mother's home; he stayed with her when he was in the big town, he would often leave his animals in the pen and his father would sometimes take them to farther cities away to sell them. Whutta was always careful when he brought home animals before taking them, there was a man who they called Kumpa, he would take animals that did not belong to him, Whutta warned me not to show him anything because he would take it for his own. I did not understand what it was to take something that was not yours. In the village everyone shared and made sure than no one was left behind.

No one was without when it came to food or things that anyone needed in the village, everyone worked together. My mother once told me that if people did not work together, then they were working against each other. I did not fully understand when my mother told me her thought, and then she took a long long rope and tied it around a tree. Me, Teeta, Loza, Pika and a few other children all tried to pull on the rope, each time the rope was pulled, someone would be pulled in a different direction, and the small tree still stood. My mother untied the rope, she tied one end to the tree and then everyone worked together and pulled on the rope until the tree bent over. All of worked together to pull the tree down, we all worked together and it was very clear to see how much more can be done when everyone works together. My mother was very kind, and very patient to help teach all of the children, nobody was quick to anger, anger never did anybody any good but fools do not see that.

Whutta told me about one time he woke up in the morning to find Kumpa removing a goat from his pen at his mother's home. Whutta confronted Kumpa and right away, Kumpa began to tell Whutta that is was not him and that the goat Kumpa had on a rope was clearly one of the goats that

Whutta had placed in the pen himself, but Kumpa shouted and yelled to make Whutta feel poorly. Kumpa put his hands up and shouted at Whutta for calling him a thief, even though he was a thief. Whutta walked towards Kumpa and demanded the goat be returned to the pen, but Kumpa continued to insist that the goat belonged to him and not Whutta, but Whutta was not a fool. Kumpa tried to make as loud of noises as possible so people would come and rush to his aid, making Whutta back down. Whutta warned me to watch out for such people, they were much like the fisi. The fisi is also called the hyena, it does not work for its own food, it waits until another animal does the work and then it shows up, making much noise and then takes the food that it wants.

Whutta did not like Kumpa, Kumpa was much like a fisi and all he did was make lots of noise. I worried that the big world was very full of men like Kumpa, men that do not work but take, take too much from the people that do work, and the workers have to work harder, it is like the animals that would drink all of the water from a puddle and let other animals to die. The Kumpa's of the world do not work but steal the rewards of the others' that do the work, it was not right and I tried to be aware and look out for them. Whutta took me into this mothers home, it was a nice home, it had electric lamps lighting the inside, there was a table and chairs like at the church. The home smelled of good food, I was so very hungry and the smells were very many. My stomach made more howlings like many of the sounds late at night in the village. Whutta introduced me to his mother, she was a thicker woman, kind of heavy set around the middle and she moved slowly when she walked. Whutta's mother nodded as she walked, she was hard to get around but she carried over a plate with some food on it, she looked up to see me and turned to get another plate.

Whutta and his mother were very kind to me, the plate she brought me had food mounded on top, I tried to eat slowly so I did not eat so much that I got sick again. The food was new to me; it had strips of crunchy greens, mushy brownish stuff but it tasted very good. Whutta used a red bottle and squirted red dots of juice onto his food. I watched as the man shook the bottle up and down, I wondered what it was he was putting onto his food, I was curious to what he was eating and I was curious to try it as well. "May I" I asked Whutta, I did not want to ask too many favors and feel like a Kumpa. Whutta warned me that it was a hot sauce, I did not know what a hot sauce was but I wanted to find out by trying it. Whutta shook the bottle very carefully over top of my plate; the red liquid did not smell very good, it made my eyes water a little when I smelled it. I took a big bite of my food and some of the red sauce was on the top.

I did not know what Whutta meant by "hot" but there was a pain in my mouth; it hurt much like I had licked a fire stick. I felt my ears turn warm, like being in the hot sun all day, I tried to breathe in with my mouth but it did not make the pain go away, after a few panicked breaths and trying to wave my hand at my mouth, my lungs began to burn and I began to cough. Whutta tried to hurry me to take a bit drink of water, he began to tell me that he was sorry for putting too much spice on my food, he said he forgot to tell me to mix in the hot sauce with my food. Water fell from my eyes for a few moments, I was too focused on the pain in my mouth to notice but Whutta turned towards me to hand me water to drink, I saw the concern in his face for me being alright. It took a few minutes to begin to feel my mouth again after finding the water, it hurt very much and then I was afraid to eat more of my food. I stared at the little red specks of liquid on my food, such big pain from such a small dot.

Once I understood what "HOT" meant when you eat it, I had to try it again without the food, I wanted to see what it was like on its own I put a small dab of the red sauce and once again I had to smell it, I wanted to smell it alone, I wanted to see what it really was, perhaps my food made it much more hot. I licked the dab off of my finger; Whutta opened his eyes big wide open when I put my finger to my tongue. My feet stomped hard to the floor, right away I felt the hot burning on my tongue and my eyes began to water again. My tongue wiggled very fast in my mouth, right away I thought I made a very big mistake. My mouth felt on fire, I tried to close my mouth on my tongue to stop the pain but even my lips, they begun to burn as well. I felt like jumping, maybe hopping would take away some of the pain in my mouth I thought. Whutta watched me, he didn't look sure why I tried the hot sauce again after I already found out that it was hot. I was not sure why I wanted to try it again but maybe I might like it like Whutta did.

I held on tightly onto the table with my hands, I wanted to see how long I could hold on, I wanted the man in me to be strong and be able stay strong and make the pain go away, it did not. My nose began to run, the liquid in my nose felt like it was trying to run down my face, water fell from my eyes and my lips were very hot like fire. Whutta slowly moved a glass of water towards me on the table, I did not hear the glass moving at first but once I blinked and the water left my eyes, I saw the water. The glass of water looked so very good, I fought my want to drink a lot of water, I could have swallowed a whole lake of water. I jumped for the water, I could not take it any longer. Whutta tried his best not to laugh but he did laugh when he told me that I did it to myself. Whutta was right, I did want to taste the liquid fire sauce, I imagined if Teeta would have tried it, he would have fought harder to be a strong man and not admit that it burned him, I tried to be that strong but it hurt so very bad. After I jumped and danced a little trying to make the  pain in my mouth go away, my cheeks were wet from the water from my eyes, Whutta made sure that I was ok before he began to laugh more.

For a moment I thought back to the night all of the men sat around and talked about Teeta and his first hunt, they laughed at him for shooting the small bird instead of the big animal and he got so very angry that some of the men were laughing at him. I felt my hands want to close to a fist to fight the pain until I remember Teeta looking so mad for very little reason so I let my hands loosen my grip on themselves and stopped being mad . My mother told me that being mad was a poor use of your mind, if you get mad that you can't find animals to hunt, it does not do you any good to be mad, become a better hunter. I did not want to be mad, at all in my life. I did not want to be mad at Whutta, he thought it was funny that I tried the hot sauce one more time, I tried to find it funny also. I began to laugh but my mouth felt very strange and tingly when I did, my lips felt much bigger and when I talked, I sounded funny, even to myself. I tried to speak to Whutta and he began to laugh more and more, I began to laugh a lot too.

The hot sauce taught me that even if something might be bad the first time that it might be all bad, sometimes trying something a different way might make it better. My lips felt very big and they hurt a little when I licked them. The hot sauce was very painful for me and even though I did not like to be laughed at by Whutta, he did also make sure I was feeling alright. I reassured Whutta that I was not going to be sick I his house like I almost was in his motor truck. Whutta continued to chuckle a little during the rest of the meal, I sat quietly for a few moments and rather than think about him laughing at me, I tried to think about what I was doing that might have made him laugh at me. I began to see why Whutta was laughing, I was bouncing on the seat of the chair and waving at my mouth, again, that must have been a sight to see. I began to try to smile but my lips were still painful but I was not hurt from being laughed at.

# CH. 5

It was very early in the morning when I woke up, my lips still felt very puffy and like I bit them a few times in my sleep. I laid awake on the small couch for a little as Whutta let me sleep a little, it was another new city and I wanted to head out to explore some more. Whutta was already sitting at the table when I sat up, I greeted him a good day and told him I wanted to go and walk around if he did not mind. I thanked Whutta very much for being kind and letting me sleep on the couch and to his mother for feeding me my evening meal. Whutta offered to walk with me a ways but told me he did not have very much time because he had to move the cows to a city to the north. Whutta gave me some folded paper and told me that it was a few moneys to use to buy lunch with; he said a strange man once gave him some money to use so now he was giving me some. I was not sure what I was going to do with the moneys but he said it should buy me a meal in the evening. Whutta told me that if I made it far enough towards the morning sun that I would make it to the ocean and get to see the boats coming into the docks.

The OCEAN, I was excited, that was the great water I had heard about. I was most excited to see it. I hurried out the door and towards the streets. There were so many more people than in the last town I visited, my journey was continuing. Whutta stopped me before I got too far away that I could not hear him. Whutta was not a man that ran very much, he lightly jogged to catch up to me, he huffed and puffed and almost had no breath to speak. Whutta ran to me and said that if I wanted to see more of the world, and that I should ask for a captain named Raza. Raza often had a boat that sailed out of the docks on the ocean and that if I told him I knew Whutta, that he might give me a job. I thanked Whutta for all of his help and headed back to the sun. The further I walked the more people I ran into, there were so many men and women, each dressed very differently than I was accustomed too. Some of the woman had large clothe wrappings on their heads, it made their hair look interesting. Some men wore long top clothing that draped all the way down by their knees; others wore button shirts like mine and tucked into their pants. I followed a street that pointed right at the morning sun, I stood up on a box to see further down the street, it was very crowded with many people but  I could see a little bit of an opening at the far end, that must have been the great water.

I passed many people, some were carrying different baskets with breads, some with colorful fruits, it was like a market but it was all on the streets, there were very many foods and small animals, and children. Some people were selling fishes while others had birds to cook and eat, there were so many people wandering about, I understood some people but most I did not. Some of the strange foods that people carried with them did not smell good, others had wonderful aromas that made me feel light on my feet as I walked near them. I had a long walk to get to the great water, and I could see where I was going to go. I saw so many different people, some woman had small babies in clothes that held them to them, other small children simply help onto their mothers as the moseyed through the streets.

I missed Teeta, I thought he should have spent a little more time traveling when he went to Teran, instead he wanted to hurry back and take his place among the men. I wanted to be the man that traveled the farthest, saw the most strange things and had some of the most interesting stories.  In all of the commotion of the streets it was hard to keep focus on one thing or another going on, people came and went from every direction, each with their tasks for the day. I tried to keep from spinning around as I noticed so many different people, there were beautiful girls, big tall men, nice small older women that smiled as they slowly walked by, and little boys that ran between people and bumping into them. There was a man that walked up to me on the street, he ran his long dirty fingers along the mud bricks of the building he walked along side of, his fingers tracing the cracks and crevices of the wall.

The man was very dirty, I did not understand the tongue that he spoke to me but his free hand tried to grab at my shoulder and my shirt. I did not like being pulled at and some of the people walking along the street began to stare. The stranger that was trying to pull at my shirt was beginning to concern me, I did not know what he was trying to get from me but he did not stop when I stopped walking for a moment and put my hand out, hoping he would stop. The man stopped walking when I did, he was wearing very dirty clothes and he did not smell very good either. I felt poorly for the man, he must not have had a home or anyone to help take care of him. The old strange man let his hand fall from the building wall, he opened up his arms to begin to wrap them around me and give me a hug. I did not want the man to hug me, he was a strange man and as more people stared at him hugging me, I felt that something was not right. I could not fend off the embrace and quickly he began acting very strange. My mother told me when I was young that nobody is the same, Teeta was always trying to prove that he was a faster runner or a farther jumper, I did not like it when he showed over and over but that was how he was and he was my friend.

I took a step back from the man struggling to keep his arm wrapped around me, it was difficult and I began to lose my balance, I tried to take another step back to keep from falling into the street but it pulled the man off of his feet. The man fell on top of me which made me fall backwards. Me and the man landed into the street, many other people were standing around us, I tried to free myself from the man and then I realized his hand was in my pocket while the other was still wrapped around me. The man continued to try and talk to me, begging and pleading but I did not understand his words. I struggled to get out from under the man, it was not easy and he did not seem to want to stand up for himself. I got my feet underneath me and raised myself back up to my feet, the man stared at me for a moment, I opened my hand and reached down to help him up and onto his feet. I reached for the man's hand to help him get up, he looked like he needed the help and I wanted to help.

The man yanked his arm from me, he began to shout and then he fumbled to his feet, but away from me. The look on the man's face was frightening and I felt that he blamed me, his eyes were open big and his smile turned to a scowl and looked very mean to me. The crowd that had gathered began to murmur, the old man hurried to his feet and ran away, he was screaming and shrieking, I tried to help the man and then suddenly he was making a commotion and I did not know why. The old man continued to flail his arms above his head as he tried to run away. I did not follow him and I did not wonder what he was making so much noise for, I focused on standing up first and then dropped my head for a moment to try to make sense of the morning. I wanted to try and help the old man, he was old like Zuda back home and everyone helps one another, but the man did not seem to want my help. Many of the people stood around me as I watched the man run away, I did not feel good about my trying to help, some people stared at me as I tried to brush off my pants, I was covered in dirt and I wanted to try and keep my clothes clean.

I restarted my walk towards the morning sun, I was close to the great water and I wanted to see it. I told my mother when I was young that I wanted to see the great water, I wanted to touch it, taste it and walk in it. There were streams and ponds back home, there were plenty of watering holes to find animals at but you could not drink from smaller ponds, animals did not know not to defecate near the water and often times the water was no good for us to drink from. One of the streams by our village was where we dragged buckets of water from many times, that water was clean to drink but there were often simba or fisi around and we had to carefully go in groups.

The air I smelled smelled different, it was hard to explain but as I walked there were many different smells, but the one smell I smelled was cool, it was a soft smell and it smelled very nice. There were so many people roaming about, men talked among themselves, woman carried children and bags of things. Sometimes it was hard to squeeze between people; some groups of people stood near the corners of buildings and made it hard to get by them. Some people had a strong smell to them, some smelled kind of like the hot sauce. My lips still felt like I bit them, but it was from the hot sauce. Some men had sticks in their mouths, but the sticks had a small fire on them and smoke was coming out, when they spoke the smoke come from their mouths and into the air, it did not smell good when I walked through it. There were men standing by small carts that had food spread out on them, some men had carts that had pots and pans on top and food cooking over a very small fire.

There were so many people but most of them looked much like me, I still wanted to find Teran and see what the different kind of man looked like, I was still curious and wanted to see the different kind of man. Sometimes I thought that maybe I would see a man that was as tall as tree or maybe a man with more arms, I did not know what to think of when my mother told me about a different kind of a man but I wanted to see plenty of them. I made good friends with Father Shumbin and his wife Arbroa, and also with Whutta, I was making good friends along my journey and I could make many many more. Some of the foods looked strange but smelled so very good, I thought I might want to taste all of them but I was not very hungry yet and if I ate full on one meal and then came across one that looked or smelled much better, and then I might not be able to eat it.

The farther I walked the cooler the air felt, the smell grew stronger in my nose and I did not know what it was, I still smelled the foods and many of the people that I passed but the one smell I smelled was smelling very good to me. I smelled fruits, food, and brightly colored spices, all whirling into the air on a faint breeze and it smelled very good. As people moved to the sides of the road I was walking  on I began to see a glimpse of the distance, it looked like the sun, but on the ground, there was a big golden circle laid out on the ground, it was sparkling and shiny. I found the great water and I was so very close to it. I tried not to bump into people as I walked, there were so many people that I thought the entire city had come out to stand in the roads and search through the foods being sold. The great big water was big and golden, it was hard to see where the water met the sky, it was all just golden and shiny. The noise and sounds of the people on the streets seemed to hush and go quiet, I hardly heard anyone and my eyes locked onto the great golden water as I walked towards it.

The hard road beneath my feet felt softer and softer as I walked, I did not hear to sounds of my feet slapping onto the ground, I hardly heard the voices of people talking; it seemed to go quiet as I walked. The glistening golden water was a bright as the sun, the closer I got to the golden water, the top edges began to turn black, the sides also turned dark. I could begin to see past the buildings at the end of the road and they gave way to the rounded edges of the suns reflection on the water, the sun made a large shimmering shiny stamp on the top of the water, the ripples glistened and sparkled inside the circle, the waves on the outside were dark with white tips on top as they moved along. I could feel more and more of the breeze on my face, it was coming straight from the great big water and it smelled different. The waves charged the edges of the land, the water splashed onto the sand and then back down again. There were small waves everywhere, some would disappear back into the rest of the water while others would rise up and course onto the shore.

From the top of the road I could see down over some wood paths that went out into the water, there were many smaller boats pulled up onto the shore, there were many men climbing in and out of the boats with nets in their hands, some men were carrying boxes and there was a lot of movement. I was amazed, the big water truly reached out until it touched the sky, there were so many people moving in and out of boats and the water, and the boats seemed to fill the shore line like grass on the plains. I felt my mouth smile, I had finally made it to the great water, my mother would be so proud. I wanted to capture what it looked like, the sight of so many people and boats moving around, and show it to her. I missed my mother and wanted her with me. I felt the sun kiss my face while the cool breeze brushed my cheeks, the same cool breeze that lifted the birds high above me.

I continued walking down the road to the great water I remembered much of the walking me and Teeta did, the tall grasses brushing along my fingertips, I outstretched my hands a little to feel the breeze blowing at me, it blew up from the great water, past me and continued to follow the road I came from. The wind blew past people working that morning, it blew past little children and their mothers, walking between food sellers, it blew past the men smoking and standing on corners watching all of the strangers move about. I wanted to be like the wind, I wanted to move about, winding and breezing through streets, seeing so many people and things so new to me. From a high enough hill back home the nyati herds could be seen moving one way and then months later they would move the other way, great big herds moved like water on the land, too many to count. The docks on the great water looked much like the paths in the tall grass back home, sticking out of the water and extending from the shore, there were so many people in the crowd that from far away the streets just looked like a moving blob of many colors and patterns.

The sun grew high when I decided to sit on a rock and watch everything that was going on, I did not know what I was going to do from then on for the night but I wanted to watch the boats float away or come back, there were so many boats and people, I was truly amazed. I watched as the sun on the water moved around and then stopped shining so brightly, the water turned blue from my seat on the hill that over looked everything. I spotted some children playing with the ball you kick, it did not look like the one I saw when I was a child but I wanted to join them for a little while. I picked myself up from the rock where I sat perched and began to walk towards the children running on the sandy dirt with a ball. One little boy was wearing orange shorts and a shirt, he kicked me the ball, he had a very big smile on his face, his smile made me smile and I gently kicked the ball back to him. The other little boy wore dark brown clothes on his legs, the three of us kicked the ball back and forth for a little while until they said something to themselves and then they headed up towards the hill together. Both little boys wave with big smiles on their faces, they reminded me of me and Teeta a few years ago when we were both that young and playful.

I turned to look back at the water, it was brown and green where it met the ground, the waves pushed around little rocks, up and then back and back up again with the edges of the water. I stood and watched the water sway up and down, the sounds of the water rushing towards the ground was a little loud, the birds overhead screeched loudly and it was all so very new and exciting. I walked to the water a little, it was cold on my feet but I bent down and scooped some up with my hand, I waited until the water was clear and I took a sip. The water was not good to drink, I coughed a little and spit it back out, the big water was not for drinking, it did not taste good at all. I stuck my tongue out and tried to use my sleeve to wipe away the no good taste, but it did not work very good.

I walked up and past many of the men working on the long wood paths that were above the water, the docks were covered with men moving nets out to fish in from smaller boats, there were some bigger boats floating out in the water and even from the shore. Many boats looked bigger than the big mountain I could see sometimes when Teeta and I walked away from the village for a day or two. Most of the men spoke words I did not understand, many of them sang or whistled with their mouths as they worked, many of the men were much bigger than me, but I could try and help move things if they needed it. Watching baskets of fish go by me on the shoulders of bigger men began to make my stomach grumble, I was growing very hungry and it was getting late in the day. I was not sure where I was going to sleep, I thought I was going to walk up the shore and maybe find a place on the grass to lay down until morning. I turned my back on the great ocean and decided to go and try some of the food I had smelled when I was walking towards the great water.

The docks on the shore were filled with men carrying boxes or other things. The sky was brilliant with colors and the sun shone on many of the men as they worked. The dark water splashed against some of the poles holding the docks up from the water, it also splashed into the air after it crashed against many of the larger rocks. The sounds of men shouting, sounds of birds calling to one another and the sounds of the city behind me all kept me alert to how many people were here, the long wood paths into the water were very busy and I wondered how hard it would be to find Captain Raza. I could not help but to sit and watch plenty of what was going on, I just walked a little to see anything I could land my eyes on, there were so many boats and people in them, as well as lots of different supplies being carried around by many men.

I found a man with some clothing wrapped around and around his head, he had some metal pans sitting on top of some clay pots that had hot fire in them, the food he was selling smelled very good and I tried to ask him if I may have some. The man gave me a look and he squished his eyebrows together, I understood that he did not understand what I was saying, we did not share a language. I reached into my pocket for the moneys Whutta gave me but found it to be empty. My stomach suddenly felt like I had been kicked, I could not breathe and my eyes began to water. I pulled my pockets out trying to make sure that I did not mistake where I placed it and I looked around, I was afraid I did not have the moneys I was given. The man began to wave his hand at me to go away. My stomach was suddenly not hungry but it was hurting that the man was shooing me away because I did not have moneys, but I understood that he had to make moneys for his family.

I hung my head and began walking back towards the great water, it did not feel as great but I was there, I was hungry and sad, I missed my friends and family in the village but I was at the great water, just like I said I would be. I made it all the way to the great water; I had a very long journey before I met Father Shumbin and his nice wife Arbroa. I cried as I walked, I had pains in my heart but I wanted to go and see the great water, and now there I was. I looked far out at the dark water as the sun changed many colors, I wondered where far beyond the water was the rest of the world, perhaps lands like in the picture books Arbroa showed me, I wanted to go back and find my mother, I missed her so very much but I was out to become a man and to see the great water, just like I said I would. My heart still had pains in it, but the pains in my stomach were very big too. As the sun got smaller and the dark sky grew bigger many of the men that walked along the docks became less and less. Many of the large boats out in the great water were still shining with lights, some of them had many colorful lights on them, and they were very fun to look at.

I roamed past many of the smaller docks as the sun began to ease behind the city. I passed some of the wooden docks that had broken boards on them, I passed some that were worn well into the dirt and others that were lined with boxes and nets. I found a large dock that went very far out into the water, I decided to walk down it a little ways, a dock of this size must have been for very large boats, like the ones sitting far out into the water in the sunset water. The wind blew harder, and much colder, I was hungry and cold and was growing tired. I did not know what to but I was still very excited that I made it all the way to the great water. I decided to sit atop one of the wood boxes on the long dock, I had nowhere to go nor anything I could do as it was growing late, I decided that I would sit on the box until I could no longer see out into the great water and then I would find a quiet place away from the cold breeze to lay down and sleep for the night.

I sat upon a wood crate on the dock; I watched the boats just sit out on the black water as the night went dark. There were a few men walking up behind me, it was hard to hear them as the waves crashed against the wood below the dock and the wind blew in from the water. One of the men said words I understood as he passed me, "the captain" I heard one man say. "Captain Raza?" I jumped to my feet, there could not be too many people with that name. Two men spun around to look at me as I jumped up behind them, one man was much bigger than me and he stood up straight to face me. I could see he had a stern look on his face and it made me feel afraid. The big man kept his fists clenched tightly, if he would have struck me it would have been mighty painful. I apologized if I offended the man; "a man named Whutta told me to locate the man named Captain Raza" I explained that Whutta thought the man could help me.

"What do you know about captain Raza?" the large man asked me again; "only that a man named Whutta said that he could help me" I again told the two men. The large man had big pants on and a shirt that did not cover his arms, his skin was not so dark like mine, he was a different kind of man, he had hair on his face and it frightened me a little when he talked. The not so big man leaned to the big man and said something I did not understand, the big man kept his eyes locked on me, I was still afraid of the larger man, he looked very mean to me. The large man stood silent, he stared at me and he seemed to grow bigger while he stood before me, I felt like if he got any bigger than he might break the wood path we were standing on and we would all get swallowed up by the great water. The not as big man kept his eyes watching me when began to speak, he said something in words I did not understand, his face eased a little bit. The not so big man said more words but in a different kind of way, I did not know what words he was using so I raised my eyebrows hoping that he would explain to me the words he was saying. Both men stared at me for a few moments, I was not sure what they were asking me, I was growing tired and was beginning to think that since the sun was going down that perhaps I should find a place to sleep and maybe try to find Captain Raza in the morning.

The large man spoke up, his voice thundered over the breeze, it made me shudder a little. "What can you do" the very big man asked me, I told the man that I had traveled a very long way and had a very tough journey away from my home, I learned to clean from Father Shumbin, learned some maps and pictures from Arbroa, worked some animals with Whutta and learned many ways to cook and make fires from my mother, and learned to hunt with my friend. The not as big man began speak in my words; "we'll take you to captain Raza, but you'll have to work" the man kept one eye a little closed as he talked to me. The not so big man wore big clothing on his body and short clothes on his legs, he was not as dark in skin like me but darker than the very big man. My stomach rumbled a little while the men talked, I thought about my stomach for a moment and then I worried, "where are we going?" I asked the two men. "To meet the captain, just like you asked" the not as big man responded to me.

I followed the two men down the wood path, there was nobody out there so I did not know where Captain may have been, I was unsure that I should be following the men, Whutta warned me about fisi men that were not good and I began to worry that the two men, that were much larger than me, they might be fisi men. "OH" it hit me, as I worried about the big men being fisi men it struck me that the old man I tried to help on the streets was a fisi man. The not as big man turned to ask me if there was something I had to say, I explained about the old fisi man and that maybe he took the moneys that I had to buy food with. The very big man turned his head to look down his back at me just before he spoke: "how do you feel about that?" I moved my lips around for a moment before I answered the man; "the moneys was a gift to me, and now it is a gift the man that must have needed it more than me."

The very big man stopped walking and turned to face me as we got to the end of the wood path that went out into the water, "I am Ngozi, I am a sailor with the captain you seek, this is Ohah and we will take you to meet the captain, but he may not let you stay." *Stay*? I did not know what he meant. Ohah began to turn and climb down the side of the wood path, there was a small boat floating on the water underneath, Ngozi opened his palm and waved it to the ladder that Ohah had climbed down, he told me to follow. The boat moved up and down very much, I was a little afraid that I would fall out and not be able to swim. Ngozi climbed down after me and when he got into the boat, it did not rock so much it seemed.

I asked Ohah what a sailor was as Ngozi pulled on the small machine on the back of the boat. Ohah leaned in to tell me but the machine began to make a loud noise and I could not hear him. The boat began to move, it drove up waves and down waves, it was like being in the truck with Whutta, and my stomach ached just like in the truck. I was too hungry and did not have any food to be ill so I wrapped my arms around my stomach and huddle down to try to stay warm. The machine was very loud and the wind was very cold. The wind was as cold as it was when the rains broke from the skies each year, but the sky was clear and many stars were coming out. I did not know where we were going and I could not see anything far out in the water, the small boat bounced up and down as we traveled for a very long time.

I did not feel very well; the buzzing noise from the machine on the back of the boat was more loud than the motors that drove through the city and town that I was leaving behind me. Teeta would never believe that I rode in a truck and now a boat, my mother would like to watch me raise and lower my hand in the air to show her how high up we drove up the waves and then back down. Nga would even sit by the fire with the other men and listen to my journey when I get back. I could not see where the water and sky touched, it was getting late and very dark out, I was beginning to worry a little, the two men I just met did not speak much, and I could not hear them over the boat machine, the waves were plenty big and it took time to drive up them and then back down the other side, looking behind me, the lights of the city were getting smaller and smaller, it very hard to see and very far away.

"Poof" suddenly there was a very bright light shining on us from the sky, I could not see it was such a bright light, it was not up high like the sun, it was not the same color or light up much of the land like the sun but it was like a white lamp, but shining right on us in the boat. Ohah was at the front of the boat and he began moving his body, I held on tightly to the boat I was afraid we were going to tip over; he blocked the light a little as he stood up and moved in the small boat. Ngozi began to stand up after he turned the loud machine off, I was very afraid that we were going to tip over into the great water. Ohah was moving at the front of the boat and Ngozi at the back, I could see that there was a great big wall of black that we were moving towards and I did not feel good about what was happening. Both men moved frantically around in the small boat, I did not know what to do and I was very scared.

Once the boat machine was off the two men spoke in words I did not understand, not even in my language, Ngozi began to shout as he stood in the boat.

The small boat rocked and moved, Ohah began to laugh, Ngozi continued to shout and I did not like it. My stomach began to really ache, the boated rocked side to side and front to back, my head began to hurt, my ears felt warm but my skin was cold. I tried to watch the bright light that was shining on us but it only made my stomach feel more sick. Ohah was laughing very loudly, between his laughing and Ngozi shouting I began to hear other voices. My eyelids felt very heavy and I could not keep my eyes open. My head began to swirl and my body began to feel very weak. I felt my body fall forward as my eyes closed, I heard Ohah laughing for a moment, until I did not hear or see anymore.  The small boat continued to move, I felt my body jerk back and forth, I felt ill and after the long day it had been, I could not stop myself from falling asleep, even in the light, everything went dark, and quiet.

# CH. 6

I opened my eyes, my head still felt ill and my stomach was also ill. There was a man staring at me when my vision returned to me. "Why do you know me?" the man asked me. "You speak my words" was the first thing I said to the man, my eyelids made it hard to keep my eyes open, my body still felt weak, there was a dim light coming from the wall to my side. I began to look around and see wood walls, pictures and maps on the walls. I was sitting on a green chair that had been padded. The man I was looking at had a thin face and looked very serious, he had short hair on his face and light skin like Ohah and Ngozi." I do not know you" I began to tell the man asking me questions," I met a man named Whutta on my travels" the man began to let up his stern look on his face, his eyebrows curved  a little and his lips straightened. I was in a room but the room still felt like it was moving a little.

"I am the captain you seek young man" Raza began to speak. I felt my mouth smile even though my stomach did not want to. I tried to smile a big smile but it made my head ill again. "I am captain Raza, you are on my boat, the Thoth" the thin man told me as he stood up from his chair. "Now my question is; what do you want?" Raza asked me right away. I closed my eyes tightly for a moment to try and think about what I was supposed to say. I blurted out to Raza that I was from a small village and wanted to be a man and went out on a hunt with my best friend Teeta and then walked until I ran into father Shumbin and rode with Whutta and got sick and then the fisi got me then there was a white light above the great water and I want to see it all. Raza turned his head for a moment as some tears fell from my eyes. Raza did not understand my rushed jumbled story, I tried to catch my breath as I began to weep, I was so far from home and missed my friend and I was not feeling well.

"I will let you sail with us if you will work, this is not a carnival ship and you will have to work" Raza spoke before he instructed that I not cry in his office, it was not good for the leather. Raza added: "you best not let the crew see you cry either, this is a man's ship and we are men" I did not know what crying and being a man had to do with not crying but it was his ship and he told me to stop crying. Captain Raza reached his hand out and asked me my name, *Ojimbo* I told him, but then he called me "boy" as he helped to pull me to my feet. I tried to tell the Raza that I was not a boy, I was becoming a man. Before I could finish what I was saying Raza lead me out of his office, there was a long hallway with several doors, there was fancy green carpet on the floor of the hallway and Ngozi was standing outside the door waiting for me. Raza looked up to Ngozi, he raised his fist by his face and he extended out a finger he said something to Ngozi, he said four things and popped out four fingers to him and turned around to return to his office.

I asked Ngozi what an "office was" Ngozi began to walk and told me to follow him. I had many questions and wanted answers, like how did Raza learn my words or what kind of name "Captain" was. Ngozi opened a small door, he told me that captain was not a name, it was his title, it meant that he was in charge. When Ngozi finally began talking to me I hurried to ask him more questions, I wanted to know what he was saying when he held up his fist and how I got to his office, and where we were. I wanted to know what a *Thoth* was, what it meant, and how many other people were on the ship with us.

Ngozi breathed out in a huff, he seemed to get a little unhappy with my questions and when he stood up straight he almost hit his head on the ceiling, he was a very big man. The room was very small and it had a sheet stretched from one corner to the other, Ngozi explained that I was to sleep in the hammock and that it was my room. He held up his fist just like Raza did, "Closet room" he said as he popped out his first very large finger, he meant that the closet with the mops and buckets was to be my room. "Rules" he said as he stuck out his even bigger second finger. Ngozi told me that the captain was in charge and that meant he made the rules, Ngozi was the first mate which meant that he made sure that everyone followed the rules and did what they were told. The captain was fair and made sure that everyone was paid and treated fairly but they traveled some rough waters and it was the captain's job to protect everything on his boat. "Fix him" Ngozi said as he stretched out his third finger, I did not understand what Ngozi meant by *fix me*, I was not broken.

Ngozi pulled a small bag from his pocket, he handed me a bit of food, and bottle of water to drink. Ngozi pulled out a small white thing from his pocket, it looked like a small round smooth pebble but it was not a pebble. "This will keep you from getting sick for a short while, you'll sleep tonight and take a few days to get used to the motion" Ngozi told me before he told me to swallow the pill. "English" Ngozi said louder than the other three rules as his smallest finger stood out from his large hand. "English?" I asked, I did not know what an *English* was, perhaps it was my job? I swallowed the pill that Ngozi instructed me to swallow before I ate the small food, my stomach was very hungry but I still did not feel well. Ngozi told me that we would worry about English in the morning, he showed me how to step up and into the hammock and told me to get some sleep and that he would be back for me very early in the morning.

I laid in my hammock, it swayed lightly back and forth but soon my stomach began to feel a little better, it felt well enough to eat what I was given. I felt very tired from the long day but it was a new place, I was lying in a strange bed and surrounded by new people, new everything. It was not easy to fall asleep, I sipped on the water I was given and I thought about my mother, my friend Teeta, and my village. There were no stars in the dark room, there was a small window on the wall behind me but it did not show anything and it was dirty. I was scared, I did not know what I was going to do, what might happen or even where I was. My stomach felt very good to have some food in it, I wanted to taste some of the foods back in the city but I had no moneys. I thought about how the great water tasted, it was very not good. I laid in the hammock and thought about a very many things. It was very hard to sleep when I was swaying back and forth but I must have fallen asleep.

"BANG BANG BANG" I awoke to the noise of someone banging on the door of my closet, it was very loud in the small room and as I jumped up, the hammock began to sway, I feared falling out. I struggled to get out of the hammock without falling; it was taller than I was so it was tricky. The voice on the other side of the door said something I did not understand. I pulled the door open to see a new man. This was a very different man, he was a short man, he had thin soft hair, very pale skin and his face was round. The man spoke to me but I did not understand him, "ENGLISH" he said very loudly. I shook my head because I did not know what an *English* was. The shorter lighter skin man waved for me to follow him down the hallway. The man had short hair, not thick curly hair like me, his eyes were a little closed and he was very different looking than me. The color of his skin was lighter than the palms of my hands, I found a different kind of man, maybe this was what Teran might have been like, I could not help but smile.

The man lead me to follow him down the hallway and then down some stairs, I stared at the ziggy-zaggy lines and gold swirls on the carpeting on the floor. The ship I was on was a very big boat, I did not want to get lost so I followed close behind. There was one big room that opened up into a kitchen and big table for people to sit at. I saw Ngozi and a few other men already sitting and eating food from bowls, it smelled very good and I was already very hungry. "You alive boy?" Ngozi asked me. "I do, but I am not a boy" I replied. Ngozi stopped chewing his food to stare at me for a moment before he told me come sit with him for a moment. I sat next to Ngozi and he began to talk: "you're a boy until the captain says otherwise, and from here on out, we only speak English." There was that word "English" again, I did not know what it meant. Ngozi gave me one last word of advice and that was that English was the language that they talked and that I would have to learn. Captain Raza informed all of his crew to speak English only so I had to learn really quick fast. Many of the words were hard to understand, I spent the meal watching the crew pick up plates, bowls, and utensils and saying the words for me to understand and learn.

After breakfast on the first day I helped a man named Nasur, he was the cook and I spent the whole day with him learning to wash the dishes and ready the next meal for the crew. Ohah came down after the midday meal to take me to tour the rest of the boat, he spoke to me in my words but also in the English so it helped me to feel less alone. Nasur was another man with light skin, he was missing hair in the very top of his head and had a few gray hairs in the short black hair that was around the sides of his head. Nasur did not say very much but he pushed his sleeves up towards his elbows and plunged his hands down into to the water to begin to scrub the dishes clean, showing me how to rub the circles on the dishes in the water to clean them. Nasur stood taller than me but he hunched his head down, his forearms showed muscles under his thin skin, which made the small bubbles dance as they held onto the hairs on his wet arms. Nasur had no wife or children, a life as a sailor was not an easy life for anyone with family, Nasur had a sister that was married and lived in some country far away. Nasur worked hard and did not always say very much but I liked to work with him some because he showed me very well what I was supposed to do.

Ohah took me to the top of the outside of the boat; he told me that as the boy it was my job to keep everything clean. The boat we drove out from the dock was hanging from a few ropes above the back of the boat. Ohah pointed to side stairs that went up to the top of the tall part of the boat, he told me that was where the captain spends most of his time and to not go up there unless the captain himself ordered me too. The boat was very big, from the side I could see the city that we left behind, it was small but I could still see it. The boat rocked side to side in the water, it made walking difficult, my legs walked more wide do keep from falling to a side, but it also was hard to not fall forward or backward. In the distance I could see the shine from the rising sun reflecting off of the windows in the city, it looked like a photograph.

Ohah waved for me to follow him to the back of the boat, on the side away from the city he pointed that way out over the distance, were more lands and if I decided to stay and work on the boat for a while, I would get to see the lands. The sun was high in the sky and the breeze was cool to my skin, I was very excited for the chance to get to see more of the world just like I told my mother and Teeta I would. I told Ohah that I would be glad to stay on the boat if I was welcome to; I knew that I had to finish working for my meals and my place to sleep so I had to get back to help Nasur wash the dishes and prepare for the later meal. Ohah told me that he would be the one to teach me most of what my job on the boat would be, everybody on the boat started out as the *boy* on a boat, there are many jobs on the boat that need to be done and I was the newest. Ohah told me that there were many things that I would have to learn but that Captain was a fair man that would be patient as long as I worked hard for him.

I liked that I would get to see more of the world, I told Teeta and my mother that I would see other lands and meet many other men, meeting the men on the boat was already a very good start. Lin was moving a bucket full of tools across the ship; I asked Ohah what kind of man Lin was because he did not look like me, or the other crew members. Ohah began to laugh, him laughing made me feel like I did something wrong, but I just wanted to know. Ohah told me that Lin was oriental, he sailed with a boat that hunted large wales and that they crossed paths in some port and Lin was offered a job because he was a master boat mechanic. I had to ask what a mechanic was, and what Oriental was.

Lin was shorter than Ohah, and everyone was shorter than Ngozi, he had a soft voice and his toes pointed out a little as he walked. Lin had more hair on his face than me or Ohah, but not as much as the captain. Lin spoke four languages and has sailed on many ships all over the whole world. Lin began sailing as a young boy, much younger than me, he learned to sail from his uncle and father on one boat near Asia, then as a teen older than me he was offered a good job on a bigger boat and he then sailed with a crew that were not people like him. Lin learned three more languages while sailing and was a very interesting man. I liked Lin, I wanted to learn the English and begin to hear all of his stories as fast as I could. Lin did not start out as the "boy" he was hired to be the mechanic and valuable crewman, and he certainly showed that he was very smart.

Ohah told me that they sailed from the southern tip of Africa all the way up to Sweden, it was a long journey but they made several stops to transport supplies. There were a few traps and a few places that the crew would often net fish between runs to different stops or when the seasons changed, they were always moving and doing things to make money for the crew, the captain was a smart man and he took very good care of his crew, and they took care of him. Ohah showed me a around the boat a little more before I headed back down the metal stairs to the kitchen to work with Nasur to prepare the meal for the evening. In the evening there was a room next to the galley that was for resources, there was a picture box that Ohah told me sit down each night, he showed me a stack of smooth shiny round discs and that it would help me to put things together to learn English much faster, and it was the only language they spoke on the ship. I did not see Ngozi very much; he worked with the captain and some of the other crew members, but not very much with me.

Ohah was in charge of teaching me most of what I needed to learn. I was shown where many of the ropes and nets were, how to walk carefully on the deck, where the floating vests were if I needed to put one on in a hurry and which button to hit if I needed the captains attention very fast. Most of the day was spent wandering around the ship with Ohah, he knew very many things and I did my best to understand everything he told me about the Thoth. I was eager to sail with the men, they each had very many things I could learn and I felt like I was joining the sailing men, instead of the hunting men back in my village. The winds were different on the ship, there were different smells and I was surrounded with dark water instead of green or brown grass.

The end of my first whole day on the boat made my legs ache, the boat moved up and down a little in the water so when I walked I had to keep stopping myself from falling from one side to another. Early the next morning Ohah woke me up instead of Lin, he told me that he had something for me to change into and that I should hurry and change before I had to go and meet Nasur in the galley. Ohah had a pair of pants and a shirt for me; I thanked the man for the clothing and did not understand. Ohah told me that there was a shower on each floor and that the crew was to shower twice a week, and that clothes should be washed as often, he thought I could use another set of clothing so he found an extra set of clothes that I could wear. Ohah told me that when Ngozi started with the captain, he was not much bigger than me; it was hard to imagine that such a large very man was once as small as me.

After the meal, Ohah told me that once I was done working for Nasur that he wanted to see me. The meal passed and the captain was missing again but I performed my duties and then headed to the top deck to see Ohah. Ohah was holding a bucket and some tools all tied to a rope, he tied the rope around my waist and asked if I had ever cleaned windows of scrubbed floors. I told Ohah about having cleaned windows at the church with Father Shumbin and how the stained windows were always covered in the dirt from the motors driving past the church. Ohah told me that it was "time to walk the boat" and walked me to one side of the boat. Ohah leaned me over the side of the boat, he made sure the rope tied around my waist was very tight, he showed me how to lean back to walk down the side of the boat and be able to wash all of the windows with my bucket and brush. Ohah tied the other rope around his waist, he leaned back and braced his feet against the side of the boat and climbed over the rail even though I was afraid, I did what I was told.

I was very nervous to step over the side of the ship, I had my wash bucket with soap in it, my scrub brush that I was to wash with and a few rags to wipe off the rubber blade. The water below was not very far but I was still a little scared. I wanted to make sure I did a good job for my captain and my shipmates so I held on tightly with one hand and tried my best to keep my feet pressed against the side of the ship so I could work with my scrub brush to clean as the water below me splashed against the side of the ship and upwards towards me. The small splashes of water shot way up high, I could feel many of the wetting the legs of my pants as I stood braced against the side of the ship as I worked to clean the sides and the windows I was tasked with

I sat on my rope and reached out to begin to wash the window when the rope that was holding me up, fell. I did not feel my own body weight on the rope around me and then I hit the water, it was cold, it was very dark below me, and I was scared. I waved my arms and tried to keep from going under the water, my floaty vest squished up under my chin and it was hard to move to struggle to swim. Water splashed my face, the bucket of soapy water hit against my head and my arm as I struggled to stay above the water. I lifted my head to take a deep breath each time the my mouth was not under the water, I looked up along the side of the boat to see Ngozi and Ohah peer over the side and look down upon me. I kicked my feet to fight to keep my head above water; I had to be careful not to smash my body on the side of the boat as the waves pushed me close to it.

The rope tied around my waist got tight, I was being pulled back up, I was much relieved that the two men were pulling me back up. I was very wet, my pants stuck to my legs, my shirt to my body, and the taste of the big water was in my mouth again. I lifted up past the window I begun to clean before I fell, the waves below me splashed into the side of boat, I was very glad I was being pulled in, I remained above the water a little but I did not have much experience swimming. Back in my village Teeta and I swam in the large ponds a few times or in the river but there were many animals that also liked to be by the water and we were not in the water for very long. I remembered what Nga was saying when he was telling Teeta about hunting, you have to remain very calm or your shaking hands might ruin the shot. I was not shooting an animal but I tried to keep my head above water and even though many thoughts were flashing in my head, I was quickly being pulled back up. Ngozi helped me over the side, his big giant hands wrapped around my upper arm and I was quickly pulled back onto the boat, I felt like a very little boy again when he pulled me up.

"I spilled my soap bucket" I muttered to the on-looking crew after both of my feet were on the deck. Ngozi and Ohah both looked very concerned for a moment, they were squinting with raised eyebrows and then their faces turned to funny and they began to chuckle a little. I wanted to do a good job for the captain and I did not want fail at my job. Ngozi laughed a big smile and began to clap his hands together. Ohah reached forward and grasped my hand and began to shake my hand and laugh too. Ohah apologized and told me that his grip on the rope slipped as he turned to talk to Ngozi, I was feeling fine and had no worries about anything. The two men laughed that I was not mad, I was not scared, and my one concern was that I dropped my bucket into the water, the two men both stood and laughed that I looked like such  mess when a horn tooted out. Both men turned to look up towards the cabin where the captain spent his days, the captain was standing firm on the side, staring down at us. Ngozi nodded his head very big and Ohah said that it was time to get back to work. "I think this time, maybe you go" I told Ohah, he turned his smile off and so I began to climb back over the side to finish washing the small windows on the side of the boat.

When I had walked around the whole sides of the boat Ohah pulled me back up again, he told me that I should go and talk to the captain now that I was starting to dry, he warned me to knock on the door and wait for permission before entering his wheelhouse. I untied the rope and helped to put all of the tools back into the bucket and then I headed towards the stairs. I was not sure what the captain wanted from me, I was curious to see what was in the room that I had not seen into yet. I began to climb up the stairs, the metal steps were rusty and dirty and they clanked as I climbed my way up, gripping the handrail that had been worn smooth from use.

The room was surrounded by windows all of the way around, I could see the captain leaning forward over a table or a desk from the inside, I raised my arm and knocked so that he could hear me then I waited to be invited in except the man lifted his head and turned to walk toward me. The captain was wearing a button up shirt, he looked a little tired but he smiled when he opened the door to greet me. The captain stepped out and leaned his elbows against the railing; "I see that you got wet" the captain asked me. I replied that I dropped my bucket washing windows and did not want to leave it behind. Raza looked at me and smiled a little. It was nice to hear more in my language, it was kind of a lonely day except Ohah speaking to me very little in my language. The captain wanted me to learn English and he told Ngozi that I would learn the best if everyone spoke it, it would make me learn it very fast.

Captain Raza asked if I was mad or upset that I was dropped into the ocean. "My mother always told me that anger or being mad was a silly waste of energy" I told the captain as he stared out over the big water. "I like that" the captain began to tell me, I looked far out into the water and watched some of the waves grow big and shiny with the sun glistening off of them. It was a grand sight and I liked that I was able to stand up high and see a little more than down on the deck. "Captain, I thank for you letting me see this sight, it is very beautiful and one day I would like to tell my mother what it was like." Captain Raza did not turn to look at me, he kept his eyes locked on the far away where the light blue sky danced with the dark water; "this is my favorite site, welcome aboard boy, we sail tomorrow." The captain pulled the door to the wheelhouse open and left me to gaze out over the great big water, the sun shimmered and sparkled on the wave tops, they were golden and the lows snaked through like serpents.

I was most excited that we were going to go off to see where the water touched the sky, there was a long way to go and I would get to explore more of the world. I thanked the captain very much and returned to my duties. I returned my cleaning supplies to where they belonged and then headed to the kitchen to assist Nasur with the evening meal. Lin walked past me, he looked very different than I did and that made me curious, I nodded and smiled to the man and he said "Hello" in English. I was excited to sail, I wondered where we were going and what we were going to do, I did not know what was involved when the boat sailed but I was very curious to find out. Nasur was not certain about what I was saying; we did not share a language. I helped to set the plates and mix the meal together. I liked helping with the cooking, I learned to mix things and how to prepare meals and sauces, Nasur was very good at cooking, he made so very many good smells in the kitchen and I got to help. I tried to ask Nasur why the captain did not eat with his crew, I liked captain Raza and he was a good man.

Nasur explained that because of what he does, that some people do not like him, he waits until his men eat lunch before he eats breakfast, just to make sure none of them fall ill, so he can take care of them, "that is very smart" I said to Nasur. I wondered how many days it would take to sail around the world, I wanted to see so very many lands, I wanted to smell more foods and see more different kinds of men. I liked Ohah, Ngozi, Nasur and I was getting to know Lin, I smiled very big thinking about the adventure I was having, I could not wait to tell my mother. Nasur said he always made the meal and that the captain came down to watch most of his crew eat and then to make himself a meal for later in the day. Raza had heard of captains being poisoned back up where he was from and he did not want to risk getting sick. Nasur said that he has sailed for many years and had seen some crews turn on their captains, I asked what he meant by "turn," then he said "KILL" them. I did not understand why anyone would kill anyone, life is very special and everyone gets one until they join the stars in the night sky.

My mother used to tell me when I was a little boy that our skin was dark because we came from the night sky and that when we no longer live, we would return. I liked to feel the wind on my skin, and the sun on my face, I used to wonder if I enjoyed feeling the sun on my face so much because if we were from the night sky, we missed the sun and maybe we came down to earth to enjoy the sun, and got night so we would not miss it too much. I liked the beauty of the sparkling night's sky, I want a very long life before I am to return to it.

Nasur told me that the sailing was not always just fun and washing the boat, there are some places where other boats bring men that want to take your boat from you, the

114

captain is very good at his job and he has made his crew very happy, but he had a big boat and many other people wanted it for themselves. I wondered if Loza met anyone like captain Raza, or Whutta, or even like Lin, there were so many people in the town and city I visited, my small village did not have that many people, but the city was full of people, like herds of nyati as they roamed for water to drink and green grass to eat. As a boy me and Teeta would watch the herds all of the time, I would watch as they blew through the plains like the winds, Teeta would hold a stick up and pretend he was bow hunting the large beasts as their hooves thundered by. I missed being a boy and running and playing with my friend, I knew that when Loza went off to become a man that it was not long before Teeta wanted to go and then it would be my turn.

Zada told me plenty that each man had their own path, a trail that they must follow and that it was up to that man to make that path theirs. I was not very certain what he meant because all of the men went down the path that lead to the morning sun and came back that same path. I did not follow that path after my first hunt with Teeta. I did not hear of any of the men talk about getting onto a boat, not even Nga, and he was the leader of the men. I tried not to think very much about my home, it made me sad to miss it and I was excited to take my stories back to everyone. I wanted more stories, I did not want one night to sit around a fire with everyone and tell my whole journey in one night, I wanted many more journeys to tell over many nights. Nasur laughed at me a little, I struggled to understand his words when he talked in the English, he spoke slowly as we worked together so I could learn but it was not easy. Between meals I cleaned the pots and pans, when I had spare time during the day I would lean against the sides of the ship and stare out into many distances, wondering where my home was, where I might go and what I might see. I was a little afraid but even men can be afraid, I was also very happy.

Ngozi walked the boat, he would walk around the sides and also down the hallways to check on everyone, he was very sure to keep everyone safe. Ngozi had bigger muscles that Loza, he was a very large man and when he walked through doors he turned his shoulders so he did not get stuck. Ngoza was the first mate, he told the men the orders he got from the captain. There were many tools and things on the boat, I did not know what many of them were or what they were for. Ohah told me that I would learn in time, I liked learning. My stomach still swayed with the boat, it turned from side to side and if I tried to stand still for very long, I felt like I would fall over. Nasur gave me a few small white pills, he said not to use more than one a day but that they would help me to get used to the moving of the boat, and keep me from being too sick. Nasur and Ohah spoke to me in my language a little, most of it was in secret so I did not feel so lonely. The night before we set sail Ohah had one more task for me, I followed him to the far galley, it was a room that had one of the picture television boxes I saw back at Whutta's mother's home. Ohah showed me how to work some of the machines and told me that he had videos for me to watch to help me learn good English. Each night after all of my work was done I was told to watch one of the disc videos and follow along.

Ohah wanted me to watch Sesame Street first, there was a big yellow bird and a hairy tembo creature, it was very funny videos and I liked them. I learned how to get to Sesame Street as we sailed, each night I learned different letters and numbers, there were songs to sing and kids to clap with. On the show I saw many different children, many unlike I had ever seen before, all on the television picture box. I like the red furry creatures and all of them were very funny. Ohah laughed that I had so much fun watching that television picture box. As I finished one picture video show captain Raza came in, I stood to greet him and ask if there was anything I could do for him.

Captain Raza asked me if I could row a boat: I told him I did not know what rowing was but I was willing to learn.

"In the morning we're heading to Comoros, it's a small island that I need to pick something up and I need your help" the captain began speaking. I did not know where Comoros was but was excited to see it. I was told that I would be joining Ohah and Ngozi on the small boat at sundown to go and retrieve a box that belonged to him before we began to sail further north. I was excited to get to join Ohah and Ngozi, they were my friends and I wanted to be able to help in any way that I could. I was excited to get to begin to sail, it was exciting and new. I finished the letter "C" and then went to sleep in my hammock. I remember trying to hop up a little into the hammock as the boat rocked a turned a little, I stepped right into the mop bucket! The water made my pants wet almost to my knee, I wished I had not done that, the water made my foot smell not good, very badly in fact. I laid in my hammock for a few moments feeling the water run down my leg a little, I hung my leg over the side so the water would drain back into the mop bucket below me. I listened to the drips drop into the bucket as I swayed a little before finally falling asleep.

It was dark; I did not get to see Comoros except from the distance of the ship during the day. Ngozi and Ohah lowered the small motor boat and climbed in, the sun was setting when we motored off to the shore. When we got close to the shore Ngozi turned the engine off and Ohah pulled out oars, and we began to row, the oars made small splashes as they pushed against the water, then they would creak a little when we would lift them from the water and put them back in to row again. Ohah explained that it was important that we were all very quiet so I rowed quietly. I climbed over the side of the boat slowly and then stood in the shallow water as Ohah and Ngozi jumped out and told me to stand firm in the water and keep the boat still until their return. Ohah told me to be weary of anyone that came near the boat and that I should be very still, perhaps even squat down a little to hide in the shadow of the boat and the water

Ohah tucked his shirt into his waist and off the two men went into the dark. Ohah told me to keep my eyes peeled and to watch for anyone that might be trying to get into the boat and to make sure that no one does. I did not know why Ohah worried that someone might try and take our boat and I tried real hard to watch out into the darkness. It was very quiet in the water, the waves tried to push me forward and backward, I tried to watch as Ohah and Ngozi slowly walked to the shore, and then I could no longer see them as they crossed the beach to the shrubs and plants on the other side. I listened to the water wash against the shore, I imagined each wave rolling over the small sharp stones until they became smooth or even smaller and turned them into the fine sand grains that I felt under my feet. I thought about how many times the small pebbles were turned over and over, grinding against each other until they were all tiny sands. The sounds of the waves were soothing, I was a little nervous to be out in the dark, I was not sure where we were or what we were doing but I was part of the crew and they needed me so I was happy to go and help. The wet parts of me grew cold from the air, but the water I was in was warm.

A bright red streak shot high into the sky, the water around me lit up with red and orange from high in the sky. I lowered my head back from watching the light streak in the air to see a few men running in the dark, they were running towards me, I did not hear anyone speak until suddenly I heard shouting. I began to panic, I did not recognize the men in the dark, I could not see their faces but there were many of them. I tried to sit in the water, if I lowered my body under the water I could hide my head in the shadow of the boat and begin to move a little, maybe I could move far enough away that the men would not see me or try to get into the boat. I lowered myself into the water, it was cold and it pushed against me, the boat rocked and tried to pull me forward and backward in the water, my feet sunk into the sand, my knees pushed into the sand and helped me to brace myself still against the tide. I heard many men yelling, the men were running along the beach shouting to each other. A few men ran to one side of the shore while the rest ran the other way, they were searching and yelling as the orange fire in the sky fell into the water.

It was hard to see in the dark, I was afraid and I did not know where my friends were. I did not know how long I should wait or how long they would take. During the day Ohah told me that he and Ngozi were going to pick up a box from the island, a box that belonged to the captain. The box was being held onto by a friend of the captains' they needed my help to hold the boat while they retrieved it. I was just supposed to hold the boat still and keep it from drifting away, a job I was certain I could do well. I tried to keep my body under the water and keep my eyes watching out for my friends. I was afraid, I did not know what the men wanted but I was certain, I did not want to find out. I crawled in the water a little ways waiting for Ngozi and Ohah to return. I saw a shiny red dot coming from some bushes, it blinded me in my eye as it waived back and forth. Two men and a big box came running from the bushes on the other side of the beach and splashing into the water towards me. I could hear Ohah shout "good boy Ojimbo, time to go." I stood up from the water and begun to turn the boat sideways so my friends could get in.

Ngozi and Ohah were trying to run with a big wooden box, they splashed and made much noise in the water. They put the box into the boat and began to run and push the boat back into the waves with me. Ohah jumped in and began starting the engine, as soon as it roared to life Ngozi stepped in, I was still pushing until Ngozi grabbed me by the collar of my shirt and hoisted me into the boat, ripping me right out of the water. Right as Ngozi began to pull me out of the water Ohah begun to speed the boat away, I thought I was going to fall out, I held on to the side of the boat as tightly as I could until Ngozi pulled me across the seat of the boat in front of the box. The boat drove up and down waves as it headed towards the ship, which was dark. I could see a small red dot light like the one that shined in my eye, one coming from the ship and the other coming from Ohah as he steered the boat.

Ohah and Ngozi clapped and cheered a little as we neared the boat. A small light from the deck of the ship shined over the side to us, Ngozi and Ohah hooked up the wires to lift the boat onto the ship like the night they brought me aboard. The boat swayed a little until it landed safely back on the deck, I was still wet and now very cold as the wind further out on the great water was very cold. There weren't many lights on the deck; I moved slowly to try not to injury myself climbing out of the boat and onto the wet slippery deck. As I turned around the captain was so close I almost bumped into him, he startled me because I could not see him well in the dark and I did not hear him walk up over the noises of the boat and the crane working. My heart was beating in my ears and the winds were whipping around me, I did not hear him walk up. "All is well and safe Mr. Ngozi" the captain shouted as I almost stepped into him. "We did well sir" Ngozi shouted over the sounds of the wind and crane moving overhead. I was glad to be back at the ship and with my friends, the men running up and down the beach did not sound very happy and I was happy to be back on the ship.

Raza turned and headed back to his wheel house in a hurry as he waved his hand in the air and shouted to Lin to "get a move on." I was beginning to shiver with the cold, Ohah slapped me on the back and told me to go ahead and get back to my room to get changed into something dry, his slap almost set me running with the push. I made my way to my room, it was the closet but it had a place for me to sleep in my hammock and keep the few clothes I had. When I opened my door I saw that some things had been moved around, I had to pull the string to turn the light on but when I did, I saw a stand-up shelf in the corner with some more clothes on it. I changed into dry clothes and left my wet ones to hang and dry, as I stepped back out I ran into Nasur, he smiled at me and nodded his head to me, I felt like my friends were liking me for my work. Nasur pointed for me to head to the galley to catch up on my picture video, beneath my feet I could feel the boat begin to move faster again.

I began watching Sesame Street again; I was supposed to watch a whole movie video disc each night so I could get better at the English. Ohah entered the area with the couches and turned to sit by me, he used the back of his hand to lightly slap my leg to the side with a smile on his face. I did not know what the smile was for but I smelled something really good. Ohah sat next to me and began watching Sesame Street with me, he also pulled up a bag of white stuff he called popcorn, I liked the popcorn. Ohah and I sat silently and finished watching the television picture movie, I was feeling very tired from being wet and cold, I did not finish my movie picture show before going to sleep for the night, the next day was another long exhausting day, I learned to fish. I had not fished before, Ohah assured me that I would need my sleep; he also told me that I did a good job holding that boat in the water and not leaving them behind.

The morning knock on my door seemed very early, I felt tired as I rolled out of my hammock, there was already a commotion in the hallway, the men were up and moving bright and early, I might have also been awaken a little later than I should have. Nasur was waiting for me in the kitchen, he nodded to me when I entered and motioned for me to begin my routine of setting out the dishes and scooping up the breakfast food for the crew. The crew was very talkative in the morning, the men doled out work and roles as they planned how they were going to work for the day. I was excited to learn to fish, back in my village some of the men used spears or rock traps to catch fish in some of the rivers, but the rivers were also full of dangerous animals so we mostly stayed away. I finished washing the dishes and then joined the men on deck, the crane was moving overhead and Ngozi was shouting over a loudspeaker. It was a bright sunny day, there were birds overhead squawking and making calls. Ohah was motioning his arms around to Lin in the crane seat while Nasur was by the side of the boat. I did not know where I was supposed to stand so I walked across the boat to ask Ngozi what my job was.

Ngozi told me to head to Ohah and help unfold the nets, he warned me to keep one hand open and ready to grab a rope or rail to steady myself as the water became more choppy the farther from land we sailed. In the distance I could see very large waves, I was a little afraid that the waves would crash us and it was frightening. I was glad that captain Raza was a good captain and that the men would help to teach me my job. Ohah was standing near the side of the ship, he had big black nets coming off of a wood roll and slowly dropping to the water below. Lin was sitting at the crane pulling levers and pushing them back to get the crane to move and help to untangle the large nets. Ohah explained what to do and I did my best to help him to untangle the nets to catch some fish to sell for money nearby. The boat rocked, some moments we were very high above the water and then the next moment I was looking up at a wall of water taller than the trees, the up and down motion made my stomach hurt a little. My legs were very shaky, the ship rolled from side to side and my legs did not stop moving and looking for a sturdy part of the deck for me to brace myself better.

The nets dropped to the water beside the boat, Lin moved the crane back and forth a little and I watched everything the men did. I was not aware of what else I was supposed to do. I could see the captain in the wheelhouse as the boat continued to sail on, the nets dragged in the water for half of the day until finally Ngozi shouted to reel them in. Ohah pulled up some long poles with shiny metal hooks on the end of them and handed one of them to me. Nasur removed small doors that opened up holes on the side of the boat that let water back out to the great water. Nasur warned me to be extra careful not to fall through one of the hatches, if I did they would not have much luck getting me back onto the boat because the ship was sailing quickly away and the crane was working the nets. I was a little afraid of falling through a hatch hole, the water was very mean that day, splashing high up the sides of the ship, and I did not want to upset Ngozi or the other men by falling over into the water. The hook poles were long and hard to hold onto, Ohah showed me how to hook the net to pull it over the boat to unload the creatures from inside.

Ohah tugged at the nets with his hook pole and fish spilled from within the nets onto the deck, many of the fish flipped and flapped around, there were so many of them and I did not know what to do with them all. There were many fish of many sizes, Nasur began sorting them into some containers as Ohah and me kept using the hooked poles to shake the animals out over the inside of the boat to the deck. My arms began to hurt from all of the net shaking, Ohah laughed that he could see that I was slowing down from being tired, Ngozi moved about on the deck helping Nasur to move around bins for different fish. Lin had a purple headband as he continued to work the levers of the crane. Lin began to bounce in his seat; he started to shout to Ngozi that something was wrong and that the crane was acting funny.

Ngozi began to hurry to help Lin; the two men began to shout back and forth, Ohah tried to shout to me from behind me just as the net above us opened up. I looked up to see a giant fish fall from the net, Nasur began to shout. With all of the noise and shouting and commotion I could not hear anyone. The large creature had a large fin on the top and two large ones on its sides, it swished from  side to side, slinging small fished through the hatch holes along the sides of the boat. All of the shouting slowly grew clear, I tried to yank my hook pole from the net but it was twisted up in it. Nasur tried to poke and pull the angry fish away from me, I was up to my knees in fish and everything was very slippery and it was very hard to stand. I kept from falling because I held on very tightly to the hook pole which was stuck to the net above me. Ngozi turned from Lin and began to hurry towards me, the shark was very mad and it had teeth in its' mouth, very sharp teeth. The shark snapped and wiggled on the deck, everyone was rushing to get it held so it did not bite anyone. The commotion on the deck was hard to make clear, everyone was running or shouting and I did not know what to do.

I turned around to see what I should do, the tail of the shark swung past me and almost hit me, it was almost as tall as I was and very powerful. I was afraid the shark would bite me or knock me down; it was thrashing wildly all around. I turned to look for Ohah, I could not see him except he was shouting. Ohah was almost out of the hatch on the side of the boat, he was trying to pull himself up back onto the boat but everything was so very slippery from the fish. Ohah had the hook pole stretched across the opening of the hatch hole and was hugging it very tightly. I let go of my hook pole and hurried to help my friend Ohah. The fish were very slimy and slippery, as soon as I let go of my hook pole I fell to the deck of the ship, fish almost covered me over. I crawled and climbed my way to Ohah, he was wriggling to try and get back through the hatch hole. I finally reached Ohah, the commotion behind me from the other men trying to wrangle the shark made it hard to hear my own voice, let alone Ohah. I grabbed onto one end of the hook pole and began to pry it away from the wall of the ship, as I braced my slippery feet against the bulkhead to try and help Ohah climb back onto the boat I was rushed with a pile of fish, my feet began to slip to the sideways and my hands were hard to hold onto the handle of the hook pole. I could see Ohah turn red in the face as he struggled to get back onto the ship, water and fish tried to go out the hatch hole he was stuck in and pushing against him.

I opened my eyes after the wave of the fish came from behind me, I looked to make sure that Ohah was still OK, I could not see him. The hatch opening was covered in fish, some still slapped and flailed their tails, others just slid around dead. I felt my heart race even harder, I was already working very hard to save my friend, the shark falling to the deck scared me very much and it was very mad as it thrashed back and forth. I found the handle of the hook pole under a mound of fish and began pulling again, it was still heavy which meant Ohah was still on the other end. The noise of the other men trying to deal with the shark made it hard to hear much. Suddenly from under the small pile of fish Ohah began to appear. Ohah had his eyes closed as he worked his way through some of the fish, he shouted to "keep pulling" and I did with all of my strength. Once Ohah got one leg back through the hatch hole he was able to brace himself back onto the boat. "Let's go Ojimbo" Ohah shouted once the rest of his body was back through the hatch hole, he was hardly standing when he turned to run and help his boat mates with the shark.

I turned to follow Ohah when the handle of my hook pole swung around and hit me in the face. My left cheek felt like the shark slapped it with the mighty tale that still swung around the deck. My arms flailed in the air, the image of Ohah sliding through the hatch hole flashed through my mind and suddenly I was stricken with the panic of going through the hatch hole also. I felt the hook pole handle tuck into my left armpit, I squeezed it with all of the fear I had inside of me, holding on for my life. My eyes watered, my ears hummed for a moment and all I could see were blurry images of my friends moving about in dim colors.

"BOOM" a loud thunder echoed out loud. I did not know what made such a noise, I blinked my eyes to make the water go out and looked around. Ngozi had the shark by one hook pole while Nasur had it near the tail with another. Ohah Froze still as his hook pole almost snagged the top fin of the angry fish, his eyes opened wide and his arms flexed as they paused. The beast laid silent, its' body straightened out as it relaxed all if its angry muscles. The tears fell from my eyes as I searched around to locate the origin of the thunder. Atop of the stairs next the wheelhouse stood the captain, his arm extended with a small black pistol aimed at the shark, a small puff of smoke rising near his head from the blast. "That's enough playing with the fish boys, Lin can't eat that much soup" the captain shouted before turning back towards his working quarters navigating the ship. Ngozi wiped his forehead with his forearm, Nasur stood up on his toes to look over the top of the creature, he wanted to see the placement of the shot that stopped the wild thrashing.

"Missed by eight centimeters" Nasur shouted, followed by a whooping howl of cheer. I was a little afraid to get near the shark, it was very powerful and much bigger than me, and all of the men began to use their hook poles to pull the shark to the far side of the ship so it was out of the way of the fish nets so the men could resume their work. I was a little afraid that the shark would come back to life and try to bite me as I walked around, I could not take my eyes off of it as I resumed sorting fish. The men picked out the rubbish that was caught with the fish, they tossed it into a large bin to throw it out with other refuse, rather than back into the water and deal with it again in the future. I helped the men sort some of the ideal types of fish they could sell at a market nearby and some of the others were sent to the kitchen with Nasur. There were so many kinds of fish, some big, some small, most felt smooth or slimy, it was a very new thing for me to sort fish. Ohah held up different fish and told me the names of them and whether or not we keep them and where are good places to sell them, and then they were placed into bins before we sent them below deck into a holding box.

We spent the rest of the day catching and sorting fish, I was given the job of catching the fish down below with Nasur in a hold and stocking them with ice. The ice was so very cold, it was white and it made my skin sting when it scraped against my knuckles. Fishing was very hard work, we spent the better part of the day catching a great many fish. After the first set of nets and fish were hauled up, Lin hopped out of his seat at the controls of the crane to assess the big shark that was brought up with the nets and onto the boat. Lin used to fish whales with other men like him; they also caught a great many sharks to sell at their markets as well. Shark was not a required food near where we were fishing so keeping the animal on ice was a waste of space for fish that they could sell. Lin used a big thick knife he pulled from a shelf on the boat and held out the very big fins, then cut them off using a back and forth motion and his large blade.

I saw plenty of animals cut up for the meat, back in the village it was everyone's jobs to help bring home the meat. Watching the shark lay still as Lin worked hard to remove the fins, I don't know what I really felt, the animal was longer than two of me; my heart ached a little to see the animal go to waste. Lin cut the fins off and then strung them up from a ling off to the side of the stairs to the wheelhouse. Lin told me that there was good money for big shark fins like that, he had a small pile in his room of dried ones and once he found the right market, he would sell them for good money. Lin showed me around some of the big shark, there were so many more teeth than a pack of simba of fisi, the animal looked very mean, it had scrapes all over its body, it was dark gray on top and white underneath. Lin said that the meat was not a bad meal but was not preferred and that he wouldn't normally take the fins, he especially wouldn't kill it for the fins, but since the captain killed it, he might as well make some money from it.

Lin tied a few ropes around the tail of the animal, he used the crane to lift it enough to drop it over the side of the ship and then drop it into the water. I found myself staring into the water, the animal was so very big and so very strong, and in a moment, one shot from the captain's pistol, and it was no longer moving. Ngozi yelled to me to get back to work once I was done inspecting the shark with Lin, I was glad to help any of my crewmates that I could and whenever I could, I even helped Lin with the shark, but it was strange. I helped Nasur carry a few bins of the discarded fish down to the kitchen, he had a large freezer to store them and taught me how to clean them first. The insides of the fish smelled a little bad, they were more slimy than the outsides and the blood seemed to be sticky. Nasur showed me how to cut the fish for the meat and then we carried the discarded parts up and threw them over the side. The day fishing was very hard work, the muscles in my legs and arms were very sore at the end of the day and I did not even try to watch my Sesame Street, I fell asleep early.

The next few days were filled with plenty of fishing and cooking with Nasur, using the hook poles to shake out the caught fish and then drop them down to the ice hold was a lot of work, using a shovel to cover the fish with ice made the tops of my arms ache each night, the hook pole made the bottoms of my arms hurt each day, and the slippery deck of the ship made my legs sore all over. The hot sun made us hurry to put the fish on ice, if we did not then they would begin to smell bad and then we could not sell them at the market when we arrived. The captain worked to make sure we had plenty of fish to sell and places to sell them, Ohah told me that they usually traveled up through to the northern parts of Europe and then back down around the bottom of Africa again. I was excited to travel all over with these sailors and I was even more excited to bring back the tales of my journey to my village. It was a lot of work to fill the holds with the fish we caught, but each fish we put in, was another fish closer to the top, then I could say I saw an entire room filled with fish! That would be a lot of fish.

Ngozi told me one night that we were going to offload our fish for a market in Zanzibar. I did not know what a Zanzibar was but he was most excited about it. Seeing the very large Ngozi smile when he spoke about the markets in Zanzibar made me a little excited to see them as well. Ngozi told me about the white sand beaches, the beautifully dressed people, the bright colors and patterns of the clothes and the foods that were very good. The stories of the people sounded wonderful, but they also made me miss my village, my friends, and my mother. I was feeling very lonely, I was out on my own to become a man, but they were still missing from me. I laid in my hammock that night and still thought back to my home, I thought about the night I went hunting with Teeta and everything that lead me to Father Shumbin and the church, and then how I got to the ship I was on. My whole life I knew my village, my home, and the way everything worked with my people, in a very few short weeks it seemed, everything was different.

The day before we stopped near the coast city of Zanzibar there was much more work to do, I cleaned much of the boat and continued to perform my cooking duties, the water was very light blue, the sun shimmered silver for a far distance, there were many smaller boats floating in the water, many of them were hauling up traps from the water below. Most of the boats were long and skinny, men standing in them were using very long sticks to push them along in the water to get around. The boat stopped a far ways out, Ohah told me that the waters were too shallow for the ship so WE had to load all of our caught fish onto the smaller boat and haul them to the market to be sold and traded. I was excited to see the city, it must have been like the city I left behind, full of many different people with their own lives, going about their own way.

I helped to load many of the caught fish into big crates, Lin used the crane to pull the large wooden boxes from the bottom of the hull and load them onto the small boat to take them to shore. Ngozi, Nasur and Ohah all traveled with the boat to take the crate ashore in the morning. I helped to fill more wooden crates by myself after I was shown how to do it, Lin worked the crane. Nasur drove the boat back and forth between the ship and the docks to offload the fish, Ohah and Ngozi moved the crates to where they belonged and then brought back food and other supplies for Nasur to bring back to the ship, for me to bring aboard. I would offload the supplies Nasur brought, and then reload the wooden crates with Lin for Nasur to take back to the docks. I spent most of the day working, the sun rose high into the sky and began t sink again. The sky turned a bright orange and with it behind me, it made the city look very alive and the boats in the water cast long shadows behind them towards the city.

When most of the fish were out of the hull and the ice mostly melted, I sat on a box along the side of the ship, and leaned onto the side and stared out over the water. When I was a young boy I would stare out over the grass plains, sometimes I would see a strange random animals wandering around looking for food or water, I thought of people like that, sure the men hunted but from far enough away, it must have looked like wandering to the animals. I heard steps on the metal stairs beside me, I didn't want to take my eyes off of the city, small dots of bright yellows reflected the sun from windows and back towards the ship. My chin rested on my wrists, the metal rail was cold on my arms but the sun was warm on my back. The wind smelled salty like the ocean, but a little sweet from the breezes bringing smells from the city. I thought very hard to think about Teeta, us as boys and the fun we used to have. After the rains broke free from the skies, we would find puddles of rain water and then run and slide into the mud, my mother always told me to wash the mud off before coming home because she did not want all that mess. My mother knew we were just children, and that children were children.

      "You can go and see it tomorrow boy," the captain began to speak as he neared the bottom steps beside me. I told the captain; "my mother always said that when something was missing, you will notice and it can make you sad, and that there was never anything wrong with being sad." Captain Raza asked me if I was missing my home, I told him that I was a little but that I chose to take this journey, and that because I made the choice as a man, that I would simply be a little sad for those that were missing from me. I made the choice to take my journey very far away, I made the choice as a man, and like a man, I would be proud of my choice. "Sounds like a good idea for any man" the captain told me. Sir.. I asked because I did not understand what the captain was saying. "That a man should have conviction in his decisions, right or wrong, good or bad, he made the choice, each choice is self-inflicted and those choices are what turn us into men."

      "Yes sir" I responded, I still had sorrow in my heart for my home. The captain walked past me and headed down to the galley. I continued to stare out into the distance, I saw the boat with Nasur, Ngozi and Ohah coming back. I shouted down the stairwell to Lin so he could come up and work the crane to bring everything back on the deck. Lin climbed up the metal stairs and out the hallway door to the deck, he was yawning and rubbing his eyes as he climbed into his seat to work the crane controls. The men brought more supplies back up with them in the boat, some drums of fuel and other assorted supplies. The men brought two drums of fuel with each trip out, and then some of them even took empty drums back with them. There were a lot of supplies moving back and forth between the ship and the city, and it was only the first day. The men offloaded and shared small stories with each other of some of the people they saw or the foods they tasted.

The men stopped off at a small fire on the beach for caught seafood, music and dancing people before they climbed back into the boat and came to the ship, Ohah was shaking his hands and moving his hips while Nasur and Ngozi both laughed at him. Ohah was always smiling and anytime he had a chance to dance with a pretty girl, he was quick to raise his arm, bow with a smile and then he would grab her hand and dance for a few minutes in any sort of music. Ohah loved to dance with girls, he said that all girls should be respected and danced with. Ohah felt that dancing with a girl was a nice way to show them that he cared that they were well and also a way to share a memory with them for a moment, a short memory that only the two of them would share, and he always got the pretty girls to smile at him, even if they did not speak the same language.

I got to travel to Zanzibar with Ohah and Lin, Ngozi watched over the ship while the captain slept, he hardly left his ship. Ohah shared some of the foods with me and we saw many people. We gathered more supplies and hauled more crates of fish to different markets, many locals caught crabs and lobsters and shells from the shallow waters while larger ships like ours brought in crates and crates of fish for people to eat. Ohah smiled very big the whole time we were on the island, he stopped along the streets to dance with very pretty girls and to say hello. Seeing all of the brightly dressed people made me miss my home even morel, many of the people were so very friendly, the woman smiled, the men greeted one another and it was all very nice. Ohah told me try many different foods, some of the crabs did not taste good, other fishes did taste very good, it seemed that everywhere I looked; someone had something cooking over a small flame while the light musical tones whispered on the breeze.

The boat ride back to the ship was much earlier than the boat ride the day before, there was still plenty of days' light left when Ohah informed us that it was time to head back to the ship. "There's still work for us to do" he said as we hauled more barrels of fuel back to the ship. In my absence the captain had a smaller fuel boat sail out to the ship to fill the big tanks in the bottom of the boat, the extra barrels were for a long journey through rough waters to make it to safer passage. Ohah explained that we were headed through waters that we not very friendly. Zanzibar was often a one day stop over to relax and spend some time on land before the time at sea, I asked Ohah if it was normal to feel kind of woozy on land, he said that I was slowly getting used to being on the boat and that it would still take time to get used to the difference between the two. I did not know what kind of dangerous waters were ahead but I knew I was with a very good crew under a caring captain so there was no need for me to worry.

The next few days were spent full steam ahead, the men did not even fish, there was plenty of time to sit around and watch Sesame Street, the men also had other video movie discs they watched on their own television picture boxes in their own cabins. Each man had to spend some time at night watching the water for smaller boats trying to sail out to our ship. On the third night of no fishing it was my turn to watch the water for other small boats. We were trying to get passed the country of Somalia, we were aiming to get into the Gulf of Aden from the Arabian sea. I was sitting on a box near the back rail of the ship, the wind was cold and I was sitting in the dark thinking about the night I went hunting with Teeta and the other men, it was making me sad. Captain Raza came down and stood beside me, he was still and quiet like the water in the distance. Raza had thin short hair around the bottom of his face, his skin was not very dark and his body was thin and tall.

"You sailing alright boy?' the captain asked me. I thought about it for a moment, I did not want to offend him so I nodded and told him that I was sailing well. I thanked the man for his kind heart to bring me onto his ship and for helping me with my journey. I told Raza that I always talked to my good friend Teeta, that I wanted to explore and have a journey, and that I could not wait to tell my mother all about everything.

Raza asked me to tell him a little about my life in the village, about my nights as a boy and then about my night hunting with Teeta and the other men before setting out to become a man, so I began my story. I told Raza about my journey, I told him about Whutta and meeting his mother, Raza laughed a little because he also has met Whutta's mother. I talked about the fisi old man that took the money that was given to me, I talked about missing my mother also. Raza could tell by my voice that I missed my home.

Raza stood up quickly from his leaning stance next to me, his jump made my heart jump as well. Raza told me to keep an eye out on the distance while he ran to the wheelhouse for a moment. I tried to look out into the distance but all I could see was pure blackness. Raza came back from the wheelhouse with a long wooden gun, it looked at little like one of the guns Nga or Ziza may have carried when they hunted. Raza told me to watch way out in the water, he saw a small light that gave him the thought that there were people out there trying to catch up to the boat. Raza told me that pirates scour the waters trying to load onto ships passing by in order to steal them or hold them for money. I did not understand why so many people needed so much money, in my village everyone worked and everyone ate, we all took care of each other. Raza knelt down to one knee and brought his face to the back of the long rifle; he closed one eye and took careful aim. "You are not going to shoot anyone are you" I begged of the captain.

The captain was a good man, a just man and I could not bear to see him take someone's life. I closed my eyes and covered my ears with my hands, I was frightened. I did not know who the pirates were but I could not have respect for a man that was going to take someone's life. "Boom" a shot rang out in my ears, I could feel the force in my chest. I felt the cold breeze on the wet tear lines on my face; I did not want to hear someone's life stop. I was very sad and all of my sore muscles tensed up after the shot echoed in my body. Raza slapped me on the shoulder; I dropped my hands and kept my head bowed down. "Take a look boy, and don't doubt your captain" Raza said as he walked away. I looked up to see a small flame on the water, I wasn't certain of what I was seeing as I tried to stop my shoulders from shaking a little. "Captain" I turned to ask. "Those small runner boats have a fast engine and require much gas to come out this far, if you shoot an incendiary round into the engine, either the gas or the oil will catch fire, if you shoot one man, the rest will keep coming, if you shoot one motor, they can't paddle fast enough to catch you."

I felt much better that the good captain did not take anyone's life. I should not have doubted my captain but I was so afraid that he was going to take a life that was not his to take. I spent the rest of the night silent and thinking about my home, it was missing from me and I was missing from it. I missed the warm nights, I missed the yelps and howls of the fisi in the distance, I missed my mother and I certainly missed my friend. It was lonely that night, the night sky was ever so bright with stars, many of them reflected down onto the water as we sailed up the Red Sea. As we passed the Gulf of Aden city lights could be seen in the far distance, the itty bitty small lights almost blended into the star reflections on top of the water at night, everything was so dark. During the days creatures could be seen down in the water, amazing fascinating creatures of all sorts.

Early in the morning the captain ordered everyone to cast nets and fish again, we were to stop at the Port of Sudan for a late evening and selling some fish would help to refuel the ship. As I took up my hook pole I realized how much fun I was truly having, I had no thought about my home nearly as much that day when I was fishing with the men and as I worked harder, they looked at me less like a boy and more like a man. With several crates worth of fish so sell to markets, the trip to Sudan was much like Zanzibar, the people were much lighter in color, like the captain and most of the crew, the clothes were not as brightly colored and some of the people wore even more dressings, like over their head. I tried to eat many different foods, Ohah and Ngozi argued over which foods were better and with Nasur and me to help to break up the arguments, the four of us ate plenty of food.

We traveled through the Suez Canal, it was a long tunnel that the ship sailed into and then the water level changed and the ship went up and then back down again, there were children playing along the sides, running as the ship sailed, some of them waved while others flew shapes in the air. I liked to see the children playing and having fun. I thought a lot of me and Teeta when we were children, we would pretend we were many different animals, even the great big tembo that walked around the plains, their big ears flapping back and forth. It was not easy growing into a man, it was much fun being a young boy but I could not be one forever. I was learning very much, I was getting better at my jobs on the ship and I liked all of my crewmates and they seemed pleased in my work.

Ngozi told me that once we reached Port Said that there might be some men coming aboard and that I should just tell them I am a sailor with the boat. I was instructed not to mention the crate that was picked up from Comoros. I did not understand why not to mention the crate but I was going to do as my first mate instructed me to. The shore in the distance had many buildings, I was becoming good at English and understood much of what was being spoken on the ship. I was getting better at fishing and still spent my time staring out into the distances, wondering what my village was doing, and then I would change sides of the ship and wonder what else I might get to explore in the world. The longer we sailed the less I thought about my home, I spoke with the captain a few times and told him more about the night I was hunting with the men and Teeta, I talked about my journey before I arrived at Father Shumbin's church.

I thought back to the day I walked with Loza toward the morning sun, he was certain he was ready to become a man, Teeta was also certain that he was ready to become a man and he wanted to hurry and be one, I was not as certain, I wanted time to explore the world a little more and now I was. Loza had Pika to become his wife when he returned to her, she was in love with him and he was ready to be her husband. Pika and Loza were a good man and wife, they complimented each other and worked very well together, my mother Bendu always said "it was a man's job to be a husband, as much as it was a woman's job to be a wife." The air smelled different as we exited the canal, there were many more boats and of many sizes around us as the captain sailed closer to the port we needed to go to.

There were long docks that stretched far out into the water when we reached the port, we did not have to load up the small boat and motor to the shore or smaller docks, and Captain Raza took the ship right to a certain dock and was able to tie off in the later hours. Ngozi and Ohah loaded the crate from Comoros onto the small boat and Lin hoisted it down to the water as the ship turned to line up with the docks. I did not understand, if I was supposed to stay quiet about the wooden crate, why it was going away on the smaller boat. Ohah left Ngozi to take the boat back out into the sea a little further, I was confused why this was happening.

140

There were some men that loaded the ship, there were men wearing blue clothes that looked the same and they spoke a language I did not understand. Captain Raza raced down the stairs to greet the men, he spoke to them in their language and they each bowed to one another. Ohah reminded me that I was supposed to tell the men that I did not know anything about the crate no matter what the men said, I was not sure why I was instructed to lie but my captain ordered it. The strangers began to speak English to the crew, there were three men, two instructed us to remain on the deck while the other one searched around down below. One man had a very long thick beard asked me my name, where I was from and where I was going. I did not know how to respond to the man so I told him the truth. The man asked me many more questions and I answered them, he then asked me what I knew about Comoros.

My heart began to thump, it pounded like thunder in my ears and I felt my fingers begin to twitch. The man had deep black eyes and his beard smelled badly. I asked the man who Comoros was, I could not think of what else to say. The man stared at me and I felt myself begin to tremble. The other man shouted to the man standing closely to me, I did not know what he said but the man standing big in front of me went away. I was much relieved when the large man turned around and headed away from me, I was a little afraid and I did not want to be in trouble. The third man came up from the stairwell and hurried to get back near the dock. Another man walked down the dock towards the ship, he was wearing tall black boots and shiny metals on his coat. Raza walked up to the man and shook the strangers hand.

Raza leaned in and spoke some words to the man with the tall black boots. I could not hear the men conversing and then the new strange man shouted aloud: "Smuggler, liar, thief," he then turned around and headed back to where he came from. The last man stood up in the captain's face, the captain stood tall and did not look the man in the face. The man reached his arm back and punched the captain in the stomach, the captain dropped to one knee, letting out a slight grunt as the men left the boat to get back on to the dock. Lin walked over to the captain and helped him back to his feet. I could not see Ngozi anywhere in the distance on the boat, I wondered where he went. The captain headed into his quarters below the deck, he told Ohah and me to stay on the deck and keep watch.

I asked Ohah what a smuggler was,he told me that the captain had a few different names and that "smuggler" was one of them. The captain loved his home country of Egypt, he also kept an eye out for treasures and artifacts from his ancestry and tried to return it to museum's in Egypt, even if the government did not approve of it. Raza often sent his finds right to safe places rather than claim them to the government, which often sells them instead of donates them. Raza is also called a smuggler depending on which country he is near, some places think of him as a fisherman, other's a pirate for stealing some ancient Egyptian sculptures and then sending them back to his home country. Ngozi had a small sacred golden sculpture of some sort of creature and was on his way to deliver it to someone that would make sure that it got to the right place, and pay him a finder's fee for doing it all.

We were told we had to remain at the dock for the rest of the day and night, the authorities warned Raza that if he tried to leave that his ship would be sunk by one of the vessels that they had patrolling the waters for pirates just like him. I was concerned, I did not want to be fired on, or sunk in the water, I did not want any of my friends to get hurt either. It was stressful to be on the boat, some guards stood tall and watchful over the ship the entire night, they stood with their arms crossed and Ohah and I stood for a while, staring back at them. The air was warm and calm; it was pleasant to be out of the colder ocean air, the warm air better reminded me of the air back home, I did not like the thought of being shot at. Nasur came running out from the doorway that lead to the below deck and ran all the way up to the Wheelhouse, his urgency was startling and Ohah gave me a strange look, a sly smile out of the side of his mouth. Ohah reached into his pocket and pulled out a deck of cards, he smiled at me and then turned to the man standing guard, they would not let us off our ship but he wondered if they might be interested in some game play since all of us were supposed to watch each other anyways.

The guards were posted to watch to ensure that no one from our ship stepped off; we were all to remain on the ship for a day. I was not sure why we were being held at the dock but I was going to do what my captain ordered me to do, it was my job. Ohah cracked jokes and spoke with one of the guards a little but got very little response from either man. I tried to be polite and not stare at the men but they were different from me, they had shiny buttons on their clothes, their uniforms were the same but their bodies were different. Both men had bushy beards on their faces; I though it must have been hot to have such thick uniforms and thick hair on their face as they stood still on the dock. Ohah warned me that they were very serious at their jobs and even though he joked a little, that they would not hesitate to fight or hurt anyone that tried to leave the boat. Captain Raza was known in many ports for one reason or another, some places he would simply give someone a ride to another country, other places he would buy or sell artifacts and make some money, this was partially why he was known as a thief or a smuggler. On rare occasion when some pirates in small boats would try to attack his ship then he might sink their small boats to avoid being taken captive; it was his job to protect his ship and crew.

The guards did not find humor in Ohah, he smiled and pleaded with them to join him in a game since I was new and did not know much about cards. The two guards looked very mean and did not trade words with Ohah, they just looked more mean if Ohah tried to get to close to leaving the ship. Ohah tried to tell the men jokes, and when they did not laugh he asked if they were being paid to not think, or think things were funny. I did not understand why Ohah was making jokes with the men, they were not very happy. Nasur came running back down the stairs from the wheelhouse and then ran up to Ohah and began to whisper in his ear. "Sorry sirs, I was informed I was being rude and I apologize" Ohah told the men that were standing guard over us. I was surprised to hear Ohah change his attitude so quickly, I had to look at him to make sure he was not goofing again, but he just winked at me.

As the night went on, Lin and Nasur took over our watch, captain Raza did not want anyone getting onto the boat at all, and the guards were supposed to make sure that no one got off either. Ohah and I made the breakfast meal, I mostly made it while Ohah slept back at the table while I made the best use of my training with Nasur, I made an easy breakfast with what I could put together and once Ohah and I ate, we relieved Nasur and Lin, whom where still sitting around watching the guards, watching them back, all with crossed arms. Lin said that Raza relieved them for a short spell overnight, that they had a three hour break in the middle before having to come back so everyone had slept a little. While cooking I asked Ohah what Nasur had really whispered to him, I was curious and not too tired to remember to ask.

Nasur is from Turkey and his sister needs his help. Nasur begged for the captain to help and the minute the
144

twenty-four hour hold is lifted from the ship, we are setting sail to help. I did not know where turkey was but I was excited to get to go. Ohah told me that his sister had met a Syrian man, his name was Ibrihim, and as soon as they were married, he moved her to his country and she had since been like a slave. Ibrihim did not respect woman, he used them for his pleasure and it did not sit well with Nasur from the beginning. Nasur got word that his sister and her two daughters finally got away from the man and needed more help to get further away to safety. The captain was going to drop everything he had to do in his home country to help out the sister of one of his crew members, he knew what she meant to Nasur and he was going to help the girls any way he could.

Lin and Nasur headed down to eat while Ohah and I stood watch, we stood two by two so it was even numbers with the guards so no one had the upper hand. Ohah went up to speak with the captain for a moment and he headed up to the wheelhouse. When Ohah returned he told me that the captain was laying on the floor stretching his back from all of standing and trying to figure out the best plan to keep everyone safe. Ohah asked about Ngozi, where was the first mate all night? Our ship was closely watched and Ngozi had no way to get back on to it. Ngozi met a antiquities dealer in a small port city nearby called Raff-El-Barr, Raff-El-Barr was very close and there (after he made the sale he was supposed to for the captain) he was informed about Nasur and he filled the boat with fuel cans and headed out before they did.

Ngozi turned right around and headed across the sea, he followed his captains' orders and knew that his crewmate needed his help. The antiquities dealer was a man named Immanuel, he was a very trusted man by the captain and he gave most of his extra money for fuel for Ngozi to make the trip across the sea. The Mediterranean Sea is wavy and choppy, Ngozi was willing to navigate the harsh sea on his own in the middle of the night for his captain, he was a brave man. Ngozi had a nights start on the rest of the crew, Raza told him that he would meet him and the girls between Tartus and Cyrpus somewhere. Ohah was gearing up for a long fast haul to catch up to Ngozi so there were no problems for Nasur's family, they were all he had. The captain knew that he owed his crew, they didn't just work for him but they were all brothers together.

A little after midday a second set of guards replaced the replaced guards, they called to the captain that he was free to go and without hesitation, the captain started the rumbling engines and began to pull us from the port. Lin joined the captain in the wheelhouse to help navigate for smaller boats and to keep slow enough in the idling traffic area crossing the traffic from the canal. Ohah and I stood near the front of the ship with Nasur, he was pacing back and forth, waving his arms to shoo boats out of the way. The crew was all involved as we set to the north, there was not much of the day and no contact with Ngozi. There was no way to know if Ngozi was able to pick up the girls he was sent to retrieve or not, it was all a waiting game. I tried to make lunch but no one wanted to eat, so I ran plates to each of my crewmates then washed the dishes. Ohah assured me that Ngozi was a skilled sailor and fighter, he always carried a large blade with him and often a small pistol that he was willing to use if it meant returning to his ship alive.

The tension was high as we neared Cyprus after dark, we had beacon lights on top of the ship and Ohah and Nasur stood at the front with spot lights searching for Ngozi. There was a great distance between the land and the island, there was a slim chance of finding Ngozi, and there was no certainty that he even made the pickup, or was able to get away with the girls, everyone was looking around in the water for the small boat, hoping we could find Ngozi. From off in the distance Nasur kept his spot light on something in the water, Ohah tried to do the same but did not see what Nasur thought he saw. There was a small twinkle in the distance, a white flashlight that got closer and closer. The captain slowed the ship down and Lin burst through the door and to set up the crane very quickly. Ohah yelled to me to take his place with the light so he could help Ngozi. I had a hard time following the small boat in the dark waves as it began to lightly rain in the dark night.

The commotion was confusing, Ohah was shouting, Lin was shouting, and Nasur was shouting even louder. Nasur and I tried to keep our lights on the boat so everyone could see. I felt my chest tighten as Ohah changed the wires on the crane so we could hoist the boat on deck. Everyone was in a hurry to get Ngozi back on deck to safety. Ohah tied a rope around his waist and then to the rigging, he needed to go down with the wires to help hook them up to get the entire boat out of the water and back to where it belonged on the deck. Lin lowered the cables to the water with Ohah tied to them. The waves raised and lowered the boat in the water and Ngozi tried to keep the boat even with the ship so they didn't bang together.

Lin slowly raised the crane, Nasur was shouting to hurry so he could embrace his sister and her two daughters. Ngozi was shouting that he got them but that they needed to get moving. Once the boat was on the deck Nasur raced to help his sister and her daughters out of the boat and rushed then to inside. Ngozi began to get out of the boat when he noticed that Ohah was not moving very much, he was holding onto the boat, leaning against the side and not talking to his first mate. Lin climbed out from his seat at the crane and ran to Ohah; it was obvious that there was something wrong. Lin ran towards Ohah to help him, he did not move. Nasur was guiding his sister and her daughters down the stairwell to his quarters so they were out of the rain, the deck was getting slippery with the light rain, the lights reflected off of the small puddles on the deck, it was hard to hurry to Ohah, and the rain hit the deck and made the sounds harder to hear.

Ngozi fell over the side of the boat trying to get to Ohah, I tried to run to help as well, but I slipped and fell onto the deck, sliding to the side. I tried to stand up and run again but as the boat tilted from side to side in the waves, I fell many times. Some of the work lights shined towards Ohah, the captain tried to get the ship out of the bay and back into open waters and on our way. Ngozi pushed and pulled the boat away so Lin could help Ohah. Ngozi pulled the boat away from Ohah and when he did, Ohah just fell to the floor. Lin dragged Ohah away from the swinging boat that Ngozi struggled to fight. Raza shouted over the overhead to get everything secured and get below deck so the ship could get back out of the bay in a hurry, Ohah did not move. As me and Lin dragged him towards the lower deck door, Ngoza continued to shout to Ohah. Lin shouted to me to pull and for Ohah to wake up, he grew more and more angry, his voice began to sound like a growl with the rain in the background

I got to Lin as he was shouting to Ohah; Ngozi was trying to keep the small boat from sliding back towards Lin as he knelt over Ohah on the deck. Ohah was not moving, Lin could be heard shouting over the sound of the rain on the deck and all of the equipment; Ngozi heaved the swinging boat to the side and tied the bow to the back bulkhead to keep it from moving more so he could finally get to his friend Ohah. I did not know what to do to help Lin help Ohah, I was worried for my friend and wanted to help him. Ngozi fell to his knees, he shook Ohah by the shirt, Ohah still did not move. Ngozi lifted Ohah from under the shoulders and began to carry him on the wet deck, he slowly and carefully stepped side to side to get his friend out of the rain. Lin shouted to me to tell the captain that Ohah was in bad shape.

I slid and fell my way to the captain; I climbed the metal stair and burst into his wheelhouse without knocking. "Ohah is hurt bad, Ngozi say he in bad shape" I shouted to the captain. Raza told me to hold the wheel and aim for the distance until someone comes back up. Everything seemed so fast in the rain, I gripped the wheel that captain Raza told me to hold onto, I did not know what I was doing and I hoped very hard that someone would come and get me very soon. I kept my eyes looking far ahead, the water was black and there were very little spots of light sparkling on the tops of the waves. The boat rocked side to side, I tried my best to hold the wheel straight and not have any problems as I tried to steer the ship, but I was much afraid, and I worried about Ohah. The rain beat against the glass windows, the noise made it hard to hear anything that was happening on the deck below.

Ngozi came into the wheelhouse, I was glad to see the first mate as I did not want to steer anymore. Ngozi looked very sad, his jaw muscles bulged in the shadows of the instrument lights, his lips were perched and his eyes hung low. "Is Ohah going to be ok?" I asked Ngozi as he entered the wheelhouse, Ngozi just shook his head slowly. Ngozi silently nodded to the door so I let myself out of the wheelhouse and towards the metal stairs back down to the deck. I could not help Ngozi, I could not help Ohah, I was going to head below deck and see if Nasur needed my help in any way. I held on tightly to the railing going down, the rain was making everything very slippery and I did not want to fall down the stairs, my legs already hurt a little from falling on the hard deck racing to help Ohah and the boat.

I got to the bottom of the stair and as I turned to the door to go below deck, I saw something towards the back of the boat, it was a man. I could not see who it was, it was too tall to be Lin, too big to be the captain and hunched over too much to be Nasur, it was a man I did not know. The man slowly stepped closer to me in the rain, the light was no good to see the man but I knew it was a man I did not know, and there was another behind him, I struggled to see in the rain. I quickly stepped to the door and I shouted with panic to the captain to "come up, there are men on the ship." I was more afraid, I wanted to try and help Ohah but suddenly there were strange men on the ship and I did not know what to do, I was scared.

I was frozen, my mind just sat blank and my eyes made out two large figures in the dark night. I wanted to run and hide in my room, I wanted to help Ohah or Ngozi, something. The rough black water below raised and lowered the large ship, but could not be seen off to either side in the night. For a moment I thought perhaps my eyes were playing tricks on me, or maybe my tired mind was fooling me as I watched two large figured saunter towards me in the dark.

The captain was quickly right behind me in the doorway, he began to shout in a language I did not understand, I tried to stay out of the way and in a moment, the captain shouted for me to move out of the way, and he pushed me to the side a little and then ran towards the first man. The captain began to swing his arms at the first man, it was hard to see the two men in the dark as they fought, I watched the captain and the first man push back and forth, a streak of light shone in the dark, I did not know what I saw but the second dark man raised his arms up over his head, I charged towards the man. When I was younger Teeta and me got into scuffles sometimes, we would push and shove each other as we grew and competed, Teeta was always faster and stronger than me and I did not ever want to hurt my friend.

I charged at the second man, he was standing over the captain and the first man in the dark and I did not know what I was going to do, but I had to do something for my captain. I struck the second man with my shoulder; I hoped to knock him down so he would leave Raza alone. When I collided with the man, my shoulder felt like it had been stepped on by a tembo, the man did not budge after I hit him, but I did. I fell onto the wet deck, I was already all wet from the rain but I felt the water splash from my body. The rain continued to fall on me and then I felt the man kick into my chest, he was shouting in a language I did not understand. My chest hurt very bad and I could not breathe in after the kick, I tried to roll out of the way but the man grabbed ahold of my shirt collar and I felt like I was being spun around like one of those kites I saw the children on the banks play with. I swung and kicked my legs as hard as I could to get the man to let me go, I felt my toes tap the deck below me and once I had a little weight on one foot, I swung the other very hard.

My foot hit very hard at the man, the grip the man had on my shirt let go and once again, I fell to the deck. In the dark I could see that the man fell over also, he groaned in agony, my chest hurt very badly, it was extremely hard to breathe, the rain made everything very hard to hear. I had a very hard time seeing with the rain in my eyes as I looked to find the captain and the first man still fighting. I held onto my hurting shoulder and ran to charge the first man to knock him off of my captain. The man was sitting on top of the captain when I lunged at him, I toppled on top of the man, he continued to shout words I did not understand. The man I was on top of used his head to hit me, I felt like he broke my forehead with his when he hit his head to mine. The first man wiggled and turned so that I was no longer lying on top of him in the rain. The first man began to stand up to his feet when BANG, a loud boom rang out.

My whole body froze, I could not breathe, the sound echoed off of each rain drop as it fell from the night sky. The sound of the bang made my ears hurt and it was hard to see as I lay on the wet deck. I was afraid to find out where the shot came from, I uncovered my ears from my hands and slowly tried to look around. The first man was still standing over top of me, the body of the second man fell to the deck. The sound of the gunshot alerted Ngozi in the wheelhouse that there was a problem on the deck, he was deafened by the rain and unaware of the commotion.

The floodlight lit up the entire deck; I looked up to see the captain standing with his arm raised and his pistol leaking smoke from the end. The captain and the man continued to exchange words back and forth; I fought to scramble to my feet, my chest still felt on fire from the kick that knocked my wind from me. The second man began to leak his blood onto the deck of the ship, he did not move. "Are you able to move boy?" the captain shouted to me, I nodded that I could, as I wheezed and gasped for my breath to return to me. My head hurt and it made my vision blurry, the captain shouted for me to go and get Nasur from below, but not his guests. I fought my way to get below deck, the swaying ship made walking on the stairs hard; I could not raise my one arm for my ribs ached too much. I slowly climbed down the stairs to find Nasur, I told him that the captain requested him; he was standing with Lin, over Ohah who was laid out on the floor, lifeless.

Nasur hung his head as he walked quickly towards the metal stairs that would take him back out onto the rainy deck. Lin looked at me and shook his head as he closed his eyes and hung his head for Ohah. I turned to follow Nasur; he was already up the stairs and stepping out into the rain before I began to climb the stairs one handed, the other wrapped around my chest. As I got near the top of the stairs I could hear shouting, I worried that there was still fighting going on so I tried to hurry again to help my captain. I stepped to the door and peered out into the lit night on the rainy deck and I could better hear what they were shouting about. The captain was pointing his pistol at the first man; the second was no longer anywhere on the deck from what I could see in the spotlight. "Mr. Nasur, this man is your problem, he is a factor in the death of Ohah, what do you suggest?" the captain shouted. The man stood near the side of the ship, he shouted and spit at the captain. Nasur shouted to the captain; "he treated his daughters like his wife, and all of them like slaves, even in the bedroom, he was not fatherly, he did not act like a husband should have, and he did not treat his daughters as a father should have." The captain walked closer to the man, he leaned in to speak to him and as the man let his shoulders drop, there was another gunshot, the flash lit up the angry face of a mustached man with clenched fists.

The captain shoved the man over the side of the ship as he began to fall after the gun shot.My strength left me and I dropped to my knees; I did not want to see a man killed. I felt lost again, I missed my home and I wanted to go back. All I could do was stare out into the rain as the captain and Nasur walked towards me to get out of the rain and go back below deck. Nasur passed and kept his head hung low, the captain stopped by my side, I could not tell what he was saying, it was a murmur as I stared out over the rainy deck, he placed his hand on my shoulder and patted a few times, then passed me as well. I knelt at the door for I do not know how long, I felt like everything in my brain was blurry, my body felt heavy and I wanted it to stop. My clothes clung to me from being wet, they made each step down the metal stairs hard to deal with, I struggled with each step.

My head hung heavy, I felt like everything had changed in a few quick moments. I felt like my months away from my home suddenly whirled away and I felt that if I ever made it back home that I would be so very different that no one would know me. I had experienced a few of my fellow tribe members that had lost their lives, everyone gets old enough that their bodies can no longer go on in their form and make their way back to the night sky, but this was different. I did not know Ibrihim, he was a mean monster man, I do not understand what would lead a person to treat any other person like a rock or a clump of dirt and not as another living person. There are no excuses not to treat people as people, women, children, elders, everyone deserves their own lives and not to be treated or turned into slaves.By the time I made it down the steps, the main galley was empty, the body of Ohah had been moved and Nasur was not around either. I walked to my small room and changed out of my wet clothes. I struggled and fought to get my shirt off of me, it was stuck to my skin and the harder I pulled and yanked, the harder it clung to me. I found myself twisting and spinning trying to rip my shirt off, I did not care if I ripped the shirt in half. I began to get very angry, I was sad and angry and hurt, all at the same time.

I was mad, angry, sad, furious and lost, and I could not change anything so I began to cry, I felt helpless and lost and wished to be a young boy again, to be back long ago before I learned and saw so many things in the world. I wanted to prove to my village that I could be the man I set out to be, I wanted to be that man for myself and all I could do was cry that I was not. I fell to the floor, I stopped struggling and for a few moments after the hard *thud*, I just sat tangled up in my wet shirt on the floor. "Knock Knock" I heard a voice through the door ask to see me when I was through. I slowed down and realized that if I took a moment to think about how I was tangled, I could untangle myself. My mother once tried to teach me the same lesson, I was a boy and did not understand but as I sat in wet clothing, crying and wasting my energy being angry.I heard my mother's voice come back to me and I stopped fighting for a moment, and just breathed. I straightened out my sore arm and slowly worked my other arm through the wet sleeve, I was upset that I got angry, I was very angry for being unable to help Ohah, or that I saw the captain take two lives, I was sad about the whole evening.

I sat on the floor for a few more minutes; I wrapped my arms around my knees and pulled them to my beating chest. My chest still hurt but it was comforting to sit and breathe and just think back to being at home.  Imagining running through the tall grasses and listening for my mother to shout for me calmed me down, it brought me peace and I finished changing my clothes. I was very sad for the lives the captain took, I did not know the men but all lives should be lived, each person is allowed to choose if they want to die, it should not be chosen for them. My mother told me when I was young that everyone has their own body in their control, that no one should decide for someone else, some people in my village had earrings and others' did not, and it was their choice, most chose to live, and others simply decided that their life had gone on long enough. I was upset and that told me that it was time to start thinking about my next adventure.

Time seemed to step between heart beats, everything slowed down, the changing of my clothes after getting stuck seemed like the moment I paused, slamming down to the floor seemed to echo through my whole body on the floor. I could not bring the many sunrises or sunsets I had seen in my life into my mind, I was lost and alone. I was afraid and wanted to close my eyes and wake up back in my bed, in my village, and with my mom. Blinking my eyes felt like a whole night of restless sleep occurred between opening my heavy eyelids, I could feel my eyes cross and shake for a moment as they refocused. My head throbbed with each heart beat from my chest, my ribs felt like they were on fire and the lungs held safely within them did too.

I stepped out of my cabin to come face to face with captain Raza, he had an unhappy look on his face, the corners of his mouth hung low and his shoulders slumped forward a bit. "Captain Sir" I greeted him as he stood against the bulkhead. The captain did not say a word to me but nodded for me to follow him, we headed towards the galley where I last saw Ohah lying on the floor, I was a very sad to have the picture in my head of how he looked, but he was not there. Raza told me that he was sorry that I had to see him do what he did, he felt bad that he had to take the lives but he was protecting his crew and as the captain, that meant doing it anyway that he had to. Raza said he saw the second man stand above me and draw a large knife, he was going try to take my life so the captain took his.

Captain Raza stood and told me that Ohah must have been crushed between the boat and the ship, he knew the dangers of tying into the boat riggings but that his friend Ngozi was on the boat and even though he did not know the three women that were with him, it was still his duty to Nasur, as a friend and crewmate, to make sure those women made it onboard safely and quickly. Ohah was a great man and it made the captain very sad to see him without life anymore. Raza said he was making plans to get Ohah back to Tunis so he could be buried at his home. Raza thanked me for running and helping him as he struggled to get the first stranger to stop fighting him in the dark. I asked Raza who the men were and what they wanted, he paused for a moment.

Raza looked around to make sure that no one could hear him, "I wasn't sure at first but once he began to shout at me to return his property, I knew it was Ibrihim." Nasur confirmed that the first man was in fact Ibrihim, a "Syrian dog that wallowed in its' own filth." Nasur whispered in his ear that the man did not deserve to live and should be put down like a mongrel. Raza told me that he did not shoot the man in the heart like he would often prefer, but rather in the gut so that if the seas show him mercy, he might survive to land, but if they not, then he did not kill the man out right, a bit of mercy he did not deserve for the life he led. Ibrihim treated his wife very poorly, and his daughters even worse, Raza did not want to talk about Nasur's business, and as captain, he did not have to explain himself or his actions to anyone but he respected his crew for their hard work, and now I was certainly one of his crew.

I told Raza I was not sure how much longer I wanted to sail with him and his ship, I thanked him for all of his leadership and for the adventures I had had with the crew but thought that maybe it was time to continue on with my adventure. Raza nodded that he understood and shook my hand; he thanked me again for having his back in the scuffle and suggested I get some sleep for the night. I did not know how to feel or what to think, I was too sad to sleep but tried to lay in my hammock and rest. My body was tired, it felt empty of energy but my mind was full. I watched the dark ceiling above me, I could not see anything. I was tired, I stirred and wanted to toss and turn a little in my hammock but I could not.

After half of the night had passed I grew restless and tired of not sleeping, I rolled to my side to slide out of my hammock and wandered down the hall towards the galley to watch some picture television movie discs. The ship was almost quiet, the sounds of the engine and the water outside was faint and quiet, there did not seem to be anyone awake other than me. I put in a movie disc and began watching some of the shows I was told to too work on my English. I watched as the big brown tembo talked with the yellow bird, even the silly creatures would not make me feel any better, I missed Ohah, I missed Teeta, and I missed my mother in my village, I was growing very lonely.

I felt a light tap on my shoulder, it startled me a little, I did not hear anyone so I did not expect anyone to be so close behind me. I turned my head to see a very little girl standing behind the couch I was sitting on, my body jumped just a little bit as I turned to see what had tapped me on the shoulder. "Hi" the little girl's soft voice greeted me; "may I join you?" she

158

asked as she walked around the side of the couch to climb onto the couch and sit with me. The little girl spoke English very well so I spoke to her in English back:" yes, please come sit" I responded to her. The little girl was very small and it took her a long moment to try to climb onto the couch in her long dress. The girl had light skin, her dress was long and light blue with brown patterns on it, her head scarf matched the light blue and she was a very pretty little girl. The girl sat close to my side, her feet barely hung over the front edge of the couch and she folded her hands and placed them in her lap. The young girl locked her eyes on the creatures on the television picture box, her face remained emotionless as she took in all the wonderment.

The girl sat quietly next to me through the letter "Y" before she turned to me and began to speak. "My name is Neely, what is yours?" the little girl asked in a weak voice. The little girl looked up to me and smiled as she waited for my response. "My name is Ojimbo Clarke" I responded to the young lady. "I'm Neely, and I'm six." The young girl sat silently for the letter "K" and then she decided I was trustworthy enough to talk to. Neely told me that her and her sister Kippa came out on a boat with their mother Ashanna, they met a very big man named Ngozi and he steered the boat out onto the water, she liked the boat but it was dark and she did not like the dark. Neely told me that she did not want to leave her home behind, she was afraid of going to a new place with her momma and sister.

Neely said that with the help of a neighbor named Uniba the ladies were moved from their home and rushed to a boat where Ngozi was ready to take them to a big ship for a trip. Neely was glad to go on the trip, she loved her mother; she loved her sister even though sometimes they fought. Neely spoke about mean people around her home where she grew up. After a few minutes of Neely talking about her childhood she began to get sad, she began to speak about her father, his name is Ibrihim and he was not nice to them. Ibrihim would lay around the home and yell and shout at the girls, her father would sometimes make Kippa wash him, Ashanna was often slapped around and made to do all of the house chores like chopping wood. Neely was very afraid of Ibrihim, she told me that he always made her mother cry and was very mean to her and her sister.

Neely spoke of one time that Ibrihim slapped around the girls, he laid with them as a husband would, even put them in small cages for days, Neely said sometimes without clothes it got very cold and her mother and sister would cry the whole time. I did not know the Ibrihim man but he treated these women poorly, I was sad that he was dead but wondered if perhaps it was a good thing for this sweet young girl and her family to be rid of him. I could not imagine what kind of a monster would treat their own family like such, I remembered my mother telling me that it takes a woman to give birth to a man, Ibrihim was no man, he was a pile of fisi waste, even covered with flies. Neely spoke through the letters "J" and "M" she would stop and giggle at some of the songs that were sung, she really liked the green guy, he was silly to her. Neely spoke of how much better life will be for her mother Ashanna to live with her brother Nasur once they reach their new home.

During the next day I was working the fishing nets with Lin and Nasur, it was hot and hard work but the pulling with the hook poles made me think about Ohah, how he showed me what to do and the laughing he would do. Raza was back in the wheelhouse, I was not sure where Ngozi was but I made breakfast alone and as the rest of the men ate, I heard Nasur speak about him steering all night long to get everyone's friend Ohah home. The morning meal was silent, there weren't many words, Lin told us that after eating we were to drag the fishing nets to make some money to send Ohah home and help set up our guests with some money for a safer life. Raza cared for the ladies he took aboard as if they were his own family, a family of one of his crew, were family to him. Nasur was very grateful to the captain for rescuing his family, he did not want to leave his place on the ship but he had to make sure his family had a safe new beginning.

I helped to tug and pull the nets with Nasur while Lin worked the crane; he was slower than usual and very tired. I asked Nasur where Ohah was because I did not see him, I was told that his body was being kept on ice to make sure he made it back to his homeland to be buried properly. Ashanna and her daughters stepped out, they wanted to earn their keep but she also knew that the deck of a boat can be dangerous and she wanted to seek permission to help in any way that she could. Raza stepped out from the wheelhouse onto the platform above the metal stairs, he shouted to Ashanna to have her girls sit on their bottoms and that she could come up and speak with him. Ashanna was wearing an all-black cloth; it covered her whole body except for her feet, hands, and face. Her face was nice, her skin was light and smooth but there were spots of red and purple near her eyes, it made her look sad.

Ashanna carefully climbed the stairs to meet the captain, her body swayed against the ship as it tilted in the waves. I continued to try to wrestle the nets over the deck to release the catch, the big piles of fish made everything very slippery and hard to stand, I remembered what the captain said and kept one hand to hold onto the boat, Ohah told me to use that hand to hold the hook pole on the net to hold myself up while walking into the piles of fish. Ohah was a very skilled sailor and he was a very funny man to have around on the ship. Ohah would dance a little or wiggly in a funny way in the fish or pick up small bits and throw them to try and hit Ngozi and then turn and whistle while trying to keep a serious face when Ngozi would turn to try to catch him. Ohah would flash a bright smile when he would turn back to throw something at Ngozi and Ngozi would still be looking at him to catch him, when Ngozi would catch Ohah, they would both laugh very loud and then get back to work.

Ashanna came back out from the wheelhouse, she had a small smile on her face which quickly disappeared when the boat tilted quickly to one side and she let her face show how afraid she was to almost fall over the railing. Ashanna held on tightly to the railing as she reached the larger area to stand on, the deck. Ashanna spoke to her daughters and they stood up and then headed back below deck. Raza had let the guests stay in his cabin while there were aboard, his was the biggest and there being three of them, he let them use it, he slept in the wheelhouse, even when Ngozi was piloting. Ashanna held on tightly to the edge of the ship as she carefully walked towards me, she shouted something to her brother Nasur and then turned back to me. "I am going to work, please show me how" she said to me. I was not a very good teacher, I had only fished over the last several weeks we had been at sea, it still felt new to me, but she wanted to learn from me. Ashanna bent down and rolled up her dress to her knees, she had a pin or something that she used to hold it up so the fabric did not rub in the fish.

Once the bottom of her dress was affixed, Ashanna then puller her head scarf backwards, she let the sun reflect off her beautiful short black hair, she had small shiny earrings in her ears and her eyes were light brown, she was very beautiful under all of the cloth that hid her away. Ashanna seemed to change when I handed her the spare hook pole, she was suddenly strong and confident. I showed Ashanna how to work the nets that came over board, we had to drag them back over the side and then look for the yellow ropes to pull them to open them to spill their bounty onto the deck below. Ashanna let her strength show after years of abuse and punishment just for being a women, she remembered that she was a strong woman that could do things on her own. Ashanna worked as hard as me, a few times I think she worked harder.

Ashanna let her smile get bigger and bigger with each net she helped to fight onto the deck, she found that she was stronger than she ever knew she could be, after years of abuse at the hands of a man that was no man, she realized she was much more than just a servant. After each net we used scoops to move the wrong fish through the hatch holes on the deck so they would go back to the water, and the rest were thrown down to me in the hull where I shoveled ice on the stacks of fish to keep them fresh until we made it to a market to sell them. Towards the end of the afternoon Ngozi joined us for the evening meal, he ate quietly and surely he missed his friend Ohah, just like the rest of us.

Kippa and Neely helped Ashanna to cook for the crew, it was very nice to get a break from the hot kitchen, but I did wash the dishes after the meal. My new friend Neely stood on a chair and helped me to wash the dishes, I let her hand them to me, I did not want her to put her hands in the water, it was very hot. Ashanna and Kippa sat on one of the couches with Nasur, they spoke quietly and looked at Neely smiling and wiggling her waist as she helped me wash the dishes. Once the dishes were done Neely pulled my hand to follow her, she pulled me all the way over to the television picture box, she wanted to see the "green funny dog" again. Neely sat with her mother and sister and asked me to play some of the show she liked, Nasur nodded his approval to me and then sat back. I sat on a separate couch and watched the show for a little while, I had things I wanted to do but I was invited by my new friend and did not want to disappoint her.

Ashanna thanked me for teaching her how to work with the nets even though my English was not so good, I worried I did not teach her very well at first but once she thanked me, I was sure I showed her well enough. Ashanna laughed a little with Kippa and Neely, Neely laughed the most. I did not know how to feel after the end of that day, I still missed Ohah, I missed my mother and Teeta and many things, I felt bad that the two men lost their lives but I also felt, not happy, but relieved that the bad men did not have their lives any more to torture the girls that sat on the couch with me and Nasur. I wondered what they were all thinking about, I was sure Nasur did not want Ohah hurt but he must have also been feeling very fortunate to have his sister back into his life and this time, he would make sure she and her daughters would be protected where ever they went.

Ngozi came down and told Nasur that captain Raza decided to head straight for Tunis, he wanted the crewmate Ohah to rest in peace quickly and then after that, we would make our way to offload Nasur and his family, then after that there was no certain route they would sail as of yet. I still wanted to get off and continue my adventure, but learning that the captain was a much nicer man than I had thought, made it less urgent to leave. I excused myself and headed up to the deck to watch the last rays of the sun sink into the western waters, the skies were tapering off with reds and blacks blending together in the horizon, the cool winds danced along my skin, the cooler temperatures made me shiver a little but it was so very nice out, it reminded me of being a boy with Teeta out in the grasses, I really did miss Teeta, and Loza and Pika and all of my friends back in the village.

"Boy" the captain shouted to me from his platform up near the wheelhouse, I did not realize where the beckoning call came from at first; I had to look around to make sure of what I had heard. The captain was motioning for me to come up and see him as we sailed on chasing the setting sun. I climbed the metal stairs and thought about walking down the long path to the setting sun on my way back to my home the night after parting ways with Loza, I had plenty of time to think about many things, one of which was maybe being out on the great water someday. Each step up the stairs clinked under my feet, looking down the side rail some of the waves fell so far down I felt like I was looking down from the top of a tall tree. The steps under my feet were lightly flecked with brown rust spots, the hand rail was worn thin from many hands running up and down it holding on. Waves splashed up some of the sides as we rode up one wave and back down only to ride back up another as we sailed. Away in the sky the birds could be seen soaring high above the water tops, the white caps of some of the rolling waves threw water splashing into the air, bits of moist mist tickled at my face and in my ear.

I knocked quickly then let myself into the wheelhouse, I greeted the captain and he again motioned for me to get closer. Raza told me to take the wheel and keep it straight, he wanted a small break and that he'd be back after a few moments of a fast shower and change of clothes. Raza stepped out for a little bit while I kept my eyes locked on the horizon. I never would have imagined steering a ship larger than all of the homes in my village, I had not been a sailor long when I was taking charge on my own, a smile broke out on my face and there was no stopping it. I liked the feeling that I was becoming the man I wanted to, my mother told me when I was young that she was excited to meet the man I would be when I was older, she would get that chance soon, I hoped. The big shiny wheel was smooth in my hands, I wondered how many hours or days or even years had Raza captained the big ship and worked his hands over and over again on the wheel. From my perch behind the wheel I could see very far away, the sky seemed to go on forever and even though it was getting dark behind me, I knew that the sun would always rise again in the next morning.

Raza stepped back in and took a seat in a long seat near the side, he laid back and pulled a hat down over his eyes, he told me to let him know if I saw anything strange or if any of the green monitors made strange noises, I had no idea what he was talking about but I certainly would if something changed. Raza asked me about my village, he asked to tell him about growing up and what it was like. I talked about Loza and Pika and turning from friends to husband and wife, I spoke about racing Teeta and having many boy adventures with him. I talked about Teeta going out with furs to Teran and coming back very fast, I spoke about many things that I knew as a child and as I did, I missed each thing.

I continued to talk to Raza, he nodded and hummed as I spoke, he did not seem to sleep but maybe he did not have to. I continued to talk about my first hunt when Teeta was gone and then the small celebration when he came back. I kept my hands on the wheel and my eyes scanning from side to side. I talked about the hunt with Teeta and what had happened. I retold my story of getting to the church and meeting father Shumbin, the walk before meeting the father was long and difficult, and very sad. Raza told me that he had friends of his and family of Ohah waiting to receive Ohah in Tunis, he had mailed people he knew and out of sincere respect for the man that sailed with him for many years, he wanted to make sure Ohah was laid to rest with all of the respect he deserved. I was very glad to know the captain for how he treated Ohah, everyone should be treated with such respect and I respected him for it. Raza stopped nodding and grunting, I could tell he was asleep by his slow breathing, I was alone to steer the big ship for a while. I was a little afraid to steer the ship but after Raza fell asleep, I grew much more confident in myself. I retraced everything that happened along my journey before meeting father Shumbin, there were many long days and lonely nights before I arrived, I think about them often.

The following morning the captain woke up just before the sun, he was impressed that I did not crash his boat, I admitted that I was very nervous at first and not knowing what the green colored glowing screens meant but I did my best. Raza told me that the engine speed was going the slowest it could go so that he could rest without worry, or burn too much fuel. Raza told me to go and get some rest; the men would do some light fishing to make sure that our stop in Tunis was as profitable as possible. I thanked the captain for his guidance and as I turned to leave, he stopped me for a moment. "I haven't forgotten about you my friend" he said to me, I paused in my steps and turned to inquire what he was talking about. "If you still want to carry on for your adventure, I can help" the captain continued to speak. Since Ohah had passed away and Nasur was going to take his family and give up sailing, Raza had to find more skilled sailors, he knew he had many good friends in almost every country around the waters, he had helped move many people and many many items which made people happy, he knew people half way around the world, and he knew some men that would help me.

I did not know why these men would help me but I thanked the captain very much for his kindness. The Mediterranean sea was very deep, the waters below the ship were black and we fished a lot of it, we often passed other ships in the water, some had large wings and others had large stacks on the top deck of metal containers, there were many ships and boats we passed along the way. Ashanna helped me to hook pole the nets and sort the fish, Nasur watched over his sister and made sure she was alright each time she stumbled, he cared for her very much. Ngozi was much more silent after Ohah passed away, he spent more time in the wheelhouse than he had before, the rest of us worked and worked very hard. We sailed passed a small island called Malta, Raza said there was very good food there and one day I should go there to see it.

We docked in Tunis, the ports were full of people scurrying about and hauling large baskets of catch up onto the docks so they could pull back out and fish more for the day, everyone dressed in their nicer clothes and together, we carried a long plastic box with the body of Ohah to the dock. Ngozi tied cables to the box and Lin swung it over the side and to the dock where there were some men waiting. One of the older men helped the coffin to lower onto a table that had wheels on the bottom and then he stood tall and waited for the captain to walk down the plank walk way to meet him. The older man had gray hair, he was wearing white clothes and when the captain reached his arm out, the man began to cry as he then shook Raza's hand. The older man was Ohah's father Amhel, Raza told him about what had happened and that Ohah gave his life to help make sure that his friend Ngozi and the girls that he helped to rescue made it aboard safely, Ohah was a good man and the captain wanted to shake his father's hand. Ngozi climbed down and hugged Amhel, they began to cry together and even though some unknown people stood around the dock and stared as others loaded and off loaded their boats, Ngozi and Amhel did not break from their embrace.

Nasur helped to prepare the fish to take to market, his nieces Kippa and Neely giggled and laughed putting stickers on some of the boxes and wrapping some of them to sell. I helped to load the crates so Lin could use the crane to swing them out of the hull and over to the dock. The offloading of the fish went smoothly, Ngozi and Amhel spoke during the entire time, both men were very sad to have lost Ohah, he was a good man and will be missed for a long time. Raza did not want to interrupt Ngozi but once everything was offloaded, he wanted to leave the port and get underway to the next destination, Ngozi vowed to Amhel to return often and visit to share more stories about Ohah. It was sad to watch the coffin with the body of Ohah get wheeled down the dock, he was with us one day and gone the next, thinking about it made me certain I wanted to continue on with my journey.

We sailed out of Tunis late in the evening, we only offloaded half of our fishing catch and the rest was bound for other ports along our journey. We sailed up the Tyrrhenian sea, Nasur was bound for Rome with his sister Ashanna and her two daughters Neely and Kippa, Raza wanted to first offload some of the fish in Naples and pick up a sailor or two to learn some of the jobs for a day before Nasur was no longer with the ship. I was going to take on the cooking responsibilities as well as teach some of the newer sailors some of the things they might need to know around the ship before I set foot on land for myself. The country was called Italy, it was known to have wonderful food and an amazing bunch of people, we delivered two crates of fish in Naples and picked up one sailor man, he had lighter skin and wore his hair cut short.

The man we picked up from Naples was named Mercurio, it was difficult for me to say it right but I practiced so I did not offend him. Mercurio was taller than me, he was also very thin and worked very hard. Ngozi was glad to have more hard workers, sailing on a boat took a lot of work. Mercurio was a nice boy, he did not speak much and did not know any English. The captain spoke to Mercurio in his language and told him to begin watching the same Sesame street pictures movie shows that I did. It was only a days' travel from the port in Naples to that in Rome, but Rome was a much more busy port and the captain also had to finish working out papers for Nasur, Ashanna, Kippa, and Neely. Neely and Kippa watched the Sesame Street with me and Mercurio, Neely often sat beside me and smiled when the green dog on the screen wiggled and moved.

Captain Raza worked feverishly through the night, we fished a little during the day to make our fish delivery larger, the money being spent on fuel for the ship was making Raza worry a little, Ngozi spent plenty of time in the wheelhouse trying to help. Raza worked with Mercurio a little, Mercurio had to learn the English like the rest of us but Raza was the only one that could speak his words to help him understand. Raza did not say much about the boy but told me to show him what I could and Ngozi would pick up the rest. Raza had two more sailors waiting in Rome, one was a man named Srestos that had sailed with him in the past, and another young man that he was going to teach to sail. Srestos was an older man, he had grey in his hair but he knew good English and he helped to teach Mercurio and the other boy. The other boy did not talk, he was smaller and younger than me, I was too busy with my jobs to learn his name and we did not meet much.

Nasur stepped off the boat with Ashanna, Kippa and Neely by his side in Rome, it was a big enough city that they could disappear and start new lives. Nasur shook Raza's hand for all of his help and told him that he would forever be in his debts for all that he had done for him and now his family. Lin showed me some pictures of the old buildings that I would not get to see in Rome, there were very old buildings from very long ago and many people liked to look at them. I smelled some of the air from the dock and I could tell I was missing some good food. Raza was very nice to help his friend and his new guests to get a new life, one that might treat them better than that bad man Ibrihim did. Raza knew that he was going to miss the council of Nasur, he already missed Ohah deeply and even though he kept his lips perched shut, you could still tell that he was saddened by all of the changed on his ship/

Ngozi waited until everyone was done eating after dinner one night and wanted to talk to me, I was surprised since Ngozi did not talk very much. Ngozi was a very large man, his shoulders were high above my head and very wide. Ngozi told me that he knew a man in a city called Monaco, the man was a friend of a friend that he and Raza knew, the friend was named Paolo and he was going to help me on my journey. Raza had mailed Paolo several weeks back after I told him about my journey, Paolo responded that he knew exactly what he could do. Ngozi told me that Paolo was once a favor of Raza's, he was picked up as a teen boy in Ragusa and sailed for a few days, he cleaned and scrubbed but the captain saw the potential the boy had and as a favor and future friend, he was to stay in touch each year and tell Raza about all that he had done with his year.

Paolo was dropped off in Monaco, the boy taught himself books and languages and was an educated man somewhere. Raza heard me talk about my journey before meeting Father Shumbin and thought that Paolo would know the right people that would also like to hear about it. Paolo was married to a woman named Celeste, they never would have met if Raza did not help the young lad, and Paolo was forever grateful. Paolo still mailed Raza every year as he promised and every so often, they would meet up for lunch if Raza was near his port. Ngozi told me that Paolo would take care of me and my needs for a few days but I should work on my English some more, I would be needing it very much soon. I was a little afraid of what I did not know, I was going to step off the ship in the next day to a land I did not know and to be with many people I did not know also. It was very difficult to sleep that night, I was going to miss my shipmates, I had met many people in my journey, many have come and many have gone, only some were with me long enough to be missed.

My mother Bendu warned me that not everyone will be in my life forever, that is what makes life such a great journey, some people cannot stay in order to make room for more and with each person you meet, the journey changes. I missed Ohah, I missed Teeta, I missed my mother and my home but I was on my journey so I would try not to miss them so much that I did not have my journey, just a little. Ngozi knew that sailing was his life, it was all he ever dreamed of and it was hard work getting to it, but once he felt the open sea air on his face, he knew he was destined to sail forever, Ohah felt the same way. Raza said that the ocean cast a spell on him, if he spent too long on solid land then he felt dizzy and sick, he loved to captain a ship and even though some countries called him a smuggler, he still brought artifacts back to his home country Egypt and he felt good about himself every night.

Monaco was a port city that called to many people from all over the world, there were so many different people there that you could feel lost standing in one place too long. The ship pulled into the port late in the morning, I hurried to help get the catch ready to offload and sell, while Lin and Ngozi worked with the new people like Mercurio, I changed my clothes and gathered my things. I looked around the ship a few more times, it was not my home for very long but it was my home for a little while. I was on the ship a month and some weeks, I learned a great many things and made good friends with the men I sailed with. There were many more large boats, the lagoon was full of smaller boats full of box traps and men with long poles to guide themselves in and out of the shallow water ways.

I stepped back to the deck to see everyone standing in line ready to shake my hand and send me off with well wishes. Raza was the last man at the side of the ship, he shook my hand very hard. I could not help but to give him a hug and thank him for the wonderful adventure. Raza told me that my adventure has just begun and to stand tall because I would always be his shipmate. Raza handed me some folded monies to put in my pocket and told me to keep an eye out for him wherever I went. I thanked Raza again for all of his help and stepped off the deck to meet a man named Paolo. Saying goodbye to Ngozi and Raza was very hard, it was harder saying goodbye to Ohah before but at least I might see Raza and Ngozi again sometime.

After all of the cities I had seen and places I had gone, I had begun to really realize how big this great world was, the great water really was great, and I only saw some of it according to Ohah. Paolo showed me the way to his motor car to take me to his home, his wife Celeste was a city official which meant they could get papers for me to be ok to travel in the country, I like the idea of traveling and seeing more lands before I headed home. Monaco is a small country and it was easy for Paolo and Celeste to make arrangements for me to begin my new set of jobs. I entered Paolo's home after he did, the home was bright and wonderful and the inside white in pastel colors were very relaxed and soothing, there was music playing in the air and the smells in the home smelled wonderful.

Celeste did not have black hair like Paolo, her hair was red, she had lighter skin that Paolo and she wore a very big smile. Paolo offered for me to sit at the table with them for a meal, Celeste explained that the papers she had for me were only good for one year and that I needed to be back home or back with captain Raza before that time. We sat and began our meal, Paolo used a little hot sauce on his food, it made me think about Whutta and his mother so I told Paolo and Celeste about meeting Whutta and helping with his cattle. I told the couple about learning to clean from Father Shumbin and his wife and the different jobs I performed on the boat when I sailed with captain Raza and Ngozi and Ohah.

Paolo and Celeste had many questions about my life in the village, I told them about joining the hunting party and about me and Teeta as boys playing in the grass or hunting chuta. I talked about the tembo in the distance and watching the herds go by year after year. I told them about one time Teeta and me were watching the tembo go by and we saw a baby one fall behind its' mother, we raced to the distance to see if we could pet the smaller creature, it was going to grow into a large magnificent creature but the baby might let us pet it. Me and Teeta ran until our legs burned like fire, then we ran some more. The further we ran the further the baby fell behind the herd; the baby could not get over a fallen tree and was crying out for the help of its mother.

As Teeta and me got near the baby, it stopped crying a little, its long nose was trying to pull on a fallen branch to help it over the tree but it could not pull so strong. The baby could not see over the fallen tree to see that its' mother had gone one without it and it was now left behind. The baby was very still as me and Teeta approached it, I wanted to help the baby while Teeta just wanted to pet it and then out run the mother before she came back. Teeta and me guided the baby tembo around the fallen tree, the baby used its long nose to pull at me and Teeta, it was as curious about us as we were about it. It had gray thick skin, but it was a little soft, its big ears flapped a little as Teeta and me showed it the way around the fallen tree so it could catch up with its' herd.

The baby tembo saw it's herd and ran to catch up, it stuck out its big ears and raised its' nose as it ran, Teeta and I ran too, but back towards our village, if the herd had caught us with the baby, we might have been in big trouble. Many animals protect their young, the fisi, the simba, and even the ndege will attack if you get near their babies, and we did not want to wait to see if the tembo would come back near us with the baby, the mommy would surely be angry. Me and Teeta told my mother that we petted the baby Tembo, she told us to always treat the babies of others' very carefully and with respect, just like we were treated when we were babies. Me and Teeta talked about the baby tembo a lot, we were the first in our village that pet a live one, we thought we were mighty hunters that we could stalk one so close and get to touch it without having had to kill it. The baby was heavy and as we pushed and pulled it, it must have been so scared, it screamed out as we tried to push it around the tree so it could run and catch up with its' mother.

Paolo and Celeste liked hearing about the baby tembo and about me and Teeta when we were young boys. Celeste did not seem to want to hear much about the men and the hunting but she listened anyways. Paolo laughed about Pika and Loza and how they grew to love each other, he said it was a little like him and Celeste. Paolo asked about Teran and carrying the skins to be traded for ammunition and things that the village needed, he asked why I didn't get to Teran, I told him about my other journey and how it lead me to meet Father Shumbin. I liked talking about my time in my village, it made me happy to remember everybody, I missed them and was so very far from them.

I spoke half way through the afternoon; they asked me many questions and were very curious about my village. I talked about the animals we hunted for food to feel our selves, I spoke about how we lived and what we studied, some of the travelers that came, like the man with the ball you kick with your feet. I talked about waiting to get to join the men and the hunting groups and how that was the most important thing to Teeta. Paolo and Celeste asked the most questions about when I went hunting with Teeta and the other men, it was all a very sad time that began my journey that ended with me talking to them at the time, remembering all of the memories made me sad again, but I also had many memories to be happy about.

It felt different to be off the ship, my bed did not swing, the floor did not rock or sway, it was hard to sleep during the first night. I was very fortunate to be a guest of Paolo and Celeste, their home was very lovely and it was a very nice home and Celeste was a very good cook too. Paolo watched some short television movie shows on his television picture box, I missed some of the Sesame street back on the ship but I was in another new land and wanted to explore and see some more, perhaps by climbing out the window onto the roof. From the roof where I sat I could still smell the sea, I missed sailing already and even though I had not sailed for years, the months I did was a part of me. My mother always told me to take a part of everywhere I went, I did not understand when she told me this when I was a boy, but I understood it after sailing with Raza, Ngozi and especially Ohah.

Paolo invited me sit with him on the second floor balcony, there was less risk of falling and from there I could still see Port de Fontvielle in the distance. I liked to see the big sails go by on the water, the shimmering gold and orange from the

178

sky bouncing off of the waves and the birds flying in and out, I was born on the land but the great water became a part of me. Paolo poured me a drink and even though it was a little sour, it was very delicious. The weather was warm and the cool breeze made me think about sailing and the afternoons when the sun began to set over the sea, I missed it already and Paolo knew it. Paolo sailed briefly with Raza, he was a deckhand just like me. Raza helped Paolo to escape his bad home and make a good new one a little ways away, where he met Celeste. Paolo bought his home with his wife so that he could always smell the sea and hear the gulls.

Paolo and me watched the sun disappear behind the mountains behind us, the darkness swallowed the whole water in the far distance, the air grew cold and every time closed my eyes, for a moment I felt like I was back on the ship and moving. Paolo chuckled a little as I flung my arms to catch myself as I felt like I was falling for a moment. Paolo knew the feeling and said it took him a very long time to not try to catch himself, especially when he was laying with his wife Celeste. With the glow of a candle on the small table in front of me being the only light left on the small balcony, I decided I was tired enough to try to sleep. I tossed and turned throughout the night, the memory of Ohah falling limp to the deck visited me in my dreams, he was charging over the side of the ship to help his friend Ngozi in the boat in the water and when he came back, his life had gone.

I had many bad dreams that night, another such dream was of Ibrihim, his body surely to get picked and eaten by the fishes in the water, he was an evil man and not even a man, I wondered where his body might be found and maybe some large fish would gobble him up and he might never be found. I was not very old in life but I knew that life was special, it was the work of a monster that would hinder someone from having a happy life, a father or mother that might interfere with the life of their child, to treat them like slaves or abuse them in anyway do not deserve to be a parent. Men should not look at children like they would their wife, women should have the right to choose their husband, a man and a woman must choose each other in order for both to be truly happy in life together, if you force someone to make a choice that you want them to make, then it is not a choice, it is forced and empty. A coward must force someone to do as they would like them too, if it is a good thing then it will be easily chosen and everyone would be happy, not angry, mean and empty.

I woke up many times during the night, the still bed scared me a few times, I grew used to the swaddling of the hammock, the swaying with the ocean was much like my mother rocking me when I was little and the sea, like my mother, was comforting. I tried to think back to when I was younger, quiet still nights of staring at the skies above and me and Teeta counting the stars or trying to see pictures or make up pictures with the stars in the sky while listening to the grasses rub together as they danced in the breeze. I found myself thinking about hunting with Teeta and the men, the sounds in the night and everything that happened.

The next morning I heard Celeste in the kitchen, there was light banging of pots and pans, I lay in the guest bed for a little while, the room was growing bright and the white walls made the light brighter around me. I felt that I was still a little tired from the poor sleep but instead of have more bad dreams, I just watched the shadows shrink and slowly go away on the walls around me. My stomach did not ache, it did not growl, I did not feel hungry, only a little sad and a little tired. I had been traveling and on my journey for months, some days I worked too much on the ship to realize how far away I was and how long it had been since I had seen my home, but I thought about it in that bed. The sun streaked in my window, it danced across the ceiling and around the room before I finally gathered the strength to get up, I found it strange that when I had work to do on the ship, I always had the strength, even when it was so early the sun had not come up yet. I stepped off the ship and onto land to continue my journey; I did not feel like a man yet and was still searching for that moment when I would be certain.

Paolo knocked on the door and told me that there was food ready when I was hungry. My stomach did not growl, it did not even feel empty, it just did not feel anything. I put my clothes on and made my way down the wooden steps to the table, Celeste had prepared a wonderful meal, there was a large fruit spread on the table, there were bright colors and many different foods to eat, for a slight moment my stomach seemed to like the smells I was nearing, I still felt dull and a little weary but with each step closer to sitting down near the food, I felt my mouth water a little and my stomach begin to crave some of the foods. The colors were bright, on the ship many of the foods were white, gray, and brown, there weren't many fresh foods other than the fish and the fruits came from cans. The fruits I was looking at were of so many colors, I did not know that most of them were but there were very many of them.

Paolo and Celeste explained what most of the many fruits were, I tasted many of them but some of the new ones did not taste good, one yellow one was very sour and bitter, a red one tasted really good and the small blue ones were also very good. Paolo spoke over the morning meal that he had a favor that he needed from me but first we had to go shopping for clothes for the job. I did not know what the job was but I was willing to work and I was also very thankful for the bed to sleep in and the morning meal to eat. Paolo was in education, he was a professor in a small building and wanted me to go with him and tell my story about my travel before meeting Father Shumbin. Celeste got me papers that meant I was allowed to be in their country, in my village any stranger that came in was given food and welcome to sleep in a bed until they moved along to where they may have been going, what kind of a world is it that keeps people out of a land that cannot belong to someone. We are born and we live, but once we die the land and great water will still be here, for many lives before and after ours, it cannot be owned, it should not be owned because we belong to it.

Paolo was wearing white cloth pants, the legs stopped above his ankles , his shirt was not white but close in color and the sleeves were rolled up to his ankles, he also wore leather sandals and he looked very comfortable and neat. Paolo had a motor car for him and Celeste to use but he often chose to drive his motor scooter, it was like a small bike you sit on and has an engine. I sat on the back of the seat where he told me too and off we went. The motor scooter buzzed and zoomed up the road, I held on very tightly. On the motor scooter we zoomed up a big hill and around some curves, I held on very tightly and was very afraid I was going to fall off or tip over. The ride was a little fun but much more scary than fun. We passed little stores where people sat at small tables and had small drinks, we saw trucks carrying goods and foods up and down the roads and very many people.

Many of the people wore light clothes as they walked back and forth across the streets, some of the men wore dark colored glasses over their eyes. Paolo had his hair sleeked back and wet looking; many of the other men also had hair that looked wet. Some of the smells I smelled were good while others smelled like smoke from the motorcars that putted past us on the motor scooter. The road was bumpy and made with bricks, it made my bottom shake on the small seat, my stomach was full of the juicy fruit I ate for the morning meal but with all of the shaking, and it was beginning to ache. Paolo looked to both sides as he drove, he tried to point to things for me to see but I could not hear him over the noise from the motor we sat on. The roads were dark grey and black, some roads were made of stones while others were smooth. Some trees lines the streets and they had small tiny leaves while others were large trees with large leaves. Many of the buildings were dark browns or light browns, each had different people wandering in or out and carrying on with their lives.

The people in this town were like so many other people in many other towns, much like the people I had seen in other ports, docks, and cities as I sailed with captain Raza through different seas. Many of the people spoke words I did not understand, I was getting better at English and with each person I met, I practiced my greetings and as many words as I could. I was happy that Raza let me learn, I was able to speak with many more people, there were still many words I did not know but I was still learning very much. Paolo pulled the motor scooter into a small space and we climbed off, my bottom was a little sore from the seat and my stomach was not feeling very well from all of the fruit in my stomach and then being shaken very much on the motor scooter. Paolo took me into a store, it smelled very badly and the smell made my eyes water. The store had fake people standing around, they were not real people, they were fake! I had so many questions about many things. The store had a potent odor, it was not a food store so I could not find where the smell was coming from, and the fake people were different, I waited for them to begin to move at any minute and I found myself stepping lightly around them trying to catch them breathing or moving, even if only a very little.

Paolo pointed to some of the clothes that were standing around inside of the store, he asked me which ones I liked and which ones I did not. There were many colors and clothes I had never seen before and I did not know what I liked, some of the shirts looked very uncomfortable and complicated with many buttons on them, other shirts had colorful patterns that made my eyes were blurry and made me dizzy. I pointed to some of the clothes and Paolo purchased them for me, I thanked him very much but did not understand what was wrong with the clothes I was wearing, the clothes that captain Raza gave to me. Paolo explained that he wanted me to speak to his lecture hall about me journey, he wanted me to stand in front of many people and speak about my journey and while doing so, I should be dressed a little better than a salty sailor.

I did not understand what was wrong with my clothes but since Paolo wanted me to dress nicer, and he purchased the clothes for me, then I would be glad to do him the favor and speak, besides, Celeste was a very good cook and had very good food. I spent the better part of the day exploring with Paolo, he took me to some of the small shops and showed me how things were in his life in the city, there were a great many people around, some sitting at small tables with small cups to drink out of, some wandering into and then back out of stores that lined the streets. Paolo took me to a market, much like the market I found before I met captain Raza, it had tables lining the streets and a great many foods on them. Paolo bought many small bits of food for both of us to sample, some were very tasty bread  and others were juicy fruits like back at Paolo's home.

Paolo had a very nice life, he seemed very happy, but I missed my home. My mother told me to take in new surroundings where ever I go, to look around and be aware and I did my best to honor to her. I looked around very much in

Monaco, it was a city rich in culture, rich in people, and very rich in wonderful cooking. I loved the smell of the sea when the winds carried it inland, the day on the motor scooter was one that made my bottom sore but my taste for adventure satisfied. So many people come in different shapes and sizes, I saw one man that was more than two sizes of me, he smiled very big and unlike Ngozi, who was big tall and big across the chest, this man was big around the middle. I saw some women with many children, some of the children stared at me as I watched them. I saw many different kinds of men, some of the small shops had music coming from them, some of the music was like I heard before when I was sailing with Raza and the crew on the ship, other music was new and did not sound very nice. Sights, sounds, smells, tastes, there were so many things to experience and I thought I had already experienced a large part of the world, I was not correct, there was much more.

I wondered what speaking in front of a lecture was going to be like, if it was like telling stories in front of the fire back home in the village then I would not to be scared. Paolo asked my permission to share my story, I felt respected as a man that he asked my permission, since it was a story about me and he thought that I would tell it better than he could. Captain Raza had sent Paolo a mail and told him about the story that I had told him back on the ship, about going out hunting with Teeta and the other men after Teeta returned from Teran and his short travels. I thought back to asking Teeta what his travels were like when he was gone, what he had seen and what he had done. Teeta did not seem very different when he returned, he came back looking the same, except he was a little different, I think he saw himself as a man and he seemed just a little different because he saw himself a little different, perhaps he just tried to stand taller.

I was excited to get to see a university, I had seen books and been taught things along my journey, Father Shumbin taught me a little and I learned a little more between the church and staying with Whutta, each day I discovered more things about the world, things I did not know before. Paolo and I returned to his home, Celeste had delicious food cooked and prepared for us one more time for the day. After the meal Celeste began to ask me questions about my journey, why I felt the need to travel so far, why I had chosen to keep traveling even though I missed my village and how, as a very young man, I had continued to make it so far from my home, on my own. I did not understand why she was so curious, in my village when a boy becomes a man, he does it on his own, and I was all by myself and meeting many wonderful people that were willing to help me, like Whutta and captain Raza.

I explained that I did not know how long I would travel or how far, but I knew I was not ready to be done yet, there were still many more places to see and even if I had to walk, I would like to see them. I had seen pictures in books at the church that Arbroa had shown me, she was afraid that she might never get to see any of the places in her pages herself and wanted me to see what was out in the world so that I might see them myself. Arbroa was a very nice lady, Father Shumbin was a good man and she stood by him as he served the people in his small town. Arbroa wanted to see the world, Teeta did not, I wanted to see much of the world, but perhaps not as much as Arbroa. Arbroa had read books and seen many pictures, the pages in her books were worn down from being turned so very much, it saddened my heart to think that she wanted something so very much and could not have it.

A man and a wife are a team and they must work together for each other, Father Shumbin had a job to do for his church but that should not have meant that his wife did not get to enjoy her life too. Pika and Loza were a silly young couple but they knew to love each other and care for one another. The evil Ibrihim man that fall to his death in the water off the side of the ship did not know how to treat women, or anyone, and that is why he was killed and would not be missed, he may have been so evil that even the ndege might not feed on him as he float in the water. There were a great many things that had happened since I left my village to hunt with the men and Teeta on that night, I thought about them very much and one day when I return to my village I would have very much to tell everyone, but I still do not have a strong desire to return just yet.

# CH. 11

Celeste knocked on my door to wake me in the early morning, I had slept better than the night before and was a little more accustomed to sleeping on still ground. Paolo was preparing for his day and was using the water closet. Celeste was already set in her work clothes and was doling out items for the morning meal for the three of us. I was offered the shower and facilities in the spare water closet after the meal and I looked forward to the shower and to putting on some of the new clothes Paolo had purchased for me. We ate a nice meal and as the home lit up in the morning hours I was told that the one stop Paolo had in store for me was to stop and visit Celeste at her work and get some photos taken for identification so I could continue on with my journey and maybe see many more places.

Celeste left the home while I was dressing for my day, I was unsure of what I had in store for me but it was going to be another day in my journey. Paolo and I climbed back onto his motor scooter, the buttons on my shirt made my shirt feel a little tight on my neck but I liked wearing the red and white shirt. Paolo started the motor on the motor scooter and off we zipped through the streets again. I learned to lean when Paolo leaned so I did not feel like I was going to fall off, I leaned to one side when I felt Paolo lean with his shoulders, and then lean back up a little when we finished the turn and drove straight again. In the morning there were many more cars and people moving about, the cool sea air blew through the streets and felt very nice on my skin.

We arrived to a grey building, it did not look very special but Paolo said that it was where Celeste worked and where we needed to stop. Raza had mailed them long ago about my story, he told Paolo that I would need some help to continue on with my journey and Paolo told him that he knew ways that I could tell my story and then get to travel further along my journey. I looked forward to lunch already, it was early and Celeste had prepared a wonderful meal which consisted of scones and jams to spread on them, they were very filling but with after eating many good foods the day before, my stomach looked forward to eating even more good foods.

Inside the building was also another new place, there were short walls that people sat behind, there were bright white lights on the ceiling and the walls were very plain grey. The bright lights were not pleasant to stand under for very long, I did not understand how Celeste remained a nice person after the lights were bright in her eyes all day. Paolo showed me to her desk and she then guided me to where I needed to stand to get my picture taken. Celeste did some work in another area before bringing me back a picture of myself on a card to use to prove who I was, I did not understand why I would have to prove who I was, who would I say I was?

Paolo gave his dear wife a small kiss and then we were off and zooming on our way to his university. There were many more motor scooters lined down a walkway when we arrived to the university. It was a bit of a long ride to get there from visiting Celeste and when we got near, I saw a very large building with so many people flowing into it, it was like a sea wave of people. Many of the people did not seem much older than me but some of them had gray hairs or face hair or even the little wrinkles by the corners of their eyes. There were so many people rushing into the building, I felt that I was in the way as people brushed into me as I stopped and stared up at the very tall building, it was taller than Raza's ship.

Paolo guided me down one such hallway and then to another before stopping at a black door with a small window in it. I could not read the sign on the door but he opened if for me and motioned to walk in. I stepped up three small steps and turned the corner to see a small stage, looking up from the stage looked like another big wave of people, they sat in rows, one higher than the other as the mounted all the way up in the back to almost the tall ceiling. I felt my eyes open wider, I could not tell if my mouth fell open or if it was still agape from seeing the university for the first time, it was all very new. There were many people and Paolo introduced them as students. I sat on a chair and listened to him speak into a small black thing that stood up from the podium and made his voice loud, it was like Ngozi's megaphone but small and made his voice much more loud.

Paolo handed me a microphone and told me to go ahead and introduce myself to his students, he suggested I tell them the short version of the story I had told him and Celeste. I told them about the village and when boys became men that they joined the hunting party and earned their space with the other men to hunt and provide meat for the village. Some of the students asked me what kinds of animals were hunted and how often. Paolo helped me to understand some of the questions and then he told me to speak about the night of the hunt. I talked about the night of the hunt with Teeta and the other men, I spoke about my journey before I met Father Shumbin and before I spoke much more about my journey after I met Father Shumbin, Paolo suggested that his students

191

take the rest of the day to think about what they had heard from me.

Some of the young students wore clothes like me, button up shirts with zigzag patterns or block squares. Some of the young girls wore long dresses or short above their knees, other boys wore short sleeved shirts or fancy dress coats. Each face I looked out at was different, blonde hair, light and dark brown hair, one boy even had blue hair, I tried to keep from staring at it but I could not stop myself from looking at it with wide eyes and amazement. One young girl was wearing a green shirt that covered her neck, she had two colors in her hair and when she asked me about one of my small adventures with Teeta, I found myself drifting off for a moment reliving my childhood. One older man was in the group of students asked a few questions about the tembo and how often we saw them when we were out hunting or gathering. I enjoyed some of the questions, for what I could understand that was, everyone seemed very nice to me.

I did not understand the purpose of the lecture, I did not really understand what the students had learned from listening to my story but  I was thankful that I got to put it in my stories of my journey to tell around the fire when I get back to my village. After speaking to the lecture I was missing my home, I missed my mother and my village. Paolo could tell that I was missing them and he showed me around some more of the university before we got back onto the motor scooter and took a long way back to his home. I got to see very large churches and buildings where they held large sport events, one of the large buildings had plants growing inside because it was so big. Paolo showed me strange buildings, and old buildings and buildings that were still being built.

Many of the buildings were very interesting to see, Paolo said that some of them were hundreds of years old which was interesting. Paolo and me even took the motor scooter high up on the big sized hill, from the hill we decided to have lunch, we ate at a small bistro and had some sandwiches as we gazed out over the sea in the distance, I asked Paolo which direction I should stare to head towards home, he pointed and I tried to think about what might have been going on in my village in the far far distance. The view from atop the hill was splendid, I could see many boats way out on the horizon, I missed Ohah and sailing on the great water, I had been far from my home for many months and even though I missed being back at home, I was not ready to go back.

I was very thankful to Paolo for taking me out to see more of the city, he took me to get new clothes the day before and I thanked him very much for that also, he was a very nice man and he helped to improve my journey very much. I always wanted to see the great water, and thanks to captain Raza, I was able to see very much of it by sailing on it. I wanted to see more lands and with the help of Whutta and now Paolo, I am seeing very much of it. Paolo and I sat for the peak of the days' sun and watched the distance, many of the ndege were small and flew around above us and larger ones could be seen out in the distance high above also. I watched as some of the things up in the sky left white tails and streams way up high. I had seen them in the sky many times and finally remembered to ask Paolo what it was I was seeing.

Paolo told me that airplanes carried people to very faraway lands, they were giant metal birds that could fly very high and carry many people very far away. I told Paolo that I wanted to see an airplane and asked if it was possible to touch one. Paolo laughed at my request, I did not make a funny joke so he confused me by laughing. I meant what I had said; I wanted to touch one of the giant contraptions. Paolo remained smiling as we both got back onto the motor scooter, the ride home was down the big hill and it seemed much faster as we zoomed back down brick roads and past bigger cars. It was fun to ride on the motor scooter, it made the wind blow passed very quickly, zooming and zipping passed people walking on the sideways looking and smiling. I wondered how many lifetimes it would take to meet everyone on the planet, I had met many nice people and some not very nice people, I wondered how many people had very different lives than I had as a child back in the village, I did not know of any of these people, the great water or of so many other lands in the world but I wanted to learn.

My mother always told me that the world was much larger than I could have imagined, she also told me that sometimes the world does not seem so big at all. I saw many colorful pictures in Arbroa's book, she had many pictures and many of them seemed painted by artists, it was hard to believe that all of that fit on this world for all of us as people to find. I wondered what else might happen along my journey but at the end of each night, I was grateful for where I had been and what I had been able to see and experience each day. Feeling the whoosh of air blow past me on the back of the motor scooter was much more fun the second day, it was a little scary the first time but it became very fun. Paolo was a very good man; he spoke highly of the captain and has made a very good life after the captain helped him out as a young man.

Once back to Paolo's home he began to start preparing the evening meal for the three of us, I was glad that I knew that I could help by cutting some of the spikey looking fruits and helping to mix together some of the food as Paolo instructed. With elegant sauces and plating, the meal was complete just in time for Celeste to walk in the door and join us. We sat and feasted once again and Celeste piped up that she had some news for me if I were interested in continuing my journey. I was already having an amazing journey so far from home and I thought about leaving in the next day or two to begin walking to see more of the world. I liked staying with Paolo and Celeste but I did not want to impose, they had their life together, mine was still my own and I wanted to continue on.

Celeste asked me what my plans might be and where I might go, I responded that I wanted to feel like the breeze and just blow from one point to another for a little while. Paolo suggested I might take a flight on one of the airplanes that I saw earlier during the midday meal. The thought of getting close to one of those machines was a little scary but very exciting, I was worried to get into a motor car with Whutta and then riding on the fast motor scooter with Paolo was also a little scary but it was good fun. I really enjoyed sailing with captain Raza, it was a rewarding way to see much of the great water and more of the world, I could earn my food and travel and make my own way as a man. Celeste told me that she had a brother in another country that was interested in my speaking for him just like I had done for Paolo. I could speak in another country if I knew their words. Celeste reassured me that I would be using the English I learned and was getting better at. Celeste had a brother that worked with a foundation and then she asked for permission to call him and ask if he would like a special guest speaker. I did not know why my speaking was so special and I tried to do my best to appreciate everything that everyone I had met had been doing for me.

Celeste told me that her brother Henry was instructing at a much larger university than Paolo, he orchestrated several groups of people and she would mail and ask him if he would be my host for a day or two in an England for me to visit him. Celeste excused herself from the table after her meal was done and began to work on her small computer box, she mailed

Henry so see if he was willing to show me around his country and help to make my journey much better. I was excited that I was able to continue my journey. I had been to many places and seen many many things, I was happy to continue on and one day tell my mother about it all. Me and Paolo put away the dishes, I was very good at cleaning the dishes, I had very much practice while I sailed, I cleaned very many dishes. I liked to help, I liked to work for what I was being given and Paolo and Celeste were so very nice to me. I sat back on the top back balcony, I liked to watch the boats far away on the great water, it made me remember Ohah. I smiled a little thinking back to being a boy and wanting to not only see the great water, but wanting to drink from it (which was not very good at all) but then getting to actually sail on it for months.

Paolo joined me on the balcony, he smoked a pipe once in a while and really enjoyed watching the boats on the horizon; "I often miss the boats, I miss sailing, sometimes I wish I had sailed more" Paolo began telling me. Paolo loved Celeste but he also loved the sea, the sea seemed to call too many men. Paolo told me that once him and his wife were done working he planned to sell his home and buy a ship to sail on, that sounded very much fun. Paolo sat quietly next to me and we both stared out at the orange sky, it was bright like a fire, there were small dots out in the air that were the birds in the far distance, they swooped and dove and curved back up high into the sky, they seemed to dance in the air and it added to the lovely late afternoon.

Celeste stepped out with us on the balcony overlooking the bay, she pushed Paolo's hands off of his chest and she curled up on his lap, she smiled that he loved her very much and she whispered in her husband's ear. Paolo grew a big smile on his face, he looked at Celeste in her eyes, he brushed her lighter brown hair from her face as it wisped in the sea wind that filled our lungs. Paolo and Celeste loved each other like Pika and Loza, you could see it in their eyes when they looked at each other, it was not a common look that you see very much, but I had seen it. Paolo had small hairs on his face and at the end of the day it made his face look dirty, his teeth looked white when he smiled or spoke, he turned to me and began to speak again; "so you want to go on a airplane?" he asked.

I did not remember what an airplane was for a moment and I looked at him, I felt my head tilt to one side as I thought about all of the English words I knew, trying to remember what an airplane was. Paolo pointed up to the sky and when he did that I remembered what he said the giant metal beast was. When I was a boy I sometimes had small bits of frightened in my stomach about something's that were new, I felt that I was a man and as a man I would be brave and happy for new things. I asked Celeste how I was going to fly on the airplane, I was feeling a little happy that I might get to see one of the new things and Celeste told me that she and Paolo were going to send me on one. Celeste told me that she was ready to send me on a airplane the next evening, I was happy to hear the news and I could not thank them enough. Paolo warned me that flying was not much fun, he told me that I would have to wait in long lines and answer questions to strangers that had bad attitudes and then sit squished in a small seat while people sneeze on you and babies cry. I did not think it was polite for someone to sneeze on me; I did not like that very much.

I hardly slept for another night in Paolo's home, the idea of lines and more new experiences left me excited and unable to sleep very well. I watched random lights flash on the walls and ceiling, I watched the shadows dance along the wall and on the windows. I finally fell asleep to the smell of the sea drifting in the window. I could not hear any waves like back on the ship but the leaves on the trees swaying in the breezes was also a comforting sound that filled my ears. I thought about speaking in the lecture, I thought about my village and about Teeta, I thought about Ohah and Ngozi and Nasur, I wondered where many people were and what they may have been doing, I thought about many things until finally, I could not think any more. In the morning I was excited to know where I was going and what I was going to be doing, I helped to prepare the morning meal for my hosts and then clean up after them, I could not thank them enough for all that they had done for me and were still willing to do. I felt much more like a man, like I had hoped I would, but sometimes I still saw a boy in the mirror, I wondered when I would begin to look more like a man.

My arms became more big with muscles after working with the hook pole for months I felt like my arms were big like Loza's, I felt a little bit taller when I stood up straight, but, when I looked in the mirror I still saw a boy looking back. When Teeta went to Teran he came back looking like himself, but just a little different, he squinted his eyes a little more and kept his jaw clenched a little more and he spoke less than he did. I felt like I was speaking more, Paolo wanted me to speak to his lecture about my adventures, captain Raza wanted me to tell him about my village, Whutta did not speak much but Father Shumbin also had many questions for me. I had seen many motor cars, I enjoyed riding on the motor scooter after being scared stopped. I cleaned up after the morning meal for my friends, Paolo read his paper and Celeste looked on her computer box for a bit. I was almost finished with the final plate when Celeste leaped from her chair, her loud holler made me almost drop the plate, I caught the plate but hugged it to my chest to make sure I had held onto it safely.

Celeste stuck her hand out from across the room to try and make sure I did not drop the plate on the floor; she stared at me with surprise for a moment and then began to share her good news. Celeste first told me that my plane was booked for the night but that there was a one day layover in a small town called Le Havre. I tried to ask what a layover was but Celeste was sharing even better news with her husband Paolo, she was *pregnant*. Paolo knocked his chair far back behind him as he jumped to his feet with excitement. Paolo and Celeste joined hands and embraced, Paolo had watery eyes as he turned to me and told me that pregnant meant she was to have a baby, he was very happy. I excused myself and let the husband and wife have some time to themselves, I stepped out onto the balcony to smell the fresh sea air. I longed for the great water as much as I longed to feel the tips of the tall grass on my fingertips back home.

I could hear both Paolo and Celeste speaking to people on their telephones back inside, I was overjoyed for them and when people like them love each other, their family should get bigger. Paolo and Celeste we extremely nice to me, they were nice people and when they hugged and smiled at each other, it was nice to hear that their love resulted in a baby. I could hear Celeste talk about wanting a boy with his fathers' sturdy build, thin frame and slick hair, Paolo wanted a girl with her mother's light brown hair and small cheek freckles, they were very entertaining to listen to, they made me giggle and smile. I set my focus on the bay in the distance, I do not know how long went by but when I finally blinked, Paolo was sitting next to me; still smiling.

Paolo told me that I had a long day or two ahead of me before I landed in England, I had to take a flight from Monaco to Le Havre, which was France, and then the next day I would have to get on another plane to England. Paolo told me that during the one day I would have in France that I would have the option to leave for a bit but to keep track of time because I would be landing very early in the morning, much before the sun would rise and my next flight out to England would be early in the next morning so I would have to keep a close watch on the time and what I was doing if I chose to leave the airport to look around. I was excited to be going on a airplane but I was also a little scared to be squished on a seat be sneezed on. Paolo could not stop smiling as he spoke, he was very much happy to become a father and he showed it with a very big smile. I was certain that Paolo would become a very good father, he was a very loving husband to Celeste and together, I was certain that they would be a very loving mother and father.

Paolo dug out an old bag of his, it had straps for me to carry it on my back to carry some of my clothes in, Paolo was very generous to me and I thanked him ever so much. When I joined Paolo back in the home it was almost time for the midday meal, I was a little scared of eating too many of the fruits that made my stomach sick on the motor scooter. Paolo showed me some of the right foods to slice up to put on small pieces of bread to serve for our meal, Celeste was still speaking in celebration and cheer on the small telephone she held to her ear as she walked back and forth in the bigger room, Paolo smiled as he snapped his fingers at her. Paolo pulled a small wad of paper from a drawer in the desk and began to unfold it onto the table. I recognized some of the green and blue lines, it was a map.

Paolo traced his finger across some of the blues and browns and reds on the paper. Paolo showed me the city that we were standing in, the city in which he lived, he then showed me some of where I had sailed and about where my village may have been back home. I liked the map, it was much bigger than the one Arboa showed me back at the small church. I looked over more of the map, there were so many lands and so much more great big water. I saw many letters and many words I did not understand but many of them were names of cities, cities like many of the ones I had visited and was going to visit.

I looked at the map at the land I was going to miss between where I was and where I was going, I wondered how many people I might meet or might not meet in between. I was curious about so many things and I asked Paolo many questions about many things. The jagged coastlines of France looked interesting; the mix of light brown and blue meant there was more great water to see. Paolo showed me some pictures of some of the things I might not see if I stayed in the airplane place, I did not want to miss my airplane to England to meet Celeste's brother Henry. I was worried a little about being squished into a small seat, I wondered how many people were squished into a airplane, I wondered what kinds of people I might meet between Paolo's city and England. I was very excited about everything, not anymore scared.

My last day in Monaco was spent with Paolo and Celeste celebrating her going to have a baby, they took me out to eat and the last meal of the day seemed to be a feast. Paolo drove me to a place that cooked your food and brought it to you, it was a very nice place, there were many kinds of people, all gathered to eat in one room. Paolo ordered spreads of food, he and Celeste told me about how they met shortly after Paolo had arrived in the city, he was sleeping in a small bus box, which is where people stand while they wait for the bus, it had rained for the 3 nights he was in the city so he wanted to sleep somewhere dry. After a few days of looking for work and beginning to question if he had made the right choice to leave behind his home country and move far away. Paolo found a small job cleaning dishes in the same restaurant we were eating our meal in. Paolo washed dishes for captain Raza, he learned how to clean very well and after a few nights of sleeping in the bus box, Paolo met a short man that was waiting for the bus.

The short man was very stocky; he was the owner of the restaurant and offered Paolo a job washing the dishes until more opportunities came along. The short man was named Vincenzo, Paolo wondered why he owned a restaurant and not a car, Vincenzo told Paolo that if he spent the money on a car, he couldn't afford a soaking wet dish washer at his restaurant. Vincenzo rode the bus everywhere, he used his money to help people that needed it, and not long after he gave Paolo a job washing dishes, he hired a small younger girl to begin waiting tables while she tried to continue on through school; Celeste. The restaurant was very special to Paolo and Celeste, it was where they first met, they worked for many years together, Paolo learned a lot about Celeste including why she was going to university, he decided that if he was going to make a good husband for such an amazing girl, that he would have to go to university as well.

Paolo took many classes and struggled to catch up with the subjects Celeste learned, and even when he felt like he was going to quit, he would see her at the restaurant and he knew he had to earn himself the right to be with her. Paolo graduated at the same time as Celeste, they sat beside each other at their commencement and once they had both finished with school, they continued to build their lives together. Paolo began to take Celeste to the restaurant once a month after they had both gotten better jobs. Paolo met Celeste in the restaurant, he asked her to be his wife at the restaurant, and both Paolo and Celeste saw Vincenzo as a father so they had to come and share with him the good news.

Vincenzo came from out of the back, he was wearing a dirty white kitchen coat, he had a white hat on over his gray hair, and he had mostly gray hairs above his mouth. Vincenzo walked slowly, he leaned over each knee as he walked out, his forearms were very big and his jacket sleeves were rolled up half way to his elbow, he had sad eyes but his mouth turned to a very big smile when he saw Paolo and Celeste. Vincenzo raised his arms and shouted to my hosts; both Paolo and Celeste stood up and yelled "POPPA" to the man walking closer to the table we sat at. Everyone in the restaurant turned to look at Paolo and Celeste. I smiled watching the loving couple hug and embrace the aging man, Paolo helped him to our table to sit with us. Paolo held his arm around his back and pulled a chair closely for him. Once Vincenzo sat back down the rest of the eaters went back to eating and talking.

Paolo turned to tell me that Vincenzo was one of a few people that came to their wedding on his behalf, captain Raza and a few other crew members happened to attend. Paolo introduced me to Vincenzo, he told the older man that I had sailed in and was only staying for a short while. Vincenzo greeted me and quickly returned to being loud and jolly with Paolo and Celeste. Once some of the boisterous laughter settled down from Vincenzo, Celeste grabbed his hand and looked at him, his bushy eyebrows raised a little and no longer looked sad. Celeste told Vincenzo of her good news, Paolo tried to hide his very big smile but as soon as Vincenzo threw his arms in the air to congratulate his guests, Paolo began smiling even larger. Vincenzo shook hands and shouted to the waiter to bring the table things to celebrate, then he began singing. In the midst of the noise and everything going on, Paolo began to speak loudly, his volume had to increase so that he could shout to Vincenzo, over Vincenzo, until he got the man's attention.

"Hey Hey Hey" Paolo continued to announce until Vincenzo was silent for a moment. As Vincenzo turned to look at Paolo, he began to smile again, he paused and began to fill his large chest with air to begin singing again, Paolo shouted to his friend that if it was a boy they planned to name it after him, and if a girl then his name would become her middle name. Vincenzo tried to begin singing again but his voice was silent, his face began to turn red. Vincenzo was silent, his face began to squint and water began to fall from his eyes and around his open mouth. Vincenzo leaned forward and grabbed onto Paolo with both of his mighty hands. Vincenzo hugged Paolo and began to cry, thanking him for such an honor. Celeste began to cry watching both of the men that she cared about the most, also crying. Celeste tried to keep wiping away her tears but once she wiped one from her eye, another would fall down her cheeks. Vincenzo reached out his arm, Paolo also reached out, to reach for his wife, both men wanted to hug Celeste and cry together for a moment. I got to see a very great love, their love for each other was bigger than the great water, and I got to see it.

Once the embrace was over, Vincenzo hobbled back to the kitchen, he stood straighter on his was way and continued to wipe his big forearms across his face, trying to dry his eyes. Paolo and Celeste finished their meal in smiles and celebration; they continued to tell me stories about Vincenzo. Vincenzo gave them a very big wedding present and with the money they were able to move from a small apartment into the lovely home that they lived in, they both worked hard and Vincenzo would never let them pay him back, but instead, helped people like me.

Paolo spoke about what he did to raise the money to pay for the wedding; he contacted captain Raza and invited him to the wedding, but also asked if he had some work for him to make money. Raza told him that he was planning to be near the city in the early summer and could have him back to return teaching before the fall. Raza was sure enough near the docks when he said he would be, Paolo said goodbye to Celeste for the better part of the summer and wondered what he was about to embark on. Celeste spent the summer still working her job for the government, but also working for Vincenzo. Vincenzo was unsure of the captain and did not want to see anything bad happen to Paolo. Celeste did not know much about captain Raza, only what Paolo had told her, she had worried many nights after long weeks of not hearing from him while he was sailing.

Paolo took a summer sailing job with Raza right after he decided he wanted to wed Celeste, he asked the captain what he could do to make enough money to help pay for the wedding and he was willing to do anything. Captain Raza had just hired a new deckhand, Ngozi, and was looking for a set of hands to retrieve some ancient artwork to take back to Egypt. Paolo boarded Raza's ship and they set sail to Ibiza, a very small island off the coast of Spain. Raza dropped anchor near the island and told Ngozi and Paolo to take the smaller boat toward the coast, they had to look for another boat in the water. The other boat was supposed to be green and yellow with a man fishing from it, it was also supposed to have a small red flag flying from it. Paolo and Ngozi spent three days sailing towards the coast and looking for the other boat, they laid out fishing nets to sleep on while they searched. Ngozi was a hard worker and wanted to make his captain proud, Paolo wanted to make enough money to marry his darling Celeste.

Paolo and Ngozi found a man named Ayllon in a boat that looked like the one they were looking for, he was an older dark tan man, he was smoking a pipe and remained hunched over in his boat when they motored towards him. Paolo said he was a little scared because in some places Raza did not always have the a good reputation, Ngozi was also ready for a fight if he needed to have one. Ayllon asked the men if they sailed with the "Pirate Raza" and as soon as he did, Ngozi was ready to turn the motor around and leave. Paolo worried that if he did not pick up what he was there to get, then he might not get the money for his wedding that he needed. Ayllon was from Sueca, it was a port town and there, Raza was known as a pirate and wanted by the authorities, which was why he docked by the island of Ibiza. Paolo stood in the boat as told the man that he had heard of such a pirate, but they were sent by a captain in search of a man in a boat with such a description. Paolo said he could tell something was not right by the way the man was acting.

Ngozi started the motor back up, it was hard to see what was in the small boat with the man but it did not look like what they were there to pick up. The water was choppy and when their boat rose above the yellow and green one, they could tell that it was all but empty. Ngozi began to pull away when the man in the other boat tried to jump into their boat with them. Paolo caught the man's arm as he tried to punch Paolo. Paolo locked one leg under the seat to keep from falling. The strange man began to swing his arms at Paolo and tried to tackle him to the bottom on the boat. The strange man swung his arms wildly, Paolo said there was no other choice than to fall backward and use the force to pull the man's head towards his and hope that when they collided, that the other man would give up his fight. Paolo curled his head down to his chest and unlocked his leg, he fell straight backward to the seats on the boat, waiting for the seats to strike him across the back and for his head to collide with the other mans.

As Paolo fell, the man fell with him, they landed on the seat of the boat and Paolo's head crashed into the other mans. Ngozi was steering the boat but also reached a fist forward to punch the man, hoping that he would stop fighting Paolo. The strange man pushed Paolo down and shook his head, Paolo braced his feet up against the strange man, Ngozi turned the boat sharply and Paolo kicked very hard, the man fell over the side towards his own boat, and out of theirs. As Ngozi and Paolo headed back to where Raza was docked, another boat was speeding towards them, it was bigger and faster than theirs and caught up to them. Paolo was still sore and ached from his fight when another strange man caught up with them, he shouted to turn the engines off and that he had to talk to them. The stranger asked if they knew captain Raza, Paolo was scared to answer the man at all. Ngozi waited a few minutes, he finally nodded and the stranger shouted to someone below the deck on his ship. A man stood up, holding a package. "I am Aurellio, I have what you need, but you have what I need" the man shouted to Paolo.

The second man came near the edge of the boats and began to tell Paolo and Ngozi that he knew the captain, or pirate depending on who you asked, he was called to get ahold of a painting for the captain and was going to be paid for it. Aurellio continued to tell Paolo and Ngozi that he was now wanted by the authorities because he was working for Raza, he now needed to be taken away and to see Raza. Paolo asked Aurellio who he knew in the boat that chased him down, Aurellio told them that after the first day of "fishing" while waiting for them to arrive, the authorities arrested him and began to take him to the docks. Aurellio saw his neighbor and jumped into his boat back on the docks. Aurellio told the neighbor to tell the authorities that he forced his way on the boat and then that he jumped off later. Aurellio left his belongings for his neighbor to sell, and that they would split the money once it was all done, now Aurellio just needed a new home to live, and he needed the captain to take him there.

Paolo and Ngozi took Aurellio to the captain, along with the package he held onto tightly as a bargaining chip. Aurellio explained the whole story to Raza, how he almost was arrested and barely escaped, he wanted safe passage where he had a good friend and asked that Raza take him there. Raza set sail to Tunis to drop off the man, and then to Egypt to deliver the painting that he had acquired for someone in the government that wanted it. Paolo was uneasy about the delivery but he and Ngozi were the men for the job. Paolo and Ngozi were given directions to find another boat out in the water down the coast a little once they got close. The smaller boat was offloaded and the two men sped down the coast looking for the delivery boat. Raza had an intricate series of pick-up and delivery men, he was careful not to step on many toes as he sailed but what he shipped wasn't always with the right papers.

Raza did his best to help people out, the more friends he made the more people he could rely on, people that knew him and would stick up for him or help to find him side work to do when he was fishing up and down the coasts. Paolo and Ngozi offloaded the painting to a red and white boat that had the right person in it, Raza spent the day in the port waiting for the port authority men to search through his boat and ensure that everything was as it was supposed to be with his ship. When Paolo and Ngozi caught up with Raza again, he was sailing back towards Tunis to drop off Aurellio, Raza was a man of his word and Aurellio was a trusted man with Raza, Raza wanted to treat him right for his service.

Paolo liked Tunis; it was a land of wild foods, late nights and fires on the beach with many people gathered around sharing stories or drinks. Paolo was in love with Celeste, but not far behind her was the sea. Paulo sailed for almost two months over the summer, he worked hard to build his muscles while fishing and found more joy on the deck than he did when he was first on the ship as a boy. Raza was a fair man, he had a thin build, he always wore nice clothes and kept a pen behind his ear. Raza treated everyone like a man, even though he called the new boys, "*Boys*." Paolo spent a day wandering the town with Raza when they landed in Tunis, he left his ship in charge to the rest of the men and spent the time catching up with Paolo and his life. Paolo assured Raza that Celeste was the love of his life and was not marrying a woman he just shared time with, he shared his life with her and she belonged in it with him.

As the two men wandered back to the ship after a long afternoon of land travel, there was a young man sitting on the docks, he was tying large knots and making jokes to them as they passed, he made the captain laugh with his quick humor and then nodded to the men to enjoy their evening. Raza asked the man why he did not ask for money, why he had not panhandled or even beg for scraps. The man said that he had many talents and in the morning, he would use them to find him some more work. Raza asked the young man what he did and why he was sitting on the dock just tying knots, the man replied that he loved the sea and that tying knots was fun to him, he had many useful skills and often times on the docks, you can find work helping to offload fish and make money each day. Captain Raza offered the young man a small room, poor pay and long hours sailing in the hot sun if he was interested; the young man happily jumped to his feet.

The captain told the boy that his name was "Captain Raza" and he shook the young man's hand. Raza told Paolo to take the boy aboard and show the young man around. Paolo planned to spend the following several days teaching the boy how to work around the boat, how to cook and clean and make sure the dishes were done after each meal. The young man was happy to work and not sleep on the docks one more night.

The boy spoke about how his father struggled to feed them both and he wanted to help his father by leaving and not having to be a mouth for his father to feed. Paolo respected the young man right away, the captain took a cold shoulder to everyone at first, he always said you can judge a man by how he works, if he was a hard worker and was honest with himself if he could or could not perform a task, then he was a trustworthy man, if he took short cuts or did not work as hard as he could, then he cheated himself and was not trustworthy. Captain Raza knew that every man did not have the same hard work, some men could work a little bit harder than others or differently, but if a man did not work as hard as he could, than he just gave himself excuses. Paolo walked behind the captain and he gave a list of jobs to the young man, the captain was ready to board his ship when he turned and asked the young man what his name was, the boy answered; "Ohah."

After the last meal with Paolo and Celeste I packed my few belongings into a bag that Paolo gave me, it was a bag that I could put on my back to carry and it fit my clothes. Celeste thanked me for the help I gave around her home, I thanked her for the wonderful food as well as congratulated her on becoming a mother and sharing some of her life with me, and then Paolo took me to the airplane place. Paolo drove me down many roads, it was late at night and I was already very tired but also excited to get to be on an airplane. Paolo reminded me that I was supposed to be on a very late flight to Le Havre and then another very late one from Le Havre to England where Celeste's brother Henry was supposed to meet me. Paolo continued to smile at the thought of becoming a father and getting to make Vincenzo a grandfather, he was a very happy and fortunate man.

The airplane port was very big, Paolo did his best to describe what I was supposed to be looking for and to remember where I was going, and I was a little scared but very excited about everything that was happening. Paolo thanked me for all that I had done but I told him it was me that was to be thanking him, we were total strangers but he opened up his home and his family to me, Paolo had a very nice life and he was very happy, the kind of happy I wanted in my life as well. I shook Paolo's hand with appreciation, and then I stepped out of his motor car and looked up at the big airplane port before walking in. I was going to miss Paolo and Celeste, they were very nice people and I enjoyed having my adventure with them.

I found the lines and stood in them with many people in the airplane port, some people looked like me from back home, some had lighter skin than me but hair like mine, and others had lighter skin and hair like Paolo or Celeste. Many people were also like me, tired and yawning in the late night. I moved slowly with many other people until I found people that knew what was going on, I was unsure of what I was doing but I knew I was supposed to go to Le Havre and I was going on an airplane. One man with very hairy eyebrows looked mean at me, he had thick black hair over his upper lip and I could not see his mouth underneath it, told me that he was not sure I could fly. "I can fly, I can squish and sneeze" I told the man, just like Paolo told me I was going to do. The man waved his hand to someone that was wearing the same blue shirt and black pants that he was, this lady had dark skin like me, her hair was big and bouncy and she had very bright red lips. The lady walked towards me, I smiled and introduced myself, I thought she might help me to find where I was supposed to go to and I was very glad for the help.

The working airplane port lady was very thick in her body, I was small and not big but she was big, she even had big hair. The lady told me to call her "Officer" and then she demanded I follow her. I was very happy to follow her because she was going to show me how to fly. I asked Officer how to fly and when I was going to be on my airplane, I was happy to go on the airplane to go to Le Havre. Officer walked me down a hallway where there were many people sitting in chairs or laying on the ground, on the far wall there were very big windows, I could see some airplanes as I looked out the windows, I asked officer if I could touch one of the airplanes out there, I asked her how to get out to them and where the door was to get out there. The sky darkened but the lights shining on the airplanes made then very shiny out through the windows.

Officer opened a door that lead to a small room, there was a table and two chairs in the room, and no window to see the airplanes. Officer told me to sit down and that Supervisor would be in to talk with me. I was happy to meet Supervisor, Officer was not very nice but it was late and she may have been tired after a long day, I know I was also. Supervisor was an older man with grey and white hair; he had white hair on his upper lip and wrinkles by his eyes. Supervisor spoke with a mean voice, he asked me where I was going and why, he demanded I tell him where I had come from and how I had gotten there. I told Supervisor about growing up in my village, I told him about Teeta and about joining the men hunting. I felt my muscles tense up when Supervisor spoke, he had a mean voice and he confused me when I told him my answers he wanted to know. I told Supervisor about meeting Father Shumbin, I told him about the hot sauce with Whutta and also Paolo. Supervisor asked about the lecture and what else I had been up to and why I was up to it in his city.

I told Supervisor about going to meet Celeste's brother Henry and getting to speak to another university, but in England. I told supervisor about what happened the night I went hunting with Teeta and the men and also about meeting Vincenzo. Supervisor told me he was going to call Vincenzo and see if my story was mine, he was very mean to me and I did not understand why. My mother always told me that a good person treats other people well, and when a person was not good, they did not treat other people good, Supervisor did not treat me good. Supervisor left the room and I was alone, the lights were bright but I was very tired so I put my arms onto the table and put my head down on them to sleep for a little while. I did not know what time it was or if I was going to miss my flight on the airplane but I was tired. I easily fell asleep because I was so tired; I do not know how long I had been sleeping on the table when Supervisor came back in. The door swung open very hard and slammed into the wall behind Supervisor, the noise startled me awake. I had to rub my eyes a little to make them focus on Supervisor, I was very tired and even though he was not being very nice to me, I tried to be nice to him because I wanted to be a nice person.

Supervisor wanted me to show him what was in my bag and in my pockets, he did not ask nicely and I told him he should have. Supervisor began to get red in the face when I told him he should be nicer to people, I even told him that he might have a nicer life if he was nicer to the people he meets, he continued to get red in the face. I opened my bag for Supervisor and removed my photo picture card to show him, I told him I got it from Paolo's wife Celeste, I showed him the other clothes I had and nothing else, I was not sure what he was looking for or why it was so important but I did as I was asked and then Supervisor told me that I could put it all back. Supervisor asked for Officer to come back in, but this officer was a much smaller officer, and this one was nice. It was funny to meet another Officer, I wonder if they knew they had the same name, I wondered if they got confused when someone called their name. The second Officer was a younger girl than the first one; she was nicer and smiled to me a few times.

I was lead to my gate by second Officer, she pointed to me where I was supposed to go and I waited in line with many other people. Some of the people were wearing sharp suits, others dresses or funny clothing and wrap. There were very many people in the airplane port and I wondered how many of them were going to Le Havre with me, I would not know anyone where I was going and perhaps I could make a friend on my way. I had made many friends on my journey, I missed all of them and there might be a day when I am on my way back across this big world that I may cross their path once again, if not, then I would just remember them in my thoughts and hope that they were all well.

I stood in line to get on the airplane, there was a man leaning on a small desk and he was waving his arms front to back, he looked very unhappy and a young woman standing in front of me turned to me and said something I did not understand. The girl was very pretty and she had very big hair. The girl standing in front of me had pale skin, she had dark black hair that was very curly and she had very red lips, almost as red as the first Officer I met at the airplane port. I walked slowly behind the young lady with big hair, she was very nice but I did not know what she was saying. There was a lady in the big airplane that showed me to my seat, many people sat very close side by side on the seats, I sat beside the young lady with the bright red lips and black curly hair. I smiled as she tried to speak to me again, I shook my head because I did not understand her, then she said more words I did not understand. Finally after a few minutes of speaking, the girl spoke in English, she asked me "how is this, is this better?" I smiled and nodded that I understood her.

The girl told me she spoke several languages so it sometimes took a few tries to find the right one to speak with. I introduced myself and reached to shake her hand, she grasped my hand and shook it back, she told me her name was Andreea and she was going to France for a few days before going to the states to become a doctor. I asked what doctors did and explained that a little about where I was from. Andreea and I talked for the whole flight, we watched the ground turn very small as the airplane rose high into sky and headed towards our destination. I told Andreea all about growing up in my village, I told her about my travels with captain Raza and even about hunting with Teeta, she listened to many of my stories as we flew. Andreea told me about growing up in Romania, she liked to travel and her mother made sure she could. Andreea had a very smart mother, just like me, her mother taught her many different languages, she had been to many middle eastern countries, she had been to England, she had been to Germany and Denmark, she named many countries I had never heard of, and then she spoke about having taken a bus through Egypt for a summer with some friends.

Andreea told me that her friends were supposed to meet her in Egypt but when she arrived she found out that they couldn't make it, and rather than get scared and go home, she still went on her adventure by herself. I was impressed that Andreea had been to so many countries, I was still learning about many of the other countries and she had been to more than I had ever heard of. Andreea told me that there were very many wonderful places to see and she wanted to see many of them since she was a young girl. I was interested to hear many of Andreea's stories, she planned to go to a university for one school, and then another one and then another after that, she knew she was going to be in school for a very long time so she was trying to see as much as she could before becoming a doctor. Andreea's mother supported her traveling around; she was worried when Andreea was left in Egypt without friends but knew her daughter was smart and brave. Andreea told me that there were many children like her in Romania, all wanting to get out of the small town and see some of the world that they had seen in picture books.

I talked to Andreea for the whole flight, we watched the sun come up through the windows and then the plane landed in France. As I followed Andreea off the plane I looked around, I thought about when I was sailing on the ship and we went through the canal on our way to Egypt, there were children flying kites and running along the canal, if I were a child and I lived near flying airplanes, I would be doing the same thing. I did not see many children, except some being carried asleep by their parents through the airplane port. I had my bag with me and I was supposed to wait until my next flight late at night, I went to go and sit down and just wait, I planned to take long sleep and then think about my mother and being back home. I took three steps and then told Andreea that it was nice meeting her and wished her luck on the rest of her adventure before going to become a doctor.

Andreea stopped me from going much further, she told me that she had planned three days in France before going on to the States and that I should join her for the day. I did not know what she meant to do but I agreed, but reminded her I had to be back by dark to make my next flight. Andreea had a big smile and then she nodded for me to follow her. Andreea had a motor car and it was waiting for her at a desk that we had to find after looking through signs in the airplane port. Sometimes it was hard to understand what Andreea was saying, the way she said her English was hard for me to hear her and I was not very good at it either. Andreea told me that she had a list of things she wanted to see in the nearby area and that I was welcome to join her to see most of it before she would take me back to the airport and then she would drive on towards a bigger city and her flight to the States.

I was happy to join my new friend, she had a small red motor car ready for her and as the sun rose, we began driving around the city. Andreea wanted me to see an art museum. I did not know what an art museum was but I was happy to spend the day with someone nice instead of being sneezed on at the airplane port. I was nervous about being back to make my flight, Henry was expecting me in England and I did not want to disappoint him. Andreea assured me that everything was going to be just fine; she told me I could trust her and that she would make sure that I was going to be back around dark. I got into Andreea's motor car, it was a little bigger than the airplane seating, and we zoomed out of the parking lot and into the city.

Andreea first drove through a very large bridge, from where we were it was higher than the ship I sailed or even Paolo's home over the water, I could see man boats out over the sea and I thought more about being back on the ship with more of my friends. Andreea sped along some of the roads; the roads were smooth like in Monaco, not dirt like the one I rode down with Whutta. There were some tall buildings in many of the cities I had seen, but as Andreea drove through some of the streets, some of the buildings were so tall that I could not even see the top of them. I watched from my seat in the small red motor car, some of the buildings reached to the clouds, I stared and tried to see the tops of some of the as we drove. I was amazed to see such buildings, some of them had fancy designs right on them, I was excited about the stories I was going to bring back to my village, I wondered if anyone would not believe me.

Andreea first took me to a museum, it was a big building that had metal and stone people, painted pictures and people that stood around quietly and looked at all of those things. In the front of the museum was a large strange cement box, but it was not a box, it had a hole in it and it looked almost like it had been flattened, but it was very big. Andreea and I had to walk to the museum before we could go inside, we drove past the large cement stone sculpture in the front and then we walked back to it. We passed a small building that was down the road, it had nice green grass and some small colorful trees, there were two benches in the yard that were around a small puddle. The puddle had gold and orange fish swimming around inside, some of the water bubbled from under the water and Andreea and me watched some of the small fish swim around in the puddle that was in the small yard in front of the small building. The small trees were topped with green leaves but the trunks were slender and gray.

Andreea and me walked into the museum, it was very quiet, and a little cold inside. The floor was brown, there were small figures and statues in clear class boxes on stands, there were some men dressed in uncomfortable looking suits and some women wearing very big hats. Andreea and I explored each floor to find more stairs and more floors, we talked a little about some of the paintings and what they might mean to us, and we asked each other some questions about what the other liked. Andreea walked a little bit faster than me, I asked her if she was rushing and she was because we only had a short day to see many things before I had to be to the airport and she had to be on her way to her next city destination. Andreea said she squeezed in as much as she could before she traveled a far ways from her home like me. Andreea was a smart girl to try to see many things, I only had one day in the town and I was glad right away that Andreea took me out when I could have just sat the whole day in the airplane port and not seen so many new things.

Andreea told me many of the things she wanted to do to become a doctor, I did not understand many of the things she talked about but she talked with a big smile on her face and happiness in her voice so it was nice to listen to her, and fun to watch her big puffy hair bounce when she walked.

Andreea showed me painted pictures that were hundreds of years old, older than Misu's fathers' father. Andreea found great beauty in the painted pictures, she spoke about the delicate hands that slowly moved brush strokes from one side of the picture to the other, layer after layer of color, one on top of the other to create a beautiful picture that lasted longer than some cultures. Andreea and me roamed through the art museum place, we walked with a hurried pace as she was in a much faster hurry than me.

Andreea and me stepped out of the art museum, she continued to smile and spoke happily about having just added more beauty to her world. There was a man pushing a metal cart out on the walkway and Andreea grabbed my wrist and told me to come with her. Andreea jumped down some of the steps that lead away from the museum, her hair bounced in many directions as she jumped down the gray hard steps, I did my best to keep up but she seemed to have much more energy than me, she was also a little better at jumping down the stairs too. Andreea ran up to the man pushing the metal cart, she greeted him with her smile still beaming on her face and her cheeks a little red from running. Andreea told the man that I was just her friend for the day and that we were out to see as much beauty as we possibly could in just one day, then she requested four of the foods he was selling from his wagon cart.

The man smiled at Andreea and me as he topped pieces of bread with vegetables and cheeses, the slices were measly topped and then lightly heated, the food smelled very good, Andreea continued to speak to the man. The food cart man was older, he had wrinkles on his face, his eyebrows were mostly gray and his hair was covered by a light brown hat that had a dark brown band around the top. The food cart man spoke softly, he was very nice and when he smiled at Andreea and me, his face wrinkles deepened. The man called himself

Porto, he lost his wife recently and chose to spend his days meeting new people and making them meals. Porto also handed some of his open faced sandwiches to some of the people that did not have homes and just asked them to tell him about their lives at the end of the day. Porto was a very nice man and he really liked to meet people, Andreea told Porto that his life was more beautiful than all of the art in the museum together, and Porto began to lightly weep.

Andreea hugged the nice man that made our lunch, she began to step away for a moment and let him return on his journey through the town when he shouted to her: "Very nice young lady, if you turn down three roads you will find a park, the park is the most beautiful in the city and you and your friend would most enjoy it." Andreea stopped and waved to the man, she took another bite of her half of slice of bread and we continued to walk. Andreea ordered four halves of slices and each one different so we each could try half of each half, she wanted to try as much as possible of the wonderful smelling foods so we shared our breads. One bread had small red vegetables with green things speckled on top, another had some cheeses and another yet had a spicy kind of meat on top, there were many good things to eat and they all smelled very good as we walked. Andreea walked very fast, she said to me that she did not often like to rush and that taking your time to take your time was a way she preferred to enjoy her life, but she was in a hurry to see as much as she could see and she wanted me to join her on her one day adventure in Le Havre.

We ate in a bit of a hurry and walked very fast back to her small red car, Andreea put her fist into the air and then pointed in the direction of the park, she then shouted "Onward" with a smile. I opened the door and took my seat in the car, I hardly had the door closed when she zoomed the car backward and then forward again to find our way out of the parking building. Andreea continued to smile as she drove, she repeated Porto's directions to go down three streets and then over one, she did not want to forget, Andreea told me that the food cart men or women are often the best people in a city to get to know, they know very many things and are always so very nice to meet. Porto was very smart with his directions, the buildings were very tall and stood into the sky, I liked to look up and try to see some of the birds way very high. Andreea turned sharply down one road and then another and then we drove down a small road that was covered in rocks, the gravel was small and gray and bits of dust into the air behind the car we drove in.

There were branches blocking out the sun from over the driveway, small spots of light bounced off of the front car window, the rest was a little hard to see. The car turned a corner and bright green grass opened up before us, the gray gravel driveway poured out into a small parking lot and Andreea began to smile again. Andreea turned the car off before we stepped out to see what we could. To one side there were large gray steps, tall cement walls and on them, were many bright and brilliant colors of paint and designs, many of them were much like the painted pictures we saw in the museum. Andreea explained that the paintings on the walls were done by local kids and most of the time many cities did not like the spray painting. I thought the spray painting was as beautiful as the museum paintings, Andreea did as well.

To the other side there was a bridge, there was more painting underneath it and a small stream that flowed underneath it. The park did not seem to be the most beautiful in the city but we decided to walk to the bridge to get a better look. The grass was very green and in the far distance we could see some small boxes with nets hanging on them. I asked my fried what they might have been for and she told me that some sports and things that children play on needed such nets, I recognized the nets from the ship I sailed on with captain Raza. The park was rather quiet, some roads surrounded the small park but the roads were up higher than the ground we walked on, the low sitting park made it quiet like it was its' own small place, away from the fast cars and high buildings. Andreea looked back over her shoulder to make sure that I was keeping up, I looked back for a moment to see how far we had walked from the car. On a small wooden bench near the opening to the small wooden bridge there was a woman lying down, she was wearing dirty clothes and must have been sleeping.

Me and Andreea tried to hush our voices as we looked around the park, we did not want to wake the sleeping lady. The morning was turning into afternoon and from the entrance to the bridge, we saw that the painted walls in the far distance had changed how they looked, the scenes of colorful names had changed into a larger picture, the picture looked like the city but with colorful swipes and swoops in the buildings, the paintings looked like a mix of cement buildings and colorful nature, instead of the separation that we saw as we drove through the city. The using one bunch of pictures close up that turned into another picture from far away was an amazing sight to see, I could not believe people were able to create such beauty, to me that was the most beautiful art I had ever seen. The big picture changed pictures, it was one picture but if you walked and stood in another distance, it looked like a different picture, it was like magic.

The lady from the bench sat up and rubbed her eyes for a moment, Andreea greeted the lady very quickly and asked her her name. "My name is Mary" the lady spoke as she began to yawn. Andreea introduced herself and me and told her that a man named Porto had sent us to the park to see very much beauty. Mary smiled and said that Porto was a very nice man, he often walked to the park to make sure her and two of the other people that lived in the park had dinner every night, at no charge. Mary and Andreea shook hands to say hello while I continued to look at the painted walls. Mary cleared her throat and with a smile told Andreea to go and stand on top of the bridge; "where the true beauty could be seen." Andreea pulled my shirt sleeve to join her and we took some steps to stand right in the middle of the bridge, the painted wall did not change much and the grass was still green, but nothing about the view had changed very much. "Look into the water sweetie" Mary shouted from her bench, she smiled and looked around the park to see if there were many other people around.

I bent over the rail to see into the water, there were some bottles standing up which the water seemed to flow over and around. The stream was not very deep, nor did it run very fast but it just looked like a stream with some bottles in it. Andreea looked at me to see if maybe I could see something that she could not, but I could not. Mary shouted one more time, "stand up on the bridge, the secret is from above." Andreea grabbed my hand and smiled at me as she began to climb up the railing. "Hold me, I trust you" Andreea said to me as she clenched my hand while she tried to find her balance. Once Andreea found her footing she began to tug at my hand; "get up here" she demanded.

I placed my feet on the rails and began to climb, the water was three body lengths below and not nearly as high as the ship, but I still did not want to fall. As I stood up tall Andreea held my hand, her eyes began to tear up a little as she looked down into the water. I looked down below the bridge to see what she was seeing. "*A Face*" I shouted out, the bottles in the water outlined a face into the water but as the stream flowed around the bottles, the water made hair ripples and the bubbles from the bottles almost brought the face to life. The bottles sunk in the sand under the stream created a portrait, the water flowed to create the hair and the air bubbles trapped in the bottles under the water released and made the outline of the face as the bubbles collected and then rose to the surface. Small swirls of water that passed the bottles creating texture to the eyes and corners of the mouth, as the water caressed the bottles in the stream, the lady face was very alive looking. Andreea let her eyes water while looking at a moving water picture of an older lady in the water. The water was mostly clear but with the light brown color sand, the portrait in the water looked like it was real and that her hair was just blowing in the wind.

Andreea turned her head towards the homeless woman Mary and spoke; "what an absolute amazing marvel of beauty, who is it?" Mary cleared her throat again and told Andreea and me that Porto lost his wife Renee Marie, she was beautiful and the love of his life. Porto met Renee before the big war, they walked over the small bridge as many times as they could and even when it was bombed, they rebuilt it by hand for the stream to flow under. Porto proposed to his wife on the same bridge as they were completing building it, and when she passed away, he spread her ashes into the stream and made the bottle portrait in her honor. The secret to the park is that Porto owns it, he gives away all of his extra food every night to the homeless and he is a very gracious man. Porto made the portrait to his wife to only be seen by those brave enough to stand on the rail, to take a higher look on life and to look for the beauty in the world around them, people that might not normally see what they aren't meant to see. Porto spent weeks constructing the bottles to make each small wave and ripples create the smile and soft eyes of his wife, just right.

Porto roamed the city to meet people, he was devastated when his wife passed away but she made him promise not to sit around the home and sulk and miss her, so he made his food cart and roamed the city to meet people and listen to their stories. I felt my heart feel both happy and sad, Andreea tried to wipe away her tears and smiled while she did. I wanted to help and felt my life fill with happiness, I was shared a secret that not many people got to see. I carefully climbed back down the railing and held Andreea's hand to make sure she also got back down safely. Andreea hugged Mary and thanked her for such an amazing story, one that she would never forget. I thanked Mary for the beautiful surprise and followed Andreea back to the car.

Andreea and me reached the car, we did not walk as fast and I watched the big gray walls with spray painting on them turn back to many small paintings from the one large painting as we walked. I reached the red car and as I opened the door, my back pack of clothes fell to the ground. Andreea looked at me with sad eyes still touched from the story, I looked down at my pack and looked back to her and smiled. I grabbed my pack and took off running, I did not know why but I felt that maybe Mary could make use of my pack of clothes, I had been given them and now they had been given to her. Mary let her eyes begin to water just like Andreea's, I began to apologize because I did not want to make the lady cry, but she hugged me very tightly and thanked me very much. I felt her cheeks smile on my neck as she thanked me, I had only given her some clothes that may wear out or tear, I was given a gift to the heart, a beautiful story of Porto and the love of his life, for me to remember all of the rest of my days in this world.

Le Havre was a fun city to visit, getting to explore it with Andreea made it much more fun, she was happy and smiley, and her big curly hair bounced around as she skipped or drove as we explored. I asked Andreea what helped her to decide to become a doctor; we had a long day full of exploring art works and big buildings. After the park we visited the very tip top of a hotel, the Hotel de Ville, the people that worked there were very nice. Andreea wanted to see the city from the top, I too wanted a view from up very high. Andreea took me to an elevator and once to the highest floor, we had to search around for a set of stairs to continue to go up. I found the small stairs the went up, there was a big red sign on it and it did not look like we were supposed to go out the door.

Andreea pulled a pin from her hair and pushed it onto a small box that hung above the door; she said it was to stop the alarm from wailing to get us in trouble. Andreea took off a cloth thingy from her wrist, she wrapped one side around the inside handle and pushed the door open, she then turned the fabric and then wrapped it around the outside handle knob. "There, now we will not be locked out" Andreea said as she smiled to me and continued her way out onto the very high roof. Andreea jumped and twirled and let her black hair bounce around in the wind as we looked around, I was not sure we were supposed to be out on the roof but she said; "how can you adventure if you do not take any fun chances, if we get in trouble we apologize and then leave." Andreea and me leaned on the edge of the roof, my heart beat in my chest and I began to feel my mouth dry, looking out over the city was very high up.

Andreea began to tell me about a time when she was a young girl, she and her mother were eating at a small café back where she was from, suddenly a big lady began to fall, knocking a glass to the floor, the shattering of the glass made everyone turn to look. As she looked the large lady was getting red in the face, she wrapped her hands around her neck and could not breathe. A young handsome man walked over, he spoke clearly to the woman and then he wrapped his arms around her and gave her a big squeeze from behind her. Everyone in the restaurant was panicking, shouting and gasping as the man squeezed the big lady, on the second try the lady bent forward and began to lose her food onto the floor. The lady's husband knelt down beside her to make sure she was well. The doctor man stepped back over the lady and continued eating his meal, he was not bothered, he was not panicked or worried like everyone else, he was a doctor. Andreea wanted to be tough and brave like the doctor man, she wanted to be beautiful like her mother too, she also wanted to be known as "Doctor Moore" the nice doctor that really helped people.

Andreea drove me in her red car back to the airplane port, she gave me a big hug and thanked me for spending the day with her, she said it was always more fun to see new places with a friendly person and to get to share the adventure. I was very thankful that Andreea was nice and took me around the city, I knew I will tell stories of my day with her back in my village when I finally return. Andreea drove off away from the airplane port and I was once again alone to sit and think about everything I had seen and done since walking away from my home. I missed my mother and knew I had been away for many months, I was not sure I was ready to begin my way back home just yet, but I thought about it.

My airplane left Le Havre and I flew to Leeds airplane port, it was a city on an island called England. Leed was another very big airplane port, there were many people all walking around, people did not seem very friendly but I smiled at everyone I passed. It was dark on the airplane and everyone seemed to be sleeping, I was still excited that I was getting to fly on another airplane, the lights of the city got smaller and smaller as it flew higher during the takeoff, I tried to watch out the windows as best as I could see but the people sitting in the seats on my side were asleep and I did not want to wake them. The flight did not last as long as the first one, I did not get to see the sun rise from the air but the sky did become lighter blue and then pink as the plane began to land. I was very tired, I tried to sleep a little but the seat on the plane was very small and it was very hard to sleep sitting up. I had flown most of the previous night next to Andreea , the nice lady with big hair and the dream to be a doctor, I had adventured all day with Andreea and now I had flown all night again.

The airplane landed and once the nice crew people began to let us out, people woke up and began to push and rush to get off the plane. I did not understand why people began to suddenly push but I tried my best to stay out of the way. I wedged and worked my way off the plane, there was so much noise, many people talking to one another or to themselves, there was very much commotion and it made me a little dizzy. There were many people pushing into each other, I tried my best to stay out of the way and find my way outside. I was supposed to look for a man named Henry, I did not know what he looked like but he was the brother of Celeste and maybe he would know how to find me. There were men in suits carrying small black box cases, ladies walking in shoes that made a clapping noise as they walked, many people had different bags off all sorts. Some little children looked like their parents were dragging them by their hands while some bigger kids just moseyed behind.

Everyone had some place to go, and in a hurry. I tried my best to not be in the way because I was not in a hurry like everyone that rushed by. I wondered if everyone in the airplane port was in a hurry or just everyone that I could see, I also wondered if maybe it was everyone in this England, or maybe I was just very tired and maybe everyone seemed to be in a rush. I stumbled towards the outwards doors, there was a man that was standing at the door and he put his hand up to stop me. My eyes were starting to sting a little as the man began to ask me some questions; "where is your baggage son" he asked me. I told the man that I had given my bags to a woman named Mary that needed my clothes much more than I did. The man let his eyebrows droop a little, his mouth opened as if he wanted to say something, but nothing came out. The man in the dark red uniform swung his arm around and he pushed the door open for me. The air was chilly when I stepped outside; I rolled my sleeves down and found a bench to wait for Henry. I sat on a cold hard bench outside, I tucked my hands under my armpits to keep my fingers from getting cold.

I did not know who I was waiting for as I sat down onto the bench. The bench was blue, it was hard but once I sat down, I felt my eyelids begin to fall. I crossed my arms to try to warm up a little and then my eyes began to tear up as I yawned. I bowed my head and quickly fell asleep. I awoke to a man shouting "Oi Bloke" startling me. I spun my head around to try to see who was shouting, I could not see much past the crowds of people moving around. I fought to stand up, my legs were sore from all of the sitting and my backside was numb. My eyes found a stocky man with a gray wool cap on his head and hair around his mouth and chin; he was standing in the open door of his motor car shouting.

"OY, you the boy?" I pointed to myself to try to ask the man if he was shouting at me. "You Jimmy? The kid from Africa?" he asked me. I began to walk towards him to hear him better over the noise from the crowd. I neared the motor car and told the man my name was Ojimbo Clarke but yes I was from Africa. Just as I began to ask him if his name was Henry he spoke up and told me that his name was Henry, he then said; "hurry up boy, the Bobby's will writ me a scratch for idling here." I did not understand what he had said but I pulled the lever on the door of the gray car and sat inside. Henry shoved himself into the car and slammed the door shut, the whole car shook. "Celeste told me to look out for you" Henry began to speak, his skin was dry and his words were hard to understand, I wondered if he was trying to learn the English too.

Henry drove for a little while, he told me a little about his country and that we were headed to Hull, a city that he lived in and where a mate that he knew was going to ask me to talk at a lecture. The motor car we drove in did not have much room, Henry had to duck his head a little and he banged on different parts of the car while mumbling to himself. The sky was gray and cloudy, I was still a little chilly so I kept my arms folded across my chest and my chin tucked a little. Each time I began to close my eyes and try to sleep a little there was a car horn honking or Henry would beat his fist against the car and shout, his words were aggressive and mean. Some words I did not know and others were hard to understand but there were also some words that Henry seemed to like to say and I was certain that they were not words that I would say. Henry raised his hand out the window to some drivers or would slam on the breaks, making my body lurch forward, it was not easy to try to sleep.

After a long drive we were finally near Henry's home, he said he had a flat and it was not very big, I did not know what a "flat" was so I did not know what to expect. Henry was too busy shouting at other drivers to talk to him, I wondered where we were going and what kinds of things I might get to see while I was with him, I asked many of my questions once we stopped driving. Henry parked his car and once the loud engine was turned off, my ears stopped ringing with the loud rumbling and I could hear without having to strain.  The clouds let out small trickles of rain, I was already tired and the chill made it very hard to focus to what I was doing so I just followed Henry into his home. Henry began to talk and tell me a little about himself but once I sat on the couch that was much softer than the bench at the airplane port, my eyes closed for good.

Later that morning there was a loud whistling in the next room, I opened my eyes and felt the surge of energy wake me up, I did not know where the whistling was coming from and being in a new place was a surprise to wake up to. Henry walked from a small hallway and into his kitchen, he glanced to see if I was awake and he nodded with a smile as he walked by. "Right on" Henry said to me before turning into the small kitchen. I rubbed my eyes and then began to try to stretch out my stiff arms and legs. My stomach growled from hunger as I stood up, I headed towards Henry to ask if he had anything to eat, I still felt a little tired but much better. Henry told me to have a seat at the table and he would bring some scones and tea for the morning meal. Henry was wearing a dark red shirt that had bits of yellow on the front; he was also wearing dark green shorts.

I sat on the chair at the table and tried to wrap my head around how long I had been asleep. Henry told me that I had actually woken up a bit and joined him for a small meal before just falling back asleep on the couch, I did not remember having woken up or even having eaten, he chuckled a little and poured me some tea. The tea was dark but it was hot, I still felt a bit of a chill in my body and slowly sipping the warm liquid helped to set me at ease from the shivering. Henry worked to clean and fix things at a university, one of the women he knew spoke to conserve things such as the elephants and rain forests, her name was Theresa Swartz, and she was looking forward to having me speak to her students about some living back in my village. Henry told me that Celeste had told him some of my story and he then continued to ask me more about my travels, where I had come from and where I might go.

I told Henry that I had missed my mother very much but I promised my best friend Teeta that I would spend much time on my journey before returning home a man and joining the hunting party. Henry asked me to tell him about Teeta, my childhood and what my journey had been like. I told Henry about sailing with the captain, I told him about the shark and about Ohah, and many of the other people I have met along my journey. I missed sailing and the smell of the great water; I missed the night howls of the fisi and other animals out in the quiet distance back home. I liked telling my story to the lecture when Paolo had invited me to speak, he wanted me to talk about my night hunting with Teeta and the journey after, until I ended up at Father Shumbin's church.

Henry asked me many questions about my journey to Father Shumbin's, he asked me how I felt, how I managed to do what I did and what it was like. I explained my sadness and how the long days alone gave me plenty of time to think about many things, especially Teeta. It saddened my heart to talk about Teeta and everything that had happened, even after having spoken about it several times with the friends I had met along the way, and even to strangers in the lectures, it still made me sad. Henry told me that he would take me to the university and to meet with professor Swartz and then he would return home, but I was welcome to come back for one more night if I needed a place to stay. I helped to clean a little of Henry's home, I did not have much to offer in regards to thanks for a place to sleep, and the food. I cleaned some of the kitchen and the dishes as well as washed the floors and some of the table for Henry, I would have cleaned some more but we then had to go.

We climbed back into Henry's small gray motor car, once again he heaved himself into the seat behind the steering wheel and slammed his door shut, it took a few tries for him to jerk back and forth in his seat to get to a comfortable position as I sat down and waited. I rubbed my wet hands on my pants to dry them and was ready to go and meet another person that wanted to hear my story. I was very grateful to have traveled so very far from home, I could not wait to get back home to tell my mother about everything I had gotten to see and do, I have had an amazing journey and done many amazing things, I was still sad about Teeta and could not decide if I had been gone long enough yet or not. Henry did not swear or shout as much as we drove, he talked about suggesting I see the Elizabeth tower in another city if I got the time and that there were many things that I would enjoy seeing along my travels if I managed to make my way around England some more.

I found myself tired, even though I was awake I still felt a little drowsy, worn down, maybe I slept too much, or maybe I was missing my home too much. As we drove to the university that I was supposed to meet professor Swartz, I began to realize how much I missed my home, the gray clouds that did

234

not stop raining and being cold was no fun, I missed the big water but more than that, I missed the tall grasses stretching out to the horizon. I missed not having to wear a shirt that choked my neck a little, I missed the sun on my skin, and I missed Teeta. I leaned back in my seat and watched the spots of water join on the window and then stream towards the sides of the car, I thought about the big herds of animals roaming to find water, they moved one way in great numbers and then a while later they moved back the other way, I thought about spending nights sleeping away from the village and also about when the men came back with meat for all.

I had a lot on my mind, I talked plenty about my travels and about what I had been through, I thought a lot about being back in my swinging hammock bed in the small closet on the ship, I liked the bed and it was very comfortable, I also liked being swayed like my mother used to do when I was young. The car motored towards the university; there were giant marble columns, big buildings and large crowds moving around in the rain. I did not feel impressed at another large cement or stone building, I was not amazed to see so many people, after the airplane port I saw the people as in a hurry and not very nice, in my small village everyone made sure they were nice to everyone else, it seems that when you get too many people in one place, that people forget how to treat other people and they just become pushy and mean. Henry parked the car and rocked a little forward and then backward to get himself to shove his shoulder into his door to open it, I took a moment to rub my hands together, my fingertips were cold, the tips under the nails were starting to blue a little.

Henry had to work but he said he would show me to the professor's office and there she would walk me through what she needed me to do. The university was very large, it seemed like a city of its; own. I looked around and noticed some of the designs on the walls and many signs and paper around, I wondered what it would be like to be a student and have to visit such a place many times. I felt my shoes and my pants become wet from walking and the small splashes kicking up, I was already cold and it was no longer fun to walk in the rain and to be so wet. I felt my teeth begin to click as my jaw shivered a little, I missed my warm home. Henry lead me into a large building and then up some stairs, he told me that the faculty offices were on the third floor so we had to take another flight of stairs up. I thanked Henry for his help and for letting me stay at his home for the night. Henry thanked me for telling him my story and wished me luck on the rest of my journey. Henry and I shook hands and I stepped into the office.

I saw a smaller older lady sitting at a desk, there was a green plant in an orange pot on her desk, she had fluffy reddish hair that had a few silver strands in it, she was wearing a red sweater and glasses that had red lines on the sides, she must have liked red. The lady held up one finger as she finished speaking into a black phone she held to her ear. The lights were bright, the sky outside was still gray and dropping rain all over, even on the windows of the university building. I nodded to the lady that I understood and I looked behind me for a place to sit down. I took a seat on a yellow chair, there was a short table that was covered in thin picture books, so I picked one up to look through. I searched through three or four of the flimsy books, there were many pictures to see but I did not find much interest in them, the pages were smooth and shiny, some pictures showed people while others were of motor cars or different kinds of animals.

"Excuse me" I heard a voice say as I looked up. I looked around to see where the voice was coming from, it took a moment to remember the lady sitting behind the short wall at a desk, she did not even look up but was calling for me. I stood back up to greet the professor, I said her name and she smiled, "I'm not who you're looking for but are you a student of hers?" she asked. I shook my head to respond, I was still feeling tired but I did my best to be polite as my mother taught me to be. The lady still did not look up to make eye contact, she picked up the black phone again and pushed some buttons before she began speaking. The lady told me that she was the secretary and that the professor would be out shortly to greet me. Professor Swartz was a tall lady, she had light brown hair that was a little curly in the font, she was wearing black pants that swung out in front of her feet as she walked. The professor reached out her hands to shake mine, she smiled to me and said "hello." I felt a little better now that I met another nice person in the country, many people did not seem very happy, I did not either with all of the rain.

The professor guided me back to her office and asked if I was hungry or thirsty, I smiled a little and told her that I was always willing to try a new food, but that I was very cold instead. The professor opened her office door and used her hand to signal for me to have a seat. I sat on a thick black seat, it was a soft cushion, and it was a little bouncy under my body. The professor opened up a small closet and removed a light brown jacket, she handed it to me and told me that her son wouldn't miss it, I looked at her because I did not know what she meant; "It's for you" she told me. I thanked her very much and quickly stood to put it on, I was still very cold and wanted to warm up. I was wondering what I was supposed to do for the rest of the day but for the moment, I was warming up and slowly getting comfortable.

Professor Swartz offered to show me some of her university, she asked if it would be too much to tell my story to three sessions of classes she had lined up for me, she really wanted many of the people to hear what I had to say. As we walked she asked me about my home, my childhood and where I had been during my travels. I spoke about many of the things I had seen and done but I really began to wonder why my journey was of such interest to so many people. I asked why my story was being told in so many places, I was happy to help anyone that I could and I liked talking about my home, I just did not understand why my story was something that could help anyone. Professor Swartz explained to me that the tembo were being killed by the hundreds, whole herds were being wiped out for their pembo, or ivory. I felt sorry for the animals I had seen along my journey before I met Father Shumbin, I told my story many times in many places and it had begun to spread that I had first-hand seen some of the things people had done.

Professor Swartz wanted me to tell her lectures full of people about the night of the hunt and everything that I had seen and been through, I was a young man with a unique story and many more people wanted to hear it. Professor Swartz had three classes to speak to and then she was also getting phone calls and emails from people all over asking that she reserve a large hall in order to take in many countrymen to hear me speak. I spoke to the three classes, the professor made sure I had lunch in my stomach and plenty of water to keep my voice from going away. The first class was full of young people mostly like me, the second and third class had a few more older adults within it and several people asked many questions, which I did my best to answer each time.

The big auditorium was going to be my last speaking of the day, I was a little tired and professor Swartz let me sleep a little in her office between speakings, I was a little nervous when she told me that she had a very large venue booked for me, she wanted me to tell my whole story in great detail and to really bring awareness to what is going on in the lands of my village. The tembo are the large elephants that people hunt that are not supposed to, I had seen many of the things that people had done to such animals and my story is a special one.

*I continued to ask Ojimbo many questions, I had half heard the story in the final lecture of the evening, I was more in a hurry for my mate to take me to the pub for a pint so I didn't pay close enough attention. It was nearing the end of the day Ojimbo and I spent hanging out and getting to know him. Ojimbo spent the better part of the day exchanging stories and I took great interest in his entire story, which I have put to paper as Ojimbo narrated. I saved Ojimbo's truly great tale until the last chapter, I wanted to capture the entire essence of this young man that seemed to carry a continent from his small village in South Africa, all the way to jolly Ole England on his strength of character, he has spoken to hundreds of interested people and encouraged many of them to really focus on the struggles near his village. Ojimbo is a bright and friendly young man, he has expressed plans to find port cities and try to work on a sail boat to make his way back home much like he did for Captain Raza, I wish him the best of luck and in the meantime, I penned his journey to reach more people for awareness of the kind beasts that roam the grass plains in Africa.*

*Here is Ojimbo's journey:*

Teeta returned from Teran , it was a small home that a man named Siwalla lived in. Siwalla was a trader man he and traded with many men from different tribes and villages, he kept his big building full of things such as medicines and other cooking supplies and things that tribes used, he dried and stretched the skins to take to a further town closer to the big water and sell to traders and to foreigners that wanted to collect pelts and furs. I was very excited to get to see Teeta again, my friend had been gone many days, and mostly I wanted to hear about his travels to far from the village. Teeta was unsure of what to expect when he got to Teran, he expected a man that did not look like the men he knew, and Siwalla did not look like the men he knew.

Siwalla was light of skin, he wore a wrapped clothe around his head and spoke our words differently. Teeta was a little nervous to meet Siwalla, he walked for five days to get to the small village, it had small boxes that played music and strange sounds. Teran had a few small homes and several animals in fenced in pens to keep for food, they did not hunt as much as we did for our meat in our village. Siwalla showed Teeta a small hut that he was welcome to get a good night's rest in and one of the villagers would prepare a big meal for him after his long journey. Siwalla introduced Teeta to Lisha, she was a young girl that was close to his age, she live with her mother and cooked for many of the villagers and travelers. Lisha had light eyes, she was most beautiful according to Teeta.

Teeta stayed one night at Teran, he sat on a small log that was near a small fire, Lasha sat next to him. Lasha asked Teeta about where he had come from, and what he liked about his home. Teeta spoke about becoming a man when he returned to the village, he wanted everyone to look at him like they did to Loza, Lasha remembered Loza, she was much younger but remembered seeing the tall and strong man with big muscles come staggering from the western path. Lasha helped make a meal for Loza but it was mostly her mother Kypi then. Kypi sat with Lasha and Loza around the very same small fire, sometimes there are more travelers, but only sometimes.

Teeta spoke with Lasha for a little while, she was a very nice and sweet girl and they exchanged smiles a little by the warm fire. Teeta spoke about his journey to Teran, he hauled many skins and pelts to trade for a list of supplies to bring back to the village, Teeta was more supposed to bring the pelts and later one of the other men from the village would come back after the skins were sold and pick up even more supplies for the village. Teeta spoke about sleeping out and alone, the worry of some of the night animals that were dangerous and how at first he was afraid even though he was trying to be strong to prove that he ready to be a man. Teeta hunted some small animals on his own to eat during his journey; he struggled to keep all of the pelts and skins hiked up on his shoulders like Loza had. Lasha began to giggle, she told Teeta that when Loza had finally made it to Teran, his arms were so tired and he was dragging the skins on two sticks that he fastened to his waist to pull like a cart, and he cried when Kypi tried to lift his arms.

Lasha apologized for giggling, one of the things the men learn is that the journey means different things to different men that make it, most want to prove how strong they can be on their own, but men also come to realize that they are stronger with the village helping to hold them up. Many of the men also learn that no matter how fast or strong they may think they are, that it is often that they need a break or a time to sit and relax. Kypi told Lasha that many of the boys that make the journey find the journey home much more of a time to grow than the journey to Teran, and many find that once they realize how big the world can be by the lonely journey, that they have a brighter outlook on their home and spouse when they get one. Teeta realized that Teran was not what he expected, in his mind the different kind of man was much like mine, maybe tall or short or different color or not like a man at all, maybe even part animal.

On our walk to our hunting grounds Teeta continued to tell me more about his journey to Teran. "Me and Lasha talked for a very long time" Teeta began another round of his adventure. Teeta and Lasha sat beside each other for a long time, she continued to help feed the weak and famished man, his measly food and long journey left him very weak and as Lasha brought bowl after bowl, Teeta would eat and eat. Teeta told Lasha that he liked her, that he thought she was the most beautiful girl he had ever seen and that even though he was on his journey to become a man, that me might think he could make her his wife.

"I am not for sale" Lasha spoke to Teeta, he did not understand what she meant by "sale" and he began to explain what he meant my liking her. Lasha stopped Teeta from talking and explained that she and her mother Kypi belonged to Siwalla and were not for sale. Teeta felt himself get angry, people cannot own other people, each person is born to be free and it angered Teeta. Teeta did not finish eating any more of the food that Lasha had brought him, as the sky got dark and the sun began to set, he shouted for the supplies he was owed for his pelts by Siwalla. Siwalla hushed and tried to calm the angry Teeta, Teeta said he wanted to hit kill the man but it was not right to take a man's life from him. Siwalla gave many of the items that Teeta was demanding and Teeta headed back towards the village.

Teeta did not sleep the first night, his anger had pushed him to walk long past when his legs ached, he had struggled to avoid vomiting but he lost the struggle, his head pounded and his fists remained clenched as he dragged the bag of bartered items away from Teran. The clinging and clanging of the pots and pans in a large white back that hung over his shoulder had pounded against his back as he marched back home. Teeta tripped and fell sometime in the middle of the next day, he said he was exhausted and angry and when he fell, he landed in a side ditch covered in tall grass, and it was soft enough to fall asleep in.

Teeta woke up itchy in the grass, he was still very angry but as he continued to walk, he turned to sad. Teeta and me camped by each other the night he got back, I riddled him with many questions and was very curious about the journey. Teeta told me all about everything he did and saw, and felt for the poor girl that let someone else own her. Teeta did not understand why such a person would do such a thing and it made his heart very sad. Me and Teeta spoke about his journey and about my trip hunting while he was gone, it grew dark and the fire had burned out for the evening, many of the other hunting men had already fallen asleep.

Sometime in the night I was woken up, there were gun shots and loud tembo calls, I had a hard time seeing for a few moments until my eyes became used to the night, the moon was bright and it created shadows that traced the other men. The ground shook and all of the men began to shout and yell. I rolled onto my back and as I tried to look, I felt a large beast step right over me, and Teeta began to scream and cry out. I was very scared, I could not see but I heard Nga shout and with small flashes of light I heard gun shots fire into the air. Ziza was shouting and running around, there were tembo stampeding through our camp in the middle of the night. When the large beast moved from over top of me I wiggled to try to move out of the way, the tembo calls echoed in my ears, their calls were so loud I hardly heard the gunshots trying to scare them away. I felt my body get hit from the side and knocked to the ground while I was trying to stand, I could hear the large footsteps but could not see where they were coming from. I fell to the ground and tried to continue to crawl to keep from getting stepped on by the giant monsters.

The loud shrieking calls from the tembo were louder than my own screams, I could not think of anything to shout but I wanted to cry out loud and make them go away. I screamed and cried and shouted and flailed my arms trying to get the beasts to leave our camp. A few clouds parted in the sky and suddenly I was standing right in front of a giant pembe colored beast, it was almost white in the dark of the night as the moon made it stand out against the black night behind it. I could not speak, I could not shout, I had no voice and my body did not want to move. The giant tembo charged at me, it was barreling down on me and I was frozen with fear.

At the last moment a small flash fired between me and the tembo, it was Teeta firing his rifle into the air to convince the tembo to change its direction. I was almost run down by a charging tembo, my legs gave away as it charged right passed me, it was so close that I felt the breeze on my skin as it passed me. I fell to my knees, I could not hear over my own crying as I was so scared. The ground was damp on my legs, my lungs burned from shouting and crying and I could not catch my breath. I huffed and puffed and my heart beat like a stampede in my ears. I inhaled, I exhaled, I struggled to get my breathing under control, my breathing was the only thing I could hear. My chest burned like fire, each breath I tried to breathe was difficult.

Nga shouted out for everyone to call out their name so he could make sure that everyone was unhurt. "Joos" was a name, "Dah" was another as I struggled to catch my breath for a moment before I was able to blurt out my own name. There were many more men that did not say their names, including my best friend Teeta. I saw a small bit of light as Nga tried to get a fire going again, it took a few moments but in the small lights of a small flame, my eyes wildly searched for my friend in the dark. I could not see against the black ground, I could barely see the shadows of the men moving around, I could only hear them stepping and moving and calling for one another.

I found Teeta's body lying on the ground, I tried to stand up to him but my legs were weak and unable to support me so I crawled to him. I could see a small bit of Nga as he tried to continue to fan the flame to make the light brighter so we could see what men needed help. Nga shouted to Joos and Dah to help the other men; "drag everyone towards the flames" he shouted out. I neared Teeta, his hands were moving a little but he was mostly still and silent. "Teeta" I shouted as I reached him, I tried to lift his head but all I heard was a little gurgling.

I could tell that Teeta was hurt badly, he did not move much as I raised his head to my lap to support him. I held his hand and tried to stop crying to try to hear if he was trying to talk. I tried to begin to pull Teeta towards the fire, maybe Nga could fix him. Teeta squeezed my hand when I tried to pull him. I was seated on the ground and unable to get a good pull to help him. "Go, Ojimbo, you are my brother, your dream is to take a long journey, for me you must" Teeta whispered to me. I
246

tried to clear the tears out of my eyes to try and see him, the light from the small fire grew a little brighter. Teeta was wet with blood on his face; it was coming from his mouth and nose. The light flickered off of the glassy eyes of Teeta, they were now still and without life. I tried to shake my friend, I did not want him gone from me, I tried to squeeze his hand while crying out his name, but it too, was without life.

I cried and shouted for my friend to be ok until Nga and Joos finally stood me up and made me realize that he was gone, he was not alone either. Nga lost his best friend Ziza. I had a hard time focusing and I was so sad and angry also. Nga dragged me to my feet and tried to help me walk closer to the fire, my legs still did not want to work and I could not catch my breath from the crying and shouting. Joos and Dah spoke between them but their words sounded muffled behind my sobbing. Nga tried to help me to sit by the fire but my body just let me drop to the dirt.

I curled up in a ball and tried to focus on the warm from the fire, I could not breathe well and I could not stop myself from crying. Nga and the two other men worked for a little while, I don't remember being tired but I did try to yawn to catch my breathing, I woke up in the morning. Joos and Dah were sleeping next to the smoking pieces of wood that was the fire I fell asleep next to, Nga was sitting up with his arms crossed around his knees, staring at the men that were his friends. In the night Joos and Dah gathered the bodies, there were six in all; Teeta, Ziza, Hyah, Auhf, Jyyr, and Gwyon, all without life, lying side by side. Joos and Dah had dug a little with very little light but it did no good so they rested a little and waited for the sun to rise.

Nga did not sleep, he stood vigilant guard and made sure there was enough fire going to fend off any scavenging animals from the bodies of our friends. I found some strength in my legs and fumbled to find my feet to rise up. My throat hurt from shouting and crying. Nga stood up to give me a hug, he looked very tired from his long night of sitting watch. I picked up a shovel and began to help dig, I did not say anything but Nga seemed to know what I would have said.

I dug and dug and switched hands when one hand or arm began to hurt. I dug a long and deep hole for my friend. When my first hole was dug for Teeta to be placed, I moved down a bit and started another hole for another member from our village. Nga began to dig and when Joos and Dah awoke, they joined in in the digging also. I thought about Loza and Teeta carrying the pelts long past when their arms would hold up, it was Teeta's anger that pushed him to walk into the night, long passed when his body had hurt and his lungs burned like the sun. I found that same anger, I dug and dug, my hands bled and the tears poured down my face. I was sad to lose my friend, I was angry to lose my friend, and I was scared to have my friend lost from me.

Once there were enough graves to bury our friends, Joos and Dah carefully placed a man in each grave, Nga and I helped also. Nga and me picked up Teeta, his head moved a little as I picked him up, his eyes did not open, his mouth did not breath in, there was no life in him. I tried not to begin crying again but Nga had a tear on his chin, we did not say any words but we all felt the same. As my friend it was my duty to bury Teeta, Nga felt the same way for Ziza. I covered over Teeta and waited while Nga buried Zizu. After all of our friends were laid into their graves, we each covered them over with dirt and sat down to miss them.

My hands bled, there were blisters and marks, my arms throbbed and I was angry. Joos and Dah spoke about going back to the village to tell everyone what had happened, they felt very sad and already missed the men they had hunted with for many years. Nga looked to me and told me that I was a man and part of the hunters now, but I did not want to be. I stood up and told Nga to tell my mother Bendu that I loved her and that I would return, but I needed my journey, I needed to make it right. I grabbed Teeta's rifle from the ground, I almost dropped it because my hands hurt so badly that I could not close my hand and my arms almost could not lift.

I put the gun on my back and the strap over my head. Joos turned to stand up when Nga put his hand on his leg to stop him from stopping me. "He must go" Nga said to Joos. Dah just watched as I stormed off into the hot day. I do not know what was in my head the first day I set out, I wanted to find that giant white beast from the night, the one that trampled into out camp and stomped on my friend Teeta. The grass was hot and dry under my feet but I did not slow my pace, I did not run but I walked very fast, the gun on my back bounced against me, the slight air on my hands relieved very little of the burning. I felt the sun heat my head, but I did not care, the sun rose high and even though my vision was blurry from the heat but I could not stop.

I marched with anger in my blood for most of the day, I could not stop thinking about the large tembo charging into my camp. I could not understand why it trampled on Teeta and not me, I was asleep right beside him. As the sun began to cool a little I decided to stop for some water and try to find something to eat, I knew that with as hot as it was and as hard as I had been trudging, my body could collapse any minute. I found a small chuta in the grass, I used a stick to beat around the grass until something edible moved. I put the food in my belly and tried to keep a small fire going through the night. It was barely light when I was packing up my small roll to lay on and a gun that belonged to by best good friend. I followed many of the signs the tembo had been there, trampled grasses and droppings were the best signs that I was following them. I had not even walked to the midday day when I came upon two dead tembo, there was a young male and an older female, there was blood all over them, their pembe had been cut from their heads and their bodies riddled with small bleeding holes.

The bodies were still warm, I must not have been very far behind them except I did not hear any gun shots. The giant beasts were rough to the touch, not as smooth as the baby me and Teeta helped when were younger. Even laying on their sides, the tembo were taller than I was, their bodies were immense. Their legs were larger around than my body, and someone killed them to cut their tusks off and left the rest of them to rot and spoil in the sun. The smaller male would have been enough meat to feed all of my village members for months, and it was now rotting in the heat. The animal laid with its' eyes open, staring at the other, they male was the smaller of the two but was still larger than the home I shared with my mother growing up.

The animal had been dead for too long to try to eat any of it, I did not want to be sick. I felt ill but the anger inside of me to go and hunt down the larger white one that killed my friend, pushed me to move on. My feet were tired, my legs weary, and my hands were still covered in blisters from digging, but I pushed forward. I followed the tracks in the dirt, there were many foot prints and I followed them all into the morning sun. I took the breaks as I could especially when I remembered Teeta saying that Kypi had mentioned the men needing breaks sometimes. I ate when I found food and I stopped for water when I could also. Some of the grass still had green bits, I ate them when I could find them. I passed mounds of droppings that spread out in the direction that the massive herd had headed.

The sun tried to beat me down but I would not kneel, I was full of anger and sadness and that monster tembo had to know my anger. The gun grew heavy being slung over my shoulders, I traded shoulders but it did not take long before the other shoulder was tired and sore also. Each step I took left grass to crunch under my feet, I kept my eyes focused on the tall grasses in search of the animal I was hunting. I was not worried about a predator like the simba or fisi, many are afraid and stay away from the very large and loud tembo. I continued to walk with a fast pace late into the day, I found another tembo that had been brutally killed and chopped up, its face was mangled and the pembe ripped from the front of it, I felt a little saddened that the animal had gone to waste but I was still filled with anger and sadness.

I ran until it was too dark to follow the trail of trampled grass, I could feel that I was close to catching the herd that killed my friend and then I would hunt the animal and become a man. I had a hard time sleeping, the grass underneath me seemed to poke through the light clothe I tried to sleep on, my body was still worn and aching and my hands hurt from the blisters. I laid awake the entire night, the stars above looked the same as when Teeta and me would also lay awake half the night and making up  what designs we could see within them. I could not help but imagine what was going through his mind as his life left his body. I was thankful that he was my best friend, and I was honored that he was mine. I watched as the small bugs of the night would cover a star sometimes, I thought about catching some of the small critters buzzing about to eat but they were small and my hands would not have worked well enough to catch one.

I was up again before the sun had broken over the horizon in the distance, I slung Teeta's rifle over my shoulder again and headed back into the direction I was headed in before I bedded down for the night. In the grass I found a small ngiri, it squealed and tried to run from me but I swung the rifle as hard as I could when it startled me. The small animal lay quiet as I began to pull it apart to begin to cook it to eat.  The heat from a small fire to cook the animal was warm but it made my hands hurt more, I began to feel a little ill and I tried to eat as much of the small animal as I could. Once the animal was cooked well enough to eat I ate most of the meat except the both back legs, I carried those to eat later as I walked, I was a little concerned with smelling of food as I walked, it might attract the nose of a dangerous animals.

As I followed the tracks and trails from the tembo I continued to find more tracks, this time there were motor vehicle tire tracks in the soft dirt. As the sun rose high I found two more slaughtered tembo, this time one was still trying to move. My stomach felt ill, the animal had been shot a bunch of times in the side and it's pembe tusks had been ripped from its' face, and yet it fought to remain alive. I spoke softly to the creature as it struggled for its' last few breaths, it blew clouds of dust away from its mouth when it exhaled, it also made a whining noise. My heart felt sad and I began to hate, I hated myself for  hating, I hated that I had pushed myself so far for hate and I wished that Teeta was still alive.

I sat on the ground beside the dying animal and tried to pet the long trunk of the tembo, it did not move from me, for nights after I sat with the drying tembo I tried to wonder why, after men had killed it and it's family, it did not fear me. I looked into the animals eye as it took its' last breath. I was tired, I was filled with remorse for what I had been part of and filled with profound sadness that I had seen so much death and dying. I hated my fellow man for their ugliness, they killed the large animals for waste, not to feed their villages or families, but to rip them apart just for some tusks. I could not understand why these strange men had done what they had done, I stumbled across five dead and desecrated tembo, and I felt disgusted and ashamed about it.

I heard a large tembo call, it was almost as loud as when it was standing over top of me as Teeta lay dying on the ground. I shrugged my head a little as the call came from the silence and frightened me. I slowly turned my head to see where the loud noise came from, it was behind me. I turned to look at the giant gray beast. The tembo opened up its' ears wide, the animal was more than three of my height, but across, it was massive. I locked my crying eyes onto the animal that had killed my best friend; it began to walk towards me. I stood tall and stared at the animal that was staring back at me. The large massive creature raised its' trunk and let out another ear piercing call, I felt my blood turn as hot as the sun, my forehead began to sweat, my hands began to clench, and my eyes widened.

I pulled the rifle off of my back, I was immediately filled with the hate that drove me to walk for days. The tembo began to come faster and faster at me, I held steady, I felt my fingers begin to tremble and shake. My hands burned as the stuck to the rifle in my grip, my blisters oozed and I could feel the grit and dirt in my open wounds, but I held firm. I did not move, I hardly breathed and I was ready to fire and kill the massive beast that killed my best friend. The tembo came closer and closer, I lined up the sights of my rifle to a point in the middle of its head, I was ready to pull the trigger and kill the animal. I focused straight and hard at the animal, I could not see anything to me sides for a moment, until the view to my sides became clear and out of the corner of my eye, I could see the dead tembo that I had sat with, just beside me.

I felt sadness fill me again, my heavy arms began to fall, my rifle suddenly felt like it was heavier than the tembo and I let it fall to the ground. The Tembo was closing in on me, I began to cry again as I thought about me and Teeta as children, my eyes began to blur with tears and with all of the anger, hurt, and sorrow in my heart, I began to shout. I shouted as hard as I cried and then cried as hard as I could shout, I don't know how close the tembo came before it began to slow down form its' charging, I could not see past my tears. I could not lift my arms and my legs no longer wanted to support me, so I fell to my knees. I dropped my head and continued to sob and cry.

In the light blurred vision of my crying eyes, I saw a great shadow come over me; I took one last breath and waited for the animal to crush the life from me, as it had to Teeta. Each moment that passed seemed longer than the days of walking, I held my breath and waited to be stepped on, it would surely kill me when it did. I blinked my eyes and cleared out some of the tears, I was still kneeling in the shadow of the beast. I began to feel weight on my arm and my back, I could not hold my breath any longer and let out a big breath. As my vision returned I realized that the tembo was wrapping its' long trunk around my back, I felt the embrace of the massive creature as I began to stand.

I continued to cry and the tembo used its' trunk to hug and embrace me, I reached forward to hug the large creature on the leg closest to me, it had massive large legs and I could not even wrap my arms around one, but I tried. I cried out how sorry I was, I was sorry for hating, I was sorry that there were men out in the world that would slaughter such animals for poor reasons and I was sorry that there was nothing I could do to help Teeta. It was cool in the shadow of the tembo, its' trunk was strong and could easily damage me, but it was soft, gentle, and caring like a mother would be to a baby. I cried for a little longer, I was embraced with an animal I wanted to kill because it killed my best friend, but killing does not make anything any better and it would not have made me feel any better.

The tembo dropped its' trunk from around me, it took two large steps and began to feel at the body of the tembo that had lay on the ground behind me, it made soft noises and blew puffs of air as it used its' trunk to feel all over the body, especially the long trunk that was out stretched in front of it. I turned to the animal and shouted kindly to it: "I am so sorry, you are now my friend and I am yours" and then I began to walk away. I had seen so much ugliness in just a few days, the ugliness of man that could do such things to animals without the purpose of feeding a village, I promised to Teeta that I would go and see the world on my journey, I had to know that there was still goodness in the world.

I walked for many days before I found the church that had Father Shumbin in it, I was worn and weary and still very sad when I showed up. I did not know where I was or where I was going, but I knew that eventually I could ask and try to find my way to Teran and from there maybe Siwalla might point me home.